HOLIDAY HEADACHES

A PLANNERS AND DREAMERS NOVEL
BOOK THREE

LYNNE HANCOCK PEARSON

ACKNOWLEDGMENTS

My heartfelt thanks to:

My walking friends, Nancy, Sandi & Rita, who meet with me three times a week at O dark thirty.

My parents, Vic & Iva Hancock for introducing me to the joy of reading.

My long-suffering husband Matt, who has never been anything but encouraging.

To everyone who has ever suggested, "You need to put that in your next book!"

CHAPTER 1

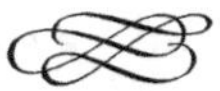

"You sure Delia doesn't want to move in with you, and I'll move in here?" Standing in front of the window with its view of Puget Sound, Sid grinned at his cousin, Cal.

"You're dreaming, pal."

Sid shrugged and walked toward the kitchen. "It was worth a try."

Cal poured the tea and handed a mug to Sid. "Who are you asking to move in with you?"

"Not sure yet. If I can, I'd like to live alone for a while." With a contract to teach wood carving at CSEC, the Coast Salish Education Center, and multiple chess set orders, for the first time in forever, Sid had money in the bank. He was taking over the lease on Cal's apartment and would have a place of his own. If he wanted to, he could run with scissors. Naked.

"Work is picking up for you?"

"Yeah. It's looking good." Delia, Cal's girlfriend, had introduced Sid to a few gallery owners in Seattle who specialized in Indigenous artwork, which led to an agent promoting his work. The reception for his carvings had blown him out of the water. No longer would he be sitting on the benches outside Pike Place Market selling hand-carved cedar totem poles to tourists for cash he'd then blow on booze. Not only did he have a steady source of income, he also had a firm grip on sobriety. He still attended meetings at ODAAT, One Day At A Time—an organization that helped Indigenous people get and stay sober—but didn't need to attend daily. And he certainly didn't need to live there anymore. It was rarely quiet as one man or another dealt with his demons. Both Sid and his mentor, Frank, thought he could handle his own demons while living independently, provided he checked in for meetings regularly.

"Good. I've already talked to the landlord, so the transition shouldn't be hard. He's a good guy, and the neighbors are nice and quiet."

Sid nodded. When Cal asked if he was interested in renting the apartment, he'd done a walk-through. The older four-story building was on Capitol Hill and had eighteen units. The apartment was a corner unit on the third floor, with bedroom windows overlooking the alley and the front window facing the street. He'd been sharing a room at ODAAT and didn't know what he would do with all that space.

The apartment Cal was moving into belonged to Delia and was quite the contrast. Almost bigger than the house Sid had grown up in, it had three bedrooms, two bathrooms, a living room, a dining room, and a big kitchen. It was light and bright, tastefully yet comfortably decorated. Cal's battered hiking boots sat near the front door, and he looked at home in his rumpled flannel shirt and worn jeans.

"I'll take your old furniture, except for the bed. Cause.…" He gave an exaggerated shudder. "I'll get my own."

Cal grinned. "Don't blame you."

She no longer worked as a concierge in the building, but it still felt weird walking into Delia's apartment for personal reasons. She wasn't there to deliver a package, oversee a repair, or listen to a complaint—not that Delia was a tenant who'd complained a lot. No, she wasn't working there anymore; Connie was an invited guest. Free to sit and relax, and didn't have to get back to the tiny cubbyhole of an office in the foyer to face the public with a polite smile fixed in place.

She, Delia, and Tommy Federov had ridden up the elevator with an older couple from the thirteenth floor, two women forever having issues with an exorbitantly expensive oven that wouldn't work. It had never been part of her job description to make repairs on appliances purchased by the tenants, but listening to tenant complaints was. Out of her uniform of navy polyester and wearing jeans, boots, and an oversized chunky green sweater selected by Tommy, a senior buyer for Nordstrom's, one of Delia's oldest friends, and now a good friend of Connie's, the two women hadn't paid attention to her at all. Strange, indeed.

Tommy continued his harangue as they stood in Delia's entrance way, "You should have put those shoes on hold."

Connie handed her coat to Delia to hang in the closet. "Tommy, even if I could afford those shoes, my lifestyle does not require sequined stilettos."

"You say that now, but don't come crying to me when it's the night of the ball and Cinderella is forced to wear sneakers."

"Yeah, yeah, yeah." She followed him into the apartment's living space.

"Hey, you." Delia walked up to a big copper-skinned man who wrapped her in a flannel hug.

Connie and Tommy exchanged grins. Cal and Delia really

were the swooniest couple. Cal moved, and Connie spotted the smaller man standing behind him. She smiled at Sid.

Not as tall nor as broad as his cousin, Sid Fraser, was a lean man with black hair tied back with a leather thong. Clean-shaven, he was dressed in jeans and a flannel shirt. The sleeves rolled up to expose sinewy forearms and a band of tattoos on his right wrist. They'd met a few times, and she'd found him to be sweet, polite, and a little shy. He wasn't hard to talk to, just a little…reserved.

Tommy pushed past her, nodding at Sid. "Is there any more tea? Connie, would you like some?"

"Oh. I didn't think we were staying."

"Yes, we're staying. You have to give us a fashion show."

Connie scowled. "You saw everything I bought. I'm not doing a fashion show." And definitely not in front of Cal and Sid. She looked over to see Sid looking at her, the corner of his mouth tucked up and his dark brown eyes crinkling. A warm tingle of awareness went through her, and she glanced away to avoid staring at the frank interest in his gaze.

"You don't have to do anything you don't want to do," Cal told her, shaking his head at Tommy and Delia. "Haven't you two tortured the girl enough?"

Delia shook her head right back. "Not everyone can work from home wearing the same clothes on repeat, frowning at their computer. Some people must meet the public and put their best foot forward while doing so."

"I do laundry and change my clothes daily. I just happen to like flannel. And I don't frown at the computer." Cal frowned down at Delia.

She pressed a finger against the wrinkle between his eyebrows. "Yes, you do. Just like this. Are your characters not behaving?"

Cal harrumphed. "Something like that."

Calvin Jimmy had been ghostwriting Regency romances for best-selling author Stacy Wrigglebottom for years. He was under contract to write a few more books and then would write under his own name: adventure fantasy stories employing Pacific Northwest Indigenous myths and folklore.

"You'll get there, babe." Delia turned to Connie. "You don't have to, but if you want to put on the new outfits, Tommy and I can help you accessorize them and suggest ways to combine them with the purchases you made last time for an effective capsule wardrobe. That should take you through to the next season without going shopping again and allow you to make minimal repeats."

"Oh, that makes sense." She still didn't want to do it in front of an audience.

As if sensing her disquiet, Sid offered, "I'm gonna get going. Cal, do you want to give me the key now or later?"

"What key?"

Cal turned to Delia. "To my apartment. Sid's taking over the lease."

"What? No! Cal, we talked about this." Delia planted her hands on her hips. "I offered the apartment to Connie."

Connie's belly dropped. Last week, Delia had asked her if she was interested. They'd discussed terms and done a walk-through, and all that needed to be done was get the key. She'd already started boxing up her things in preparation for moving out of her childhood bedroom. Her mother had initially protested, saying Connie was too young to be living on her own. At twenty-eight, Connie disagreed. She was tired of staring at the unicorn wallpaper and was too old to be sneaking into the house to avoid an inquisition from her parents. Delia suggesting Cal's apartment was the perfect solution. But if it was going to Sid, she was screwed.

"You did not talk to me about this."

"Uh, yeah," Delia responded. She stalked to where she'd left her purse and pulled out a leather-bound planner. She flipped through the pages, then held it up triumphantly. "See?

Last Tuesday, there's a note about Connie taking over the lease."

Cal was shaking his head. "Tuesday was the day I had to drive up to Tulalip. A pipe burst and flooded Mom's office. Sid and I went up to help move things. Remember?"

Delia stared at Cal and then down at her planner. She groaned. "There's an X beside the entry instead of a check mark."

Shifting her gaze from the arguing couple, Connie looked at Sid. He seemed just as unhappy as she felt. He opened his mouth, but Tommy intervened before Sid could speak.

"Let's go make the tea." He led Sid and Connie into the kitchen. They watched Cal and Delia bicker from the other side of the peninsula. "Sorry, Sid, but my money's on Delia."

Sid sighed. "You're probably right."

Connie wasn't certain what his housing situation was. She knew he'd been staying at a mission near Seattle Center for alcoholics but didn't know if that was still the case. A part of her wanted to be the bigger person. Step back and let Sid have the apartment. Another part wanted to be selfish. That part was in the lead at the moment, so she kept her mouth shut. She had no desire to be the adult child still living with her parents.

"I've never been to Cal's place." Tommy filled the kettle and put it on the stove. "What is it? A studio? One bedroom?"

Ramrod stiff and looking as uncomfortable as she felt, Sid said nothing, so Connie spoke. "No, it's a two-bedroom corner unit." She went on to describe the place, trying to keep the wistfulness out of her voice. In her mind, she'd already painted the living room a sunny yellow and positioned the secondhand furniture her mom had bought and was storing in the garage.

"So consider sharing. At least temporarily." Tommy glanced between her and Sid. "That would give you both time to figure things out and smooth things over for them."

He jerked his head toward where Delia and Cal were still going at it nose to nose.

Connie blinked. She'd lived at home her entire life with her parents and two younger siblings. She could handle a roommate. Her mother would probably like that better than Connie living alone. But living with a man? She looked over to see Sid watching her. If possible, he looked even more unhappy. She knew it wasn't ideal, but would it be so bad to be roommates? They didn't have to be friends. Just agree on some simple ground rules. Heat rose from her neck, and she was sure her cheeks were beet red. Other than her father, she'd never lived with a man, never spent the night with a man. What would it be like to share a place with someone as attractive and interesting as Sid?

In contrast to her incredibly boring home life, he'd bounced around while growing up, lived on the streets, and battled addiction. Other than his apparently horrid mother, his family loved him and helped nurture the talent that had landed him contracts with major art galleries in the city. One of his chessboards was on display at CSEC, and she'd marveled over the intricacies of the cuts and the imagination of the design. The hands that had painstakingly taken a block of wood and turned it into a piece of art for which people willingly paid a lot of money.

Catching his eye again, she realized that he held himself differently. Head high and shoulders back, a confidence radiated from his lean form. Not a look-how-awesome-I-am confidence, but like he was at peace with himself. A quiet hum of energy came off him, pulling her toward him. Did he feel it too? She didn't think so. While he was openly studying her, she didn't think he was imagining intimate exchanges over coffee in the kitchen. He was probably trying to figure out how to say, "Thanks, but no thanks."

Now would be a good time for the ground to open up and swallow her.

His hands were jammed into his front pockets, and his Adam's apple bobbed. His phone rang, and he frowned, pulled it out of his pocket, and headed toward the entryway, frowning even harder.

"Are you opposed to a roommate? Can you even afford a place on your own?" Tommy made the tea and pulled two mugs down from the cupboard, clearly at home in Delia's apartment.

"I can afford the place by myself," Connie revealed. "But I won't be shopping for more clothes anytime soon, and ramen will be a regular meal item. And I don't mean that bougie stuff you and Kevin like to eat. Restaurant meals will be few and far between.

"As for a roommate, that's not off the table. It would certainly make my mother happy. She thinks I'm too young to be living on my own." Connie watched Cal and Delia trying to talk over one another. She should probably let Sid have the apartment. He was Cal's cousin, after all.

Before she could say anything, Sid strode back to the kitchen, looking directly at her. "Let's do it," he said. "If you're up for it, let's share the apartment."

Seriously? It was such an about-face she almost looked over her shoulder to see if he was talking to someone else. Hope rose to the surface. "Are you sure?"

He held her gaze and nodded once.

She cleared her throat as relief swept through her. "Let's try it for six months and see how it goes."

Sid nodded again, looking more resigned than happy.

"Excellent!" Tommy beamed.

Sid pointed to the living room. "Shall we tell them?"

"In a few minutes." Tommy's eyes twinkled. "I'm kind of enjoying the show."

CHAPTER 2

𝒰sing his key, Sid opened the door to the apartment. He dropped his duffel in the hall closet and walked into the living area, his steps echoing on the old hardwood floors. Empty, the space seemed much larger than the last time he'd been there. From where he stood by the window, he took in the dining area and the half-height wall behind which was a countertop in the galley kitchen. He didn't bother looking but knew the appliances and cupboards would be empty and clean. Cal wouldn't have left a mess behind.

Sid headed down the short hallway. On one side was another closet and the bathroom. The vanity had four drawers and a mirrored medicine cabinet over the sink. He had no idea how much space Connie would need, but one drawer would be enough for him. He smiled when he saw the bathtub and shower combo. It would be nice to have a little more room than the tiny shower stalls at ODAAT. The bedrooms looked to be about the same size, and neither one appeared to have an obvious advantage. After sleeping rough for over a year and living first in a dorm and then a shared room at ODAAT, a room to himself, regardless of size, would be a luxury. His brand new bed and mattress would arrive today, and in his duffel, he had sheets, pillows, and a comforter from Cal's mom, Aunt Angie.

He glanced at his phone. The text from Connie said she'd be there around noon. Nothing against her, but he'd wanted to try living by himself. But then Violet had called. Sid shuddered, remembering the conversation.

"Hey, what's up?" Even from an early age, his mother had insisted she call him Violet. It was hard to attract a man when you had a kid in tow.

"Angie just told me you're moving into Cal's apartment. Make sure you get one of those beds so that the head of the mattress moves up and down. I've always wanted one."

"What are you talking about?" From where he stood in the entryway of Delia's apartment, he could see his cousin running his hands through his hair.

Violet tsked. "When I come to stay with you, I want one of those deluxe beds. Actually, just give me your credit card number, and I'll order it myself."

That got his attention. "You are not coming to stay with me."

"Why not? It's got two bedrooms. Plenty of room for both of us. I want to...."

Alarm bells went off in his head. There was no way he could live with his self-centered mother. She'd turn the place into party central, and his sanity, not to mention his sobriety, wouldn't be able to stand it. Violet rambled on about thread count and goose down while he scrambled to find a way out of it. Movement near the dining room table caught his attention. Connie had placed her mug on the table. The light went on in his brain.

He stared straight at Connie. "You can't stay with me because I have a roommate already."

"What?" Violet screeched.

"Yep. Sorry. Gotta go." He'd disconnected without one bit of remorse.

After agreeing to a six-month trial period, things moved

quickly. Papers were signed, keys handed out, and phone numbers exchanged. For the first time in forever, Sid had a woman's name in his contacts list who wasn't related to him or to a family member. Separately, Delia and Cal had pulled him aside, each warning him not to screw it up. Sid thought Delia might be referring to Connie rather than the apartment, though.

How could he possibly screw up? They barely knew each other. She'd given him a ride once, and they'd had a few conversations. To be fair, Connie did most of the talking. Sid had pretty much nodded in all the right places. She was too damn cute for words. Full of ideas and enthusiasm, he went tongue-tied when she turned her attention on him. His hands were suddenly sweaty, so he rubbed them down his legs. He could make conversation. He would be a good roommate. He'd remember to put the toilet seat down and rinse the sink after shaving. Before he could wind himself up into a panic, a noise drew his attention.

"Ta-da!" he heard from the front of the apartment. Damn, he'd been so caught up in his thoughts about Connie that he hadn't even heard her arrive.

Quick footsteps followed her declaration.

"Don't fuss, Mom, the truck will be fine. Come and look at the apartment. See? The appliances work, and everything is sparkling clean."

Sid blew out a breath. Connie's mom was there as well. "Let's do this," he muttered.

✳

"Hi."

Connie whipped around. "Oh! Hey. I wasn't expecting you this early."

"I wasn't expecting you either."

"Right." Her cheeks felt like they were on fire. "We have to get the truck back by six, and I didn't know what traffic or parking would be like, so we left earlier."

"Not a problem. Where are you parked? I can give you a hand."

Feeling a tug at her shirttail, Connie turned. Her mom glared at her.

"Right! Umm, Sid Fraser, this is my mom, Julia Ortega."

Sid stepped forward, his hand extended. "Mrs. Ortega, it's a pleasure to meet you."

Connie held her breath. She knew Sid was close to her age, but he seemed much more grown-up than she was. Perhaps because he'd been on his own for so long. Her mother gave him a closed-lipped smile but accepted his hand. Good manners went a long way, but that didn't mean her mom wouldn't watch him like a hawk.

Sid returned the smile then looked at Connie. "My bed's arriving sometime this afternoon, and I'll take whichever room you don't want."

"You sure?"

At Sid's nod, Connie turned to her mother. "I'll let you choose."

Her mother walked away, and Connie faced Sid. The watery November sunshine hit his blue-black hair, making it shine. This close, she saw the fine lines around his eyes and bracketing his mouth, a tiny scar on the right side of his upper lip. She lifted her chin to meet his gaze. It appeared he was studying her as well. She refrained from biting her lip and willed herself not to blush. Makeup wasn't a daily thing, and apart from plucking stray hairs, slapping on moisturizer was the extent of her beauty regimen. Mentally, she gave her head a shake. Sid was her roommate, not a potential boyfriend, so it didn't matter what he thought about her looks.

Footsteps signaled her mother's return. "Take the back

bedroom. The closet is bigger. You probably have more clothes."

"Umm…probably?"

Sid's lip twitched. "Definitely."

"The back bedroom it is." First hurdle down. They could do this.

Outside on the sidewalk, Connie introduced Sid to Tarik and Jamal, two college students she'd hired to help her move. Jamal unlatched and raised the moving truck's loading door, revealing Connie's belongings, which had been loaded under her mother's supervision. With effortless grace, Sid swung himself up into the truck, the muscles in his thighs bunching and flexing as he looked things over.

"The boxes are labeled with a room designation, and the furniture is self-explanatory," Connie pointed out, swallowing the saliva that had pooled in her mouth when he bent over to inspect the writing on one box.

"How about I stay here and unload. The guys will deliver, and you and your mom can unpack?"

"Sounds good." She accepted a box of linens from him and headed up to the apartment.

Her belongings were transferred from the truck to the apartment with few missteps. Her mother had found a secondhand couch and matching side chair in a muted burgundy and a recliner in dark brown. While they weren't Connie's choice of colors, they were clean and in good repair. With bright throw pillows she'd picked up, they'd work nicely. After much discussion, she and her mom had decided on a square bar-height table and four chairs. Pushed into the corner, it fit nicely into the dining alcove, giving them more room to move around, and could double as a workspace.

Through texts, Sid had said he was happy to let her furnish the place her way. He expected to be gone most of the day carving at ODAAT. While Connie was employed by the Coast Salish Education Center, it wasn't necessary for her to be physically in the building, and she anticipated working from home frequently.

The movers took off just as a delivery van arrived with Sid's bed. Connie left him to supervise the unloading and setup, and joined her mother in the kitchen. A cupboard door was open, revealing neatly stacked dishes and glassware. "Thanks, Mom, you're a godsend." She didn't have to check to know that the utensils and pots would be stored in locations similar to her mom's own kitchen.

Her mother nodded briskly, collapsing a box and adding it to the pile near the table. "The boy brings nothing with him? Not even a coffee mug?"

Connie rolled her eyes. "We've been over this. He said he'd be buying some things after he got settled. I don't mind if he uses my kitchen stuff."

"Just as long as he cleans up after himself."

"Speaking of cleaning up," Connie pushed her hand through sweat-damp hair. It might have been a cold November day, but she was sweating like crazy. "I'm gonna do that right now."

From a box on the bathroom vanity, she withdrew a clean, folded hand towel and pressed her face into it. A towel she had bought and her mother had laundered for her. She might not say it aloud, but her mother showed her love with each one of her actions.

Connie washed up and scowled at her reflection. Her dark hair was growing out from the short, spiky cut she'd worn for the past two years. Now, it flopped over her forehead and curled around her ears. Tommy had suggested a hairstylist, and Connie was tempted to take him up on it but worried about salon prices. Hearing voices coming from the kitchen, she pushed that thought aside and went to investigate.

She stopped where the hallway to the bedrooms intersected with the short hall to the front door. Through the entry to the kitchen, she could see her mother's back. She and Sid spoke in Spanish, too quiet for Connie to understand them. Whatever it was, it pleased her mother because she chuckled and pulled him in for a hug. Sid's arms circled her in what looked like a reluctant embrace—at least on his part.

Walking loudly on the hardwood floor, Connie approached the kitchen from the dining area. "What's going on?" she asked.

Her mother smiled broadly. Sid stood pink-cheeked with his hands in his front pockets.

"Nothing," her mother replied, then turned and patted Sid's arm. "I left a pot of chili in the fridge, and the cornbread is on the counter. Just heat it up when you're ready to eat. I'm going to head home before traffic gets crazy."

Connie narrowed her eyes at the pair but decided to let it go. If Sid had her mother's blessing, that's all that mattered. She walked her mother to her car, hugging her and thanking her profusely. Julia Ortega's unflagging energy was exhausting at times but incredibly useful; the move had gone well because of her drive and organization. Connie headed back to the apartment where dinner awaited. And Sid.

CHAPTER 3

Sid looked around at the stocked, tidy kitchen and shook his head. He was welcome to use everything. Connie had told him that, but it wasn't until Mrs. Ortega hugged him that it became clear.

From his duffel bag, he'd pulled out the one thing that mattered to him. Unwrapping it from a T-shirt, he'd carried the chipped and battered teapot into the kitchen and asked if there was a place for it. It didn't need to be on display, just someplace he could access it.

Mrs. Ortega had taken it into her hands and looked it over. "It has a history, yes?"

He'd looked down at the floor, then up into her perceptive eyes. The lie died on his lips before it had a chance to form. "It belonged to my grandparents. They passed a while ago." He didn't say that his best memories involved sitting in their old diner turned bookstore, drinking tea. Somehow, the woman in front of him understood.

She nodded once and pointed at the cupboard over the fridge. "We will put it there. You can reach it, and it will be safe."

"Thank you, Mrs. Ortega," he said in Spanish. He wasn't

completely fluent, but he'd picked up the language over the years from working construction and in restaurant kitchens.

Her smile lit up the room. "Please, call me Julia," she replied in the same language. "I want you to have my phone number. In case," she lowered her voice and looked toward the hallway. "In case she needs something. Connie is my oldest and very responsible. She never needed to be told twice how to do something, and perhaps I took advantage of that. Now, she tries to do too much by herself, and it's a struggle to get her to accept help, let alone ask for it."

"I understand." Sid pulled out his phone, and she rattled off the number. Her look of relief made him feel like he'd hung the moon. What it must be like to have a mother who cared that much for their child.

Connie's footsteps brought him back to the present. "Hey," she said. "Give me a second, and we can discuss the house rules."

"Sure," he said to her retreating back. House rules? What the hell? She was back before he could wrap his head around what she meant.

She settled at the table in the corner, a notebook in front of her. His face must have reflected his confusion because she chuckled. "That came out wrong. I figured we should talk about expectations so there won't be any misunderstandings or confusion."

His shoulders relaxed. Her mom wasn't wrong; Connie was a take-charge individual. "That makes sense." He hesitated momentarily, then opened the fridge and pulled out the pitcher of water Julia had placed there to chill. "I'm gonna have some water. Would you like some?"

"No, thanks." She was flipping through pages, not even looking at him.

He filled one of her glasses and brought it to the table. "This is really okay? Me using your stuff?"

"Yeah. I mean, if it's something precious that I don't want

you to touch, I'll let you know." She waved at the contents of the kitchen. "I got everything at Goodwill or on a free site, so it's not like I spent a ton on it. If you break something, replace it. Does that work?"

"Sure."

"That being said, I am attached to my Kraken travel mug. There will be consequences if that goes missing."

"Got it." Sid grinned and pulled his phone from his pocket. On the notes app, he typed in HOUSE RULES. Under that, he wrote, "Don't touch Connie's Kraken mug," and showed it to her. "Ready for the next one."

Her eyes sparkling, the room lit up with her laughter, and he grinned again.

Connie put her pen down and looked at the list. It was going smoothly. She'd found a site with suggestions for roommate rules. Sid was remarkably amenable and seemed used to cleaning up after himself; she'd peeked into his bedroom to see he'd made the bed. She wondered and hoped that it was something he did every day. In her mind, there was something satisfying about a neatly made bed.

There was one thing they hadn't yet discussed. She felt her cheeks warm. "So, overnight guests of the um, romantic kind."

"That won't be happening for me."

"Really?" she squeaked out, unsure if she was surprised he didn't have someone in his life or relieved that she wouldn't have to put up with a woman falling all over him in front of her.

"No," he said firmly and then waggled his eyebrows. "At least, not anytime soon."

Disappointment settled like a weight in her belly. Well,

crap. Did that mean he was a player, or did he have his eye on someone and was getting ready to make his move? Again, she barely knew the guy, which was why they were having this conversation. Setting boundaries so the other person wouldn't be blindsided.

"Right." She stared down at her notebook, not wanting to see the knowing look in his eyes, and chose her words carefully because she had no idea if he had a sexual preference. "So, when you *do* have someone stay overnight, I think that—"

A snort interrupted her train of thought, and she looked up to see his eyes dancing with amusement. "I'm sorry." He held up a hand until his laughter subsided. "I know this is awkward and uncomfortable because we barely know each other, but I just had to tease you. I'm not looking for a relationship, and I'm not into causal sex, so I won't be bringing any women back here. Now, if you're seeing anyone.…" He looked at her with one eyebrow raised expectantly.

She sat back and crossed her arms, trying to figure out if she was offended, annoyed, or pleased. She couldn't remember the last time a man had teased her. Could she reciprocate? Looking at Sid toying with his water glass and watching her while waiting for an answer, she thought that maybe when she knew him a bit more, she might be brave enough to try teasing him, but now she would just stumble over herself and look like an idiot.

"I'm not seeing anyone, either. In the future, if one of us is.…"

He responded as if reading her mind. "We let the other know in advance?"

"Agreed. And, um, try to keep the noise down."

This time, *his* face was pinkening. "I sleep with earplugs anyway."

Connie slapped the table. "Me too! My dad's snoring sounds like a freight train."

"It was never quiet at ODAAT. My last roommate talked in his sleep." Sid grinned and then turned serious. "Speaking of, I don't want alcohol in the house."

She was so glad he'd brought it up. She'd known it was an issue but hadn't written it down. "That won't be a problem."

Sid folded his hands in front of him. "I've been sober for almost a year. I can be around people who are drinking, like in a restaurant, but if it's here in the apartment, I'm afraid I'll be tempted. Does that make sense?"

"I think so. But, hang on, you were at the party when the bookstore closed down. There was booze there."

"Yeah, that was hard. I stuck close to my uncle most of the time. That made it easier. And then, I was talking to you and didn't think about it." His eyes crinkled with his grin.

"Oh." She didn't know what to say. She remembered the conversation; it was the first time they'd met, and they'd talked about books. She'd been surprised to meet a man who read romance novels and suggested authors for her to check out. They'd been interrupted when one of Sid's cousins came to talk to him, and he'd left earlier than Connie. The party wasn't nearly as fun after that.

She closed her notebook and shoved it away. "I'll type this up and send you a copy. We can make amendments as things come up."

"Sure."

He seemed so cavalier about the whole situation. Obviously, he hadn't lain awake at night worrying whether his pajamas were presentable.

"I'm gonna finish unpacking and hang up my clothes."

"I'm done. It's easy when all your belongings fit into one bag." He tipped his head to the side, indicating the pile of what was supposed to be a complete bookshelf. "I can put together that bookshelf and hook up the TV."

"Would you?" She smiled her thanks. "And then, shall we have supper together? Mom's chili."

"Sounds like a plan."

He refilled his glass of water and took it into the living room. Placing the glass on the coffee table, he squatted to make sense of the disassembled shelves. The movement drew her attention to his perfect backside filling out his worn jeans like they were made for him. Seeing that perfection every day would make it awfully hard to remember they were roommates, and only roommates. Something had nagged at her since they agreed to share the apartment.

"Hey, Sid."

"Hmm?" He peered at her over his shoulder.

"Why did you change your mind?" At his furrowed brow, she went on, "I mean, you obviously didn't want to share the apartment with me, but then you did. Why?"

He rolled his eyes. "My mother assumed the second bedroom would be for her. You were a *much* better choice." He turned back and started putting the shelves together.

"Oh." Connie headed into her bedroom and closed the door. A better choice than his mother. What a ringing endorsement that was. She stuffed all thoughts of a mutual attraction deep inside and wrenched open a suitcase, the well-being that had suffused her moments ago leaking away like a deflated balloon.

Insomnia had never been a problem for her. Connie checked the clock on the bedside table. One a.m., which meant she had five hours before she needed to get up. The room was dark and relatively quiet. Heavy curtains blocked out street noise, and she had her trusty earplugs. It had been a busy day, and her body drooped with exhaustion, but her mind churned like a hamster on a wheel. Each image in her brain featured the face of the man in the room next door.

After dinner, he'd cleaned up the dishes, taken a shower,

and left for a meeting. She'd puttered around, pleased to have the place to herself, but grew restless after a while and had to remind herself that they shared an apartment—reluctantly on his part, apparently—and she should not expect him to hang out with her. She'd grabbed her laptop to work on the grant she was applying for and got lost in the minutia of filling out forms. When she'd heard Sid's key opening the door, she'd perked up. He'd murmured a greeting, then retreated to his room, and she'd gone to bed shortly after that.

She punched her pillow and shifted. The bed was new, and she wasn't used to the mattress. It was firm and lacked the body-sized divot she'd spent years creating. And she had to pee.

Hauling herself out of bed, she debated the necessity for a bathrobe. All the goods were covered by her baggy, red plaid flannel pajamas. Besides, Sid was asleep. She snuck out of her room and down the hall to the bathroom, closing the door behind her before turning on the light. She'd finished her business and was washing her hands when she heard a noise. She listened. Sid was up and moving around.

Go back to bed or go see what he was doing? She was awake and far too curious. On silent feet, she crept down the hallway.

He sat on the couch, hunched over the coffee table. A newspaper was spread before him. The lamplight was too low for her to see properly, but it looked like…filling a pipe? Oh God! They'd talked about booze but not drugs. This would not do.

"What are you doing?"

He reared back. "Shit! You scared me."

Something clattered to the table, and he fell back against the couch. His long hair hung loose, and he pushed it back from his face. "You nearly gave me a heart attack."

Connie crossed her arms. "I repeat. What are you doing?"

They turned when the tea kettle started whistling. Sid rose and brushed past her. "Right now, I'm making tea. After that, I'm gonna go back to carving." He turned off the stove and poured the water into a teapot sitting on the counter. He twisted around, crossing his own arms. "Is that okay with you? Should it be added to the house rules? No carving after dark?" His shirt hung open, exposing a smooth bronze chest, and he hadn't tied his hair back. With the thick slash of his eyebrows and his flattened lips, he was no longer the easy-going man she'd come to expect.

Salivating over his lean frame right now was a bad idea. Heart thumping, she stared down at her bare toes and then up at his hard, unsmiling face. There was nothing relaxed or amused in the way he looked at her. Gesturing at the coffee table, she murmured, "I'm sorry. I couldn't see properly and I…."

"Jumped to conclusions?" he supplied, his words clipped.

She winced. "Maybe."

Sighing, he turned away and pulled two mugs from the cupboard. "It's decaffeinated. Do you want some?" At her nod, he filled the cups. "I said I'm sober, and I meant it. Besides, drugs scare me."

"Yeah?" She took the mug he proffered, cradling its warmth.

"Yeah. I'm afraid to try them. I'm afraid I'll like them too much." He walked over to the couch and sat.

She took a seat next to him and pointed. "That *is* a pipe, though."

He picked it up, holding it for her to see better. "Yeah. Uncle Dan, Cal's father, smokes a pipe. I'm making this for him."

Taking in the intricate cuts, she was impressed. "Wow. That's really good. Is it a bear claw?"

"I'm glad you figured that out. Otherwise, I haven't done a good job." He put the pipe on the table and sipped his tea.

"Do you normally work during the night?"

He shook his head. "This place is a big adjustment. The bed, the room to myself, the quiet. I couldn't sleep. You?"

"Same. I've always lived at home."

"You didn't go away for college?"

She huffed. "I wish. No, I did two years of community college before switching to UW. My family lives in Ballard, so it didn't make sense for me to live in the dorms. It's a three-bedroom house with one bathroom, and I have two younger sisters." She looked around the tidy living room. Other than Sid's carving tools, everything else was hers. "I'm kinda used to chaos, and this is just weird."

"I moved around a lot when I was a kid," he said quietly, looking down at his cup.

"Oh. Was that good or bad?"

While Sid took his time replying, the sound of a truck accelerating up the hill came through the window.

"Both, I think. My mom is—hopefully, you won't have to meet her. She's a narcissist. The world revolves around her, and I was in the way most of the time. I stayed with Uncle Dan and Aunt Angie off and on until I finished school. Then I worked wherever I could. Fishing boats, gas stations, tree trimming. I was at Cal's grandparents' place a lot."

"The bookstore?"

"Yep, and their house. They and Cal's parents kind of adopted me. Gram invented jobs for me to do, things she said required a strong back, in order to keep an eye on me. I even had my own bedroom." He picked up the pipe and a tool that looked like an icepick and made deft strokes, leaving divots and swirls.

Connie relaxed against the cushions and watched him work. His hair had fallen forward, and he'd push it back over his shoulder only for it to fall forward again. She got up, went to the bathroom, and came back. "Here," she said. "A leftover from when I had long hair."

He accepted the hair tie and pulled his hair back into a tail. "Thanks."

She watched him work for a while longer in the quiet intimacy of the lamplight, thinking she could get used to it. She gave her head a shake. Those thoughts wouldn't do her any good at all. "Thanks for the tea. I'm gonna try to get some sleep." She took her mug into the kitchen and put it in the sink. "Are you gonna stay up for a while?"

"For a while. I don't have to be anywhere until late afternoon." He sat back until shadows covered half of his face. He looked relaxed yet watchful, watching her.

She waited, hoping he would ask her to stay, wanting to continue their conversation. But it was the middle of the night, and they were just roommates, so she lifted a hand in a little wave and said softly, "Well, good night."

His reply was equally soft. "Good night."

When she got to her room, she peeked back over her shoulder. He was still watching. Catching her eye, he nodded. "Sleep well, Consuela."

It wasn't until she snuggled under her comforter, sleep overtaking her, that she realized he'd used her full name and had spoken in Spanish.

She smiled and drifted off.

CHAPTER 4

The laundry facilities were on the first floor of the building. Three washers and a large sink against one wall. Four dryers were facing them, and in the middle was a big island with a flat countertop for sorting and folding items. The machines were coin-operated, and Cal had warned Sid to stock up on quarters, saying that if he wanted to avoid the other tenants, to do his laundry around noon. He was about to start the washer when a quavering voice scolded him.

"You didn't separate your laundry! The whites will come out dull and dingy if you mix them in with colors."

He turned to find a tiny, round woman scowling at him. Favoring her right leg, she walked in and hefted a laundry bag onto the island. "Young people treat everything like it's disposable. Get a hole in a sock? They toss it out. They don't darn. They don't know how to treat a stain. Pah!" She muttered away without looking at Sid, separating her laundry like it had offended her.

Sid didn't argue. He'd been doing his own laundry since he learned to read. He'd once washed a red washcloth with his white socks and underwear, turning them pink. His mother told him it was his own fault, refused to buy him new ones, and the other kids at school laughed at him. Aunt Angie bought him new socks and underwear in gray. To this day, Sid didn't own anything white and washed everything together, calling it his "unified laundry method."

He started the washer but whipped around when he heard a gasp. The woman was bent in half, clutching the edge of the island in a white-knuckled grip. "What? How can I help?" He rounded the counter to see something had fallen to the floor. He picked up what turned out to be underwear and put it on the counter. The woman snatched it away.

"Pervert! You leave my panties alone." One hand pressed against her hip, she glared at him.

Raising his hands in surrender, Sid backed away. "Just trying to help."

"I don't need any help."

Under her narrow-eyed glare, he left the room, hoping the other tenants in The Firs were less cranky. Maybe he could pay Connie to take care of his laundry to avoid future run-ins.

After running a few errands, he shook off the rain before entering the lobby of the apartment building. One wall was lined with a bank of mailboxes. A container for recycling junk mail stood underneath them, as well as parcels that had been delivered. Sid didn't bother to check his mailbox or look at the parcels, knowing that Connie would have done so already. He ignored the ancient elevator and took the stairs, his steps muffled by the carpeting. He let himself into the apartment. It was dark and quiet, and he knew he was alone. He hadn't really wanted to talk to her, but he was oddly disappointed. Their agreement was to share the apartment for six months and then go from there. It was even in the house rules that they would discuss the situation after six months. At first, living with a woman he wasn't related to had been awkward.

After a couple weeks, they were slowly getting into a routine.

He liked her. She was the tidiest individual he'd ever met but didn't fuss at him. Unlike his mother, who'd practically lived in front of the bathroom mirror, Connie didn't take forever in the bathroom. She smelled good and looked even better. Her baggy pajamas couldn't hide her figure, and Sid made a point of only looking at her face. One day, she'd left a lacy pink bra hanging on the back of the bathroom door, and he'd just about had heart failure. She didn't need to know the thoughts running around in his head. She'd think he was a pervert, just like the laundry room lady.

He hung up his jacket, left his boots in the closet, and headed into the kitchen to make tea. And stopped. His teapot, his grandmother's teapot, lay in pieces on the counter. Beside it was a note.

I'm so sorry!!! If I can't fix it, I'll get you a new one. Sorry!!!

He swallowed past a lump in his throat and picked up what used to be the handle. He knew it was an accident and that it was just an object, but Gram's memory lived in it. She'd be the first to tell him not to get sentimental over an old piece of old pottery, but sadness washed over him anyway. He'd liked looking at it, cupping the round belly in his hands, and remembering the many times Gram made him a pot of tea and encouraged him to talk. Pops would be sitting at the counter listening and carving away. Gram wasn't always patient and could be gruff, especially with a scruffy, scowling teenager who was angry at the world. Sid missed her every damn day. He found a paper bag under the sink and dropped each piece of the broken teapot inside. He tucked the bag in the back of his closet, stripped off his clothes, and climbed into bed.

❋

"He'll understand, and he's not going to be mad," Connie repeated the words as she got out of the car. From where she'd parked, she could see their apartment. None of the lights were on. Was that good or bad? Sid didn't have a routine or a set schedule, and it wasn't her business what he did during the day or what hours he kept. He was clean and quiet and agreeable and easy on the eyes. He'd understand.

She hadn't meant to break it. She didn't even know it was there. Which was stupid. She'd seen him make tea multiple times without thinking that he had to put it somewhere. She'd blindly shoved a bag of rice in the cupboard above the fridge only to have the teapot come crashing down. And shatter. It broke into so many pieces she wasn't sure that she'd collected them all.

Climbing the stairs to the apartment, she muttered, "He'll understand."

She slid a key into the door lock, then turned at a noise behind her. The hallway was empty. The murmur of a TV came from a few doors down. She glanced at the door opposite and saw a shadow move in the gap where the door met the floor. Someone was watching her through the peephole. She was tempted to stick her tongue out or flip the bird. Instead, her concierge training kicked in, and she waved cheerily. She hadn't met any of the neighbors yet, and she crossed her fingers, hoping it wasn't a creepy old guy who'd stare at her chest every time they met.

The apartment was silent and dark. She closed the door softly behind her and turned on the lights before opening the closet. Sid's jacket was hung up, and his boots were on the floor. She passed the kitchen and looked down the hall. His bedroom door was closed, and the lights were off. Releasing a soft sigh of relief and frustration, she returned to the kitchen and spotted the sticky note. The pieces of the teapot were gone. They weren't in the garbage or the recycle, and she wondered what he'd done with them. Walking the short distance from the kitchen into the living room, she stopped and looked at his bedroom door again. Was he asleep? She checked the clock on the kitchen stove. Eight p.m. Her gaze drifted down to the floor and snagged on something that looked like a button. Crouching down, she picked it up. The shiny brown ball was the finial from the lid of the teapot. Should she leave it on the counter for Sid? Deciding to give it to him face-to-face, she called it a night and headed for her own room.

Connie crossed off an item on her list and closed the planner. "That's it," she said to the faces on her Zoom screen. "I'll be sending in the grant application tomorrow and hopefully will hear back from them by the end of the month."

The executive director for CSEC raised her hand for a virtual high-five. "Good work. If we can secure that grant, we can hire two mental health counselors to liaise with the high school. All right people, meeting adjourned. Have a good afternoon."

Connie waved at the others and clicked out of the meeting, sinking back into her chair. She ran a hand through her hair. Staring at herself on a Zoom screen made her realize she needed to find a hairstylist. The curls were getting out of control but weren't long enough to pull back into a hair tie.

Footsteps sounded, and Sid entered the kitchen wearing another flannel shirt and jeans.

"Oh, I didn't know you were here. I hope I wasn't too loud." She made a mental note to find her earbuds and use them for future Zoom meetings.

"It's fine." He didn't look at her as he poured a glass of water and downed it.

"I'm so sorry about breaking your teapot. I didn't know it was there and knocked it off the shelf and—"

"It's fine."

"—if you give me the pieces, I can put it back together. I've got some great glue, and you won't even be able to see the cracks. Oh, and I found—"

Tension radiated off him, and he snapped, "I said it's fine. I know it was an accident, so just leave it." He rinsed out the glass and put it in the drain tray, then stalked out. Minutes later, the front door opened and closed.

Connie was alone, feeling worse than when she'd broken the stupid teapot.

CHAPTER 5

"Earth to Connie." A hand waved in front of her face.

"Oh." She blinked. "Sorry about that." She looked around the coffee shop, then back at her friend-slash-client.

Delia sat back, head tilted. "No problem. I was just saying I like your suggestions and to go ahead and update the website."

"Good." She nodded, folding and unfolding her napkin before stuffing it into the empty coffee cup on the table before her.

The beautiful blonde across from her flicked a hand at the open laptop between them. Connie did technical support and maintained the website for Delia's organizing business. It had grown to the point that she now had a waiting list months long. She specialized in older people needing to downsize, usually to prepare for entering assisted living. She had a knack for being diplomatic and tactful, often suggesting to clients that they keep photographs of their treasures instead of the treasures themselves.

"That's all? You've been nagging me for weeks to look at them, and all I get is 'Good'? What's up? Something's bugging you. Is it that handsome roommate of yours? Did you leave your underwear in the bathroom again?" Delia grinned.

Connie hid her face in her hands and shuddered. Sid hadn't said a word but would not look at her all that day. "I wish. No, I broke his teapot. I apologized and offered to replace it or fix it. He accepted my apology, but I know he's still angry and he has every right to be but...." She looked up to see Delia's wide-eyed look. "What?"

"Was it a big ugly Brown Betty teapot?"

Connie nodded, feeling something like dread crawl up her spine.

"Honey, that belonged to his grandmother and was the only thing he wanted when they cleared out the shop." Sympathy dripped from Delia's words, and Connie wasn't sure if it was for her or Sid.

"Really?" she breathed out on an unhappy sigh.

Delia nodded. "He told me once that his best memories revolved around drinking tea with his grandmother."

Family and traditions meant a great deal to Connie. Neither set of grandparents lived close, and if she were to lose the photographs and keepsakes she had from both her grandmothers, she'd be devastated. "And I broke his memory keeper?" She didn't think she could feel any worse.

Delia winced. "Maybe I shouldn't have told you that."

Connie's throat got tight as she fought back impending tears. She stuffed her planner and laptop in her bag and rose from the table. She was out the door of the coffee shop without saying goodbye.

"*Y*our girlfriend is standing in the dumpster."

"Excuse me?" Keys in hand, Sid turned from the apartment door to the voice behind him.

The tenant from across the hall, a tall, angular woman in

a Snoopy sweatshirt, stood in her open doorway, leaning on the frame of a walker. "I said," she spoke louder, enunciating each word carefully, "your girlfriend is standing in the dumpster." Not waiting for a response, she shuffled around and closed the door behind her.

"Girlfriend?" He gaped at the apartment door until realization dawned on him. "Connie?"

Stuffing his keys in his pocket, he rushed down the hallway and down the stairwell, turning right at the bottom, down the first-floor hallway, past the laundry room door, and out into a narrow courtyard. The graveled area held dumpsters and recycling bins for Sid's building and its neighbor. It was just big enough to accommodate the large trucks that came by each week to empty the containers. The sun was going down, and he squinted into the growing shadows. The place seemed empty, and he wondered if the old bat was imagining things. A clang told him otherwise.

"This should be in recycling. Honestly, what is wrong with people? Too darn lazy, that's what it is."

A piece of cardboard flew out of a dumpster, narrowly missing him. He moved closer and peered over the edge. Connie was bent over an open garbage bag, lifting out each item with a gloved hand, examining it, and then placing it in another garbage bag. Piled behind her were a bunch of unopened bags, while in front of her was a neatly stacked pile of what he assumed were the bags she'd gone through. "What are you doing?"

"Gah!" Connie leaped back, the beam from her flashlight swinging around wildly.

Sid raised his hands to block the light. "Connie, it's me. Sid."

"Oh," she said, one hand going to her chest. "It's you."

"Yep, it's me. And I repeat, what are you doing?" He almost gagged as a waft of decayed something came toward him.

She twisted around, went to put her hands on her hips, must have thought better of it, and let them hang loose by her sides. "I'm looking for the pieces."

"The pieces?"

She bobbed her head, brows scrunched together. "So I can fix it. I know it's not going to be perfect, and you may not be able to use it anymore, but I can glue it back together so it at least resembles what it once was." She gestured to the bags behind her. "I've only got a few more to go through. And I want to know why everyone uses black garbage bags. From now on I'm buying a different color. If I ever have to do this again, I'll be able to identify ours."

He forced himself not to smile. It was possibly the nicest yet dumbest thing anyone had done on his behalf. "It's not in there."

"What?"

"I said it's not in there. Here," he extended a hand, "let me help you out."

She stuffed the flashlight into a pocket and shuffled toward him, peeling her gloves off and tossing them behind her. Taking her hand, he guided her to the side, and she clambered over the edge of the dumpster to stand in front of him. "Thank you." She peeked up at him from beneath long lashes, then looked away.

"You're welcome," he replied, resisting the urge to point out the food stains on her clothing. He took a tentative sniff. Was the smell coming from Connie or the dumpster itself?

"What did you do with it?"

"I collected the pieces into a paper bag and put it in my room. My closet, to be specific."

Her shoulders slumped. "I never thought to look there."

"My room?" Putting a hand on her elbow, he led her toward the door.

"No, the closet. I did look in your room." She shot him a guilty look. "You're awfully neat and don't have much stuff, and I didn't really touch anything. I'm sorry, I shouldn't have done that."

"No, you shouldn't have." He didn't point out that was an item on their agreement. "Why didn't you just ask me?"

She stopped in front of him, twisting her hands together. The light over the door picked up the sheen in her brown eyes. Tears? "You were so upset, and Delia told me the teapot was all you had from your grandmother, and the garbage gets picked up tomorrow, and I wanted to fix it so you'd still have your memory keeper."

A memory keeper. He'd never thought of the teapot that way, but it was an accurate description. He did smile at her this time, at her perception, and to let her off the hook. "I've got all the pieces. We'll figure out something to do with them."

She sniffed. "You're not mad?"

"No, I'm not mad." Things were crap right now, but they had nothing to do with Connie. *Her* mother helped them move in, stocked their refrigerator, and frequently called Connie. Just to check in, see how her day had gone, and if they had enough food. On the other hand, Violet had run up her credit cards and wanted Sid to pay them off. No wasn't a word she was used to hearing, and she'd hung up after screeching that Sid was an ungrateful little shit. To top it off, a friend from ODAAT who'd maintained his sobriety for many years fell off the wagon and hadn't been seen for a while. The broken teapot was the least of his concerns right now.

He opened the door and guided Connie into the laundry room. "How about I go get your bathrobe and laundry detergent, and you can throw those things into the washer?"

"Oh." She glanced down at her clothes and then back up at him, looking both embarrassed and grateful at the same time. "Thank you. My robe is hanging behind my bedroom door, the detergent is under the bathroom sink, and there's a bowl of quarters on my dresser."

"Got it." He closed the door before heading down the corridor.

All the things that could have gone wrong went through his mind. What if she'd gotten injured or bitten by a rat? What if 3B hadn't seen her? They were so new to this roommate thing; would Sid have paid attention if she wasn't home? Shit. She could have really hurt herself, yet she'd climbed into a dumpster to find the broken pieces. She'd done that for *him*. He didn't know how, but he would let her know how much that meant to him.

He hesitated at the door to their apartment, then crossed the hall to knock. The sounds of slow footsteps and the clanking of a walker came through the door. It opened. "Yes?" Sparse eyebrows peaked above smudged glasses.

"Thank you. I appreciated that."

The woman grunted and then closed the door.

CHAPTER 6

After retrieving her bathrobe, Sid stood outside the closed door of the laundry room so she could change without an intrusion. She came out in the ratty old flannel robe to find him waiting, hands shoved in his pockets. The fluorescent light directly over him created more shadows than illumination. She couldn't see his eyes, but the hard line of his mouth seemed to soften. He narrowed the distance between them and raised a hand. Her breath caught, and then he pulled a tiny piece of Styrofoam out of her hair.

"Oh," she said with a shaky laugh. "Thanks."

His lips twitched. "Not a problem."

They walked back to the apartment in easy silence. She showered and emerged from the bathroom wearing clean clothes to find Sid watching TV on the couch. He rose when she entered the living room.

"Would you like some tea?" He glanced over his shoulder as he walked into the kitchen.

"Umm, sure." Connie plopped down in a chair at the table to watch him. "You got a new teapot!"

He nodded. "I did. And this one is metal. You can't break it."

Her shoulders stiffened then relaxed when he turned to her with a smile and a wink.

"I picked it up at a thrift store and got these at the same time." He held up two white mugs. One embossed with a bold C and the other with an S. He delivered the cups of tea to the table and went back for a plate of cookies.

"Oh," she said, taken aback by the simple gift. "That's... that's so nice. Thank you."

He sat across from her, picking up a shortbread cookie and dunking it in his tea before eating it.

Outside the quiet apartment came the sounds of people walking down the corridor, heading to their apartments. Connie had lived in the same house in the same neighborhood her entire life. It was strange for her to live so closely with others and not know who they were. When she'd worked as a concierge, even though she didn't live in the building, she had spoken to most of the residents or at least knew them by name.

The alarm sounded on her phone, and she turned it off. At Sid's questioning look, she said, "The washing machine should be done in a few minutes. I didn't want to forget about my clothes."

She sipped her tea, thinking about the circumstances that led her to be doing laundry at this time of the day. She got up, went to her bedroom, and returned. "Here," she said. "I found this."

Sid accepted the finial for the teapot lid without a word. He cupped the round ball and moved his thumb back and forth across the rough texture of the broken edge. His Adam's apple bobbed, and he nodded once. "Thanks."

She waited to see if he'd say more. He'd accepted her apology and said it was fine, but she hated disappointing people. "Would you *please* let me put it back together?" she pleaded.

"It really is all right." He stuffed the finial in his pocket. "This is just fine."

"No, it's not." She waved a hand around the apartment. "It's the only thing you have from your grandmother. Now you don't have anything to remember her by."

"That's not true. Remember all that junk in the back room of Jimmy's Joint?" Sid's eyebrows went up.

Connie nodded. Delia had shown her photos of the mounds of stuff accumulated by Cal's grandparents that Delia sifted through on Cal's behalf.

"Delia found this for me." He pulled out his wallet, extracted a folded photograph, and handed it to her. A scrawny young man stood with his arms around a much older man and woman. All three wore big smiles.

Connie giggled. "Oh my God. Is that you? And is that Gram and Pops?"

"Hey, give me a break. I was seventeen," Sid protested with a mock-scowl. "Yeah, that's Gram and Pops. Delia found a bunch of photos and is going to digitize them for me. But this one I wanted to keep with me."

Handing the photo back to him and feeling better than she had in hours, she watched him study it with a fond look before putting it away. "I'm glad you've got pictures of them, but I still want to fix the teapot." Then she switched gears and asked, "How did you know where I was?"

He tipped his head to the side. "The lady across the hall told me."

"Oh."

"I think her apartment overlooks the alley. She could probably see you."

"I'm sure that was entertaining. Have you noticed her watching you through the peephole?"

"No." Sid frowned. "That's weird."

Connie shrugged. "I wave at her door before I come

inside. I think she's lonely and doesn't get out much. What did she say to you?"

"Only that you were standing in the dumpster." His cheeks went pink, and he reached for another cookie.

"Have you met any of the other tenants? I saw an old woman collecting her mail, but she just grunted when I said hello."

"A lady scolded me for not sorting my laundry," Sid said in a flat voice. "And then she called me a pervert and accused me of trying to steal her underwear."

"Seriously?" she gaped. "Why would she do that."

"She dropped something, and it looked like she was in pain, so I picked it up for her. Turned out to be a pair of underwear."

Connie laughed.

"For a tiny woman, they sure were big."

He spoke just as she was taking a drink, and her laughter turned into a choking cough. Looking alarmed, Sid got up and came back with a paper towel. He thrust it at her.

"You all right?"

She wiped her eyes. "I will be."

A muffled expletive came from the front door, and they rose from the table, entering the hallway in time to see a folded piece of paper slide under the door. Sid lengthened his stride and pulled the door open in time to see their land-lord, Fred, rising from a crouch.

"Oh, hi," he said, straightening up. "I wasn't sure you'd be home, so I was going to leave you a note." The sixty-ish balding Black man addressed Connie over Sid's shoulder, then nodded at Sid.

Fred retrieved the paper from the floor. "I'm glad you're here. This will be easier to explain in person." He rushed on. "Nothing bad. May I come in?"

Sid opened the door wider, stepping aside to admit Fred.

He raised an eyebrow at a shrugging Connie, and they turned to follow Fred into the living room.

Their landlord indicated a colorful poster of the Skagit Valley tulip fields, then the furniture. "I've owned this building for many years, and I always find it interesting how tenants furnish their apartments." He chuckled. "You two have made this real cozy. I don't think Cal ever put anything on the walls."

Sid shoved his hands in his pockets and gave the man a small smile. "My cousin was a minimalist."

"I'll say." Fred ran a pink-palmed hand over his dark, gleaming head, looking around the apartment. "You settling in okay?"

"We are, thanks. The building is in really good shape, and the tenants we've met seem…nice." Connie remembered her manners. "Please, sit down. And would you like a cup of tea?"

Fred sat on the couch, shifting to settle his bulk after putting the folded paper on the coffee table. "No, thank you."

Sid gestured for Connie to take the armchair, and he leaned against the side of it.

"Did Cal ever tell you about the arrangement we had?"

Sid and Connie looked at each other and back at Fred, shaking their heads.

"I live on the top floor of this building, and I own two others here in Seattle. I also have a house in Maui. I like to go away for the winter months, and while Cal was living here, he was the building super while I was gone. A janitorial team comes in once a week, but Cal kept an eye on the building, let me know if there were any problems, and fielded tenant complaints." He looked directly at Connie. "With your experience as a concierge, I was hoping you two would take that on. I have a list of plumbers, electricians, etc., to take care of repairs, so there isn't any heavy lifting on your part except for depositing rent checks. All but four tenants pay by bank transfer. Two don't like computers, and one had an issue with identity theft."

"That's only three," Sid stated.

Fred chuckled, looking sheepish. "The last is my ex-mother-in-law. When I made the switch, I sent letters to each tenant explaining the process. Evelyn returned hers to me with a note that said, 'I don't think so.' We've never talked about it again."

Connie looked up when Sid nudged her shoulder. His eyebrows were raised in a silent question. She shrugged imperceptibly then looked over at Fred. "We've noticed that it's all older people living here, and they seem to be all women."

Fred bobbed his head. "We're close to the senior center and on a major bus route. Both those things are important to older people. I used to contact the director of the senior center when I had a vacancy. That hasn't happened for a long time. Except for Cal and now you, Sid, I haven't had a male tenant in years. These old gals like it here and aren't ready to move on."

"Do they all live alone?" Connie asked.

"Yep. They've outlived their partners or never had one in the first place. Two of my aunts live one floor down. They each have their own apartment. They're practically inseparable but would no doubt kill each other if they lived together. I have emergency contacts for each of the tenants and will give that to you if you decide to do this."

"Can we get back to you? We need to talk this over."

Fred nodded and rose from the couch. "Certainly. I do have a property management company I've used before, but the tenants like it when there's a person on-site to talk to. The details are on that paper, as well as my contact information. Can you let me know in the next few days? I'll be leaving for Maui in a couple weeks and would like to get this settled."

"Will do." Connie followed Fred down the hallway. When he opened the door, he waved at the peephole across the corridor. Connie did so as well before closing the door behind Fred and heading back to join Sid.

He held up his cell phone, telling her, "I texted Cal to find out his experience. You've done this kind of thing before, what do you think?"

She picked up the paper to look over the details. "Fred says none of the tenants are ever late with the rent, so we won't have to hunt them down. He's given us names and numbers for the contractors he uses. Other than having to make a deposit at the bank once a month, it shouldn't be hard. And the compensation is—" Her eyebrows winged up.

"What?"

Connie gulped. "Our rent would be reduced by half."

"Wow." Sid's eyes rounded. "That's kind of hard to turn down." His phone dinged, and he looked at the incoming message, then grinned. "Cal said it was the easiest money he ever made. The worst thing he ever had to do was unclog a toilet."

"Pfft." Connie waved a dismissive hand. "Been there, done that. I guess we're in."

CHAPTER 7

If there was a twelve-step program for people addicted to writing in planners, Connie would be an ideal candidate. She was often up before Sid, and he'd find her sitting at the table with one of many planners open in front of her and different colored markers spread out on the table. He'd find her drinking her coffee and staring off into the distance. Assuming she was journaling, Sid made as little noise as possible. Different planners seemed to have different purposes.

After accepting Fred's offer, Connie put together a binder for the apartment building and proudly showed it to Sid. She'd used colored tabs to divide the sections into tenant information, contractors, a repair log, tenant complaints, Fred's to-do list, and his contact information. Sid made polite noises but otherwise ignored the binder; he was pretty sure he'd never have to use it.

Besides agreeing to be on board, Sid hadn't done a darn thing. Fred communicated with Connie, giving her the lowdown on each of the residents, gave her a master key, keys for emptying the coins in the laundry machines, and instructions on making bank deposits. Fred showed her and

Sid the maintenance room with its furnace and hot water tank. It contained the industrial vacuum and cleaning supplies the janitorial service used when they came by weekly to vacuum the hallways, clean the laundry room, and wash the plate glass windows of the lobby. Connie sent Fred off to Hawaii with a breezy aloha and told Sid she wanted to have an open house and invite the tenants to stop by their apartment for punch and cookies.

"No," he said.

"What?" Connie stood in the doorway to his bedroom, looking surprised. Like making small talk with strangers and letting them wander through their home was the greatest thing in the world.

He inserted a bookmark and put his book on the bed beside him. "No."

"But this is a great opportunity to introduce ourselves. These ladies are used to Cal and Fred. We're unknown quantities, and if we want them to trust us, they need to get to know us. They're older women living alone and we need to—"

"No we don't. We don't need to do anything besides what Fred asked us to."

"But—" Connie sputtered.

"I did not hear Fred ask us to do wellness checks." Sid rose from the bed and brushed past Connie.

She followed him into the kitchen. He opened and closed first the fridge and then the cupboards. He wasn't hungry. He wasn't thirsty. He wasn't interested in having this conversation. Turning to glower at Connie, he found her smiling beseechingly.

He pointed at her. "That's not going to work. You can't just give me big eyes and a hopeful smile and expect me to go along with your harebrained ideas."

"It's not a harebrained idea. Neighbors get along better when they get to know each other. The same thing can happen here. When we become friends with the tenants, our interactions will have less tension."

The woman in the laundry room who'd accused him of stealing her underwear came to mind. Connie might have a point.

"Not only that," Connie continued, "the pandemic has been hard on seniors. Especially those who live by themselves. Isolation becomes a habit that isn't healthy. Socializing is good and helps to build community."

He couldn't argue with her. COVID kicked everyone's ass, and no one came through the pandemic completely unchanged. He gave in. "Fine. But not here."

"But—"

He held up a hand. "Host it in the laundry room. It's neutral territory, and people are in and out of there all the time."

She glared at him through narrowed eyes, drumming her fingers against the kitchen counter. A smile slowly appeared as she turned to pick up one of her planners. "That's actually a really good idea. I'll print up a notice to put under each apartment door so tenants can drop by for a few hours."

Sid choked. "A few hours? No. Make it a coffee hour." He could see a protest forming on her lips and added, "I will be there for one hour. That's it."

"Excellent!" she said, bouncing on her toes. "This is going to be great."

Sid hoped so.

The storage closets of the old apartment building were a veritable Aladdin's Cave of Wonders. Connie had dashed off an email to Fred, telling him what she intended and asking if she could expense the cost of the food.

He'd given his blessing and told her to use whatever she could find in the closets.

Connie dug up an old coffeemaker that made up to forty cups. Next to it was a big glass punchbowl and a stack of metal trays. Someone in the building used to entertain. She scrubbed everything in the huge sink in the laundry room, debating whether to buy regular or decaf coffee.

Except for his promise to attend, Sid did not get involved at all. He eyed the stack of trays but didn't say anything. He perused her shopping list but didn't comment. When he saw her ironing a brightly colored tablecloth, his eyebrows shot up, but he remained silent. It made Connie anxious and defensive. Was it too much or not enough? She wanted to talk to Delia, but she knew Delia would talk to Cal, who might mention it to Sid. Instead, she texted Kevin, one of the partners in Grand Gestures, a premier event planning company in Seattle. A friend of Delia's, Kevin was generous, business-savvy, and got right back to her.

"How many people are you expecting? What are their dietary restrictions? What is your budget, and what is the purpose of the event?"

"Why, Kevin. I'm fine, thanks for asking," Connie teased.

Kevin groaned. "You're a friend. I thought we were beyond the need for social niceties."

"Not all of them. Did I catch you at a bad time?"

"Not really. I told my mom I'd help out with a function at her church, and it's snowballed." He sighed. "She knows I can't say no to her."

"Is she taking advantage of you?" Connie had met Eleanor Armstrong once and thought that if she didn't already have a wonderful mother, she'd want Eleanor to adopt her.

"No more than usual. Now, pull out your planner 'cause here are my suggestions."

The day of the get-together came, and with it, her climbing nerves.

With a testy, "I'll be there. I promise," Sid left the apartment.

Connie didn't blame him for being testy; she was a bit of a basket case. She flitted around the apartment impatiently watching the clock, with nothing to do but wait. She was all caught up with work, the apartment was clean and tidy, and her laundry was folded and put away. She tried reading, but the book didn't hold her interest, and she had too much energy to stream a movie or TV show. She looked at the closed door to Sid's bedroom, tempted to go in and organize his underwear drawer. Finally, *finally*, it was go-time, and she set to work transforming the laundry room into party central.

Tenants came through and set upon the food like locusts. Two women brought Tupperware containers that they filled with cookies from the trays. Another brought a thermos that she filled with punch right from the bowl. A few muttered hellos and suspicious glances were directed at Connie. Otherwise, no one spoke to her. Then they were gone, leaving a smattering of sandwiches, scones, and cookies in their wake.

Connie blinked back tears as she surveyed the decimated buffet. She didn't know what she expected, but it certainly wasn't this. Part of her was glad that Sid hadn't shown up. He probably would have smirked and said I told you so. She set about cleaning up. She gathered all the goodies onto one platter and picked up the empty cups and plates. At least the laundry room was close to the dumpster, and she didn't have to lug trash bags from her apartment. At a quarter to four, she considered calling it quits when she heard voices in the hallway.

Moments later, three women entered. One was tall and thin, leaning on a walker, a bright orange scarf that complimented her umber skin wrapped around her head. Beside her was a smaller woman with the same dark skin, small wireless glasses, and gray hair scraped back into a tight bun. With them was a much younger woman, closer to Connie's age.

"Hi," Connie chirped. She leaped up from where she'd been sitting beside the coffee maker and waited to see if they would speak to her.

The two older women directed tight-lipped smiles at her while the younger woman smiled openly. She had warm, light brown skin and soft, kinky curls in a mixture of browns and golds. "Hi," she greeted Connie with a smile. "I'm Vivian Thompson. Fred is my father." She indicated the taller woman. "This is my great-aunt, Jean Sinclair," then the shorter woman, "and my great-aunt, Grace Thompson."

"It's lovely to meet you all." Connie clasped her hands in front of her, inclining her head at each woman.

Vivian nodded at the empty trays stacked neatly behind the punch bowl. "It looks like you had quite the party. I'm sorry we couldn't get here sooner."

"I told you to avoid the Arboretum," Ms. Thompson muttered.

"I'll remember next time Auntie," Vivian replied. To Connie, she explained, "I drove my aunts to a meeting at their church, and traffic was heavy."

Connie nodded her understanding. "Do you live in the building as well?"

"My aunts are on the second floor. I live in Columbia City."

Ms. Thompson eyed the platter and spoke in a belea-guered voice, "It would be better for everyone if you lived here with your father, but no one listens to me."

"Yes, Auntie." Vivian rolled her eyes like she'd heard that before, then turned back to Connie. "Dad told me that your fiancé is Cal's brother?"

Connie poured coffee while the women filled their plates with sandwiches and scones. She answered Vivian with a chuckle, "No, there's been a misunderstanding. Sid and I aren't a couple, we're just roommates, and Cal is his cousin, not his brother."

"That Cal was a handsome man. If his cousin is as good-looking, maybe you should introduce yourself." Ms. Thompson nudged her great-niece with a gleam in her eye. "Wouldn't that make your gran happy?"

"Auntie!" Vivian scolded.

"Grace!" Mrs. Sinclair hissed.

Ms. Thompson shrugged and sipped her coffee. "Just saying."

Vivian shook her head and explained to Connie, "My grandmother on my mother's side lives here as well. Not everyone…gets along in the family."

Ms. Thompson snorted while the others pretended not to hear her.

There was the sound of running feet, and then Sid burst through the door.

"Sorry I'm late," he said, meeting her gaze directly and looking contrite.

A collective sigh went up from the others. His cheeks were flushed, and his hair had come out of its ponytail. He looked windblown and…yummy.

"Oh, my," Mrs. Sinclair murmured.

"Um hmm," Ms. Thompson agreed.

Vivian smiled but didn't say anything.

Connie pressed her lips together. "Ladies, this is my roommate, Sid Fraser."

He nodded at the others and came to stand by her side. "An accident was blocking the West Seattle bridge. I'm sorry I missed most of the party."

Connie smiled tightly. "Well, the best people are here now."

Sid had the complete attention of the women. Mrs. Sinclair and Ms. Thompson eyed him with open appreciation as he removed his wet jacket and hung it on the door-knob to dry. He rolled up the sleeves of his flannel shirt, exposing sinewy forearms, and turned toward Vivian. "I was at the Coast Salish Education Center."

"I don't believe I know where that is." Vivian looked at him with a frown on her pretty face.

"It's next to the Duwamish Long House and Cultural Center on West Marginal Way."

Vivian shook her head. "I must have driven past and just not noticed it."

Shoving his hands in his pockets, Sid rocked back on his heels. "It's umm, fairly new." The three women looked at him expectantly while he stared down at his shoes. Waiting for him to continue, Connie noticed the wet sawdust clinging to his jeans and dusting his shirtsleeves. The others had clearly noticed as well. Ms. Thompson murmured something to her sister, who nodded. Connie thought that it served him right for being late. They would have fielded the stares together if he'd arrived on time. But no, he'd taken off and left her to handle everything.

Keeping her exasperation to herself, Connie said, "Sid is an instructor in Indigenous carving. My family isn't Coast Salish, but I work for CSEC as well. I work with small busi-nesses and do grant writing. What do you do, Vivian?"

"I'm an insurance inspector."

"She travels the country making sure buildings are up to code to ensure employees are working in a safe environ-ment," Mrs. Sinclair said proudly.

"Safety is important," Ms. Thompson chimed in.

Vivian grinned at her aunts. "You make me sound like a superhero."

Keeping an eye on Sid, Connie further engaged the women. She learned that the two aunts had once been next-door neighbors but sold their suburban homes a few years ago and moved into their nephew's building. Vivian had an older brother who lived in Hawaii, and she had never lived in The Firs. Connie got the idea that with her grandmother, father, and two great-aunts living there, she would have little alone time.

Sid didn't actively participate in the conversation but made appropriate noises and facial expressions, indicating he was following along. An alarm went off on Connie's watch, and she silenced it, saying, "It's four o'clock." She indicated the nearly empty platter and asked the ladies, "Would you like to take some things with you?"

"Thank you, but no," Mrs. Sinclair replied. "We really appreciate you doing this. It was lovely to meet you both and put a face to a name. Right Grace?"

Ms. Thompson had stuffed one last cookie in her mouth and nodded vigorously. She swallowed and bobbed her head. "Yes. Are either of you readers? We have a book group that meets monthly, and you're welcome to join." While she addressed both of them, she looked directly at Sid.

Feeling him stiffen beside her, Connie jumped in, "That sounds lovely. Let us know the dates, and we'll see what we can do. What kind of books do you read? I'm a fan of romantic suspense but don't care much for thrillers."

"I like historical romances. Lynn Winchester is a favorite," Mrs. Sinclair declared. "Your cousin introduced us to a lot of authors. For some reason, he didn't care for Stacy Wrigglebottom. I don't know why because I quite like her books. Especially the most recent ones."

Vivian ushered her aunts out the door, telling them she'd join them shortly. Turning back, she told Sid and Connie, "Once they get going on books and authors, they can go for hours. It was great meeting you both. Thanks for doing this." She sent a dazzling smile in Sid's direction before leaving.

Connie slumped against the island as Sid gusted out a breath beside her.

"Was everyone like that? Full of questions?" he asked.

She shot him a narrow-eyed glare. "They were the only ones who spoke to me. No, wait, someone asked me where, and I quote, 'that long-haired young man' was. I couldn't answer." She unplugged the coffee urn and made to pick it up, but he got there first.

"Do I dump it down the sink?"

She nodded then watched him pour out almost the entire urn. The punch had been a hit, but hardly anyone drank the coffee. Sid emptied the remainder of the punch and asked, "Do you want to wash or dry?"

That was unexpected. She'd figured that if he didn't have the courtesy to show up on time, he wouldn't bother helping with the cleanup. "I'll wash." Scrubbing something would be therapeutic. Sid took the leftover food up to their apartment and returned with a couple of dish towels, a dishcloth, and dish detergent. They cleaned up the laundry room and returned the urn and party supplies to the closet without speaking.

Sid returned from taking out the garbage and recycling and stood in the doorway. "Anything else?"

"No."

"Fine."

"Fine," she echoed.

"Good." He tugged his jacket on and went out the back door into the growing dark.

Picking up the cleaning supplies, she stomped up the stairs to the silent apartment. The door to the hall closet was ajar, and she slammed it shut, but it bounced back and caught her in the forehead. "Ouch!" Tears filled her eyes as she rubbed the tender spot. Just great. A perfect ending to a perfect day. She dropped her things in the kitchen and went into the bathroom. A red mark bloomed above one eyebrow and would turn into a beautiful bruise. Her hair wasn't long enough to cover it, and it would no doubt lead to questions.

The truth was too damn embarrassing. She could just see the conversation.

"Yeah, I slammed the door in a snit."

"And why were you in a snit, Connie?"

"Because the tenants in my building were rude, and my room-mate showed up late to the coffee hour, and then he helped me clean up and left."

"Where did he go?"

"I don't know."

"Why was he late?"

"I don't know!"

There was the rub. When Sid left that morning, she had no idea where he was going and hadn't asked. He worked for himself and didn't have set hours. She sniffed and caught the scent of cedar. Following her nose, she went back to the hall closet. Inside, she found Sid's backpack, fragrant with cedar.

Crap! She pulled out her cellphone and scrolled to find the calendar for CSEC. What she saw there made her groan in self-disgust. She'd scheduled the coffee hour Sid hadn't even wanted to do for the same day as the first woodcarving class he was teaching. He hadn't said anything, and she didn't know how he felt about leading a class.

Connie drew energy from being with people. Speaking in front of others did not bother her in the slightest. She thought back on all her interactions with Sid when other people were around. He didn't hide or run away. If work was to be done, he took care of it. He was always a quiet presence who didn't draw attention to himself. Today, he was supposed to teach a class—for what she assumed was the first time—and then rush home to smile and interact with more strangers. No wonder he'd been testy. This was her idea, and she'd all but guilted him into doing something he didn't enjoy, then treated him like crap for arriving late. If she were in his shoes, she wouldn't want to hang around the apartment, either.

How could she make it up to him? Chewing on her bottom lip, she stared into the fridge for inspiration. Left-over tea sandwiches and cookies were not going to cut it. Fortunately, the last time she'd visited home, her mother had given her many containers of soup. Connie pulled one from the freezer. While that thawed, she set about making biscuits.

It was fully dark by the time Sid returned. He entered and quietly hung up his things. From the corner of the dimly lit living room, Connie saw him pass the kitchen without a glance and head toward his bedroom.

"Hey," she said quietly, relieved he was finally back.

"Shit!" He jumped and placed a hand over his heart. "What the hell?"

"Sorry!" Connie hurried over, clutching her hands in front of her. "So sorry. I didn't mean to startle you."

He let out a shaky laugh. "Well, you did." He shot her a glance then turned away.

"I made supper. Well, I mean, I heated up supper, but I made biscuits."

"I'm not hungry," he said, opening the door to his room and turning on the light.

The dismissal hurt, but she pressed on, eager to get them back on an even keel. "How was your day?"

The light from his bedroom highlighted the droop of his shoulders and the lines on his face. He'd pulled his hair back into a ponytail, and she could see the tightness in his jaw. "My day was fine."

"Was it fine," she gestured broadly, "or was it, you know, FINE?"

"I have no idea what you're talking about." He wasn't tall, but there was enough of a height difference for him to look down at her.

"You know, FINE the acronym: F'd up, Insecure, Neurotic, and Emotional." She knew she sounded like an idiot, but at least she had his attention. If she held on to it long enough, she would apologize, he would accept it, and she'd be able to go to sleep not feeling so pushy and self-centered. Because she wasn't. At least, she didn't *try* to be.

He stared impassively at her for a beat, then spoke through gritted teeth, "The first fine. My day was okay."

While baking the biscuits, she'd envisioned them sitting at the table while he told her about the students in his class and what he planned to teach them. He'd ask her about the women who'd showed up for the coffee hour, and they'd laugh.

"Okay. Well, good." She gestured at the living room. "Do you want to tell me about it? And I'm so sorry I scheduled the coffee hour for the first day of your class. If you had told me, I would have rescheduled. In fact, why don't you give me your schedule so I can put it into my calendar?"

His mouth set into a hard line. "Look. Our agreement was to share the apartment and now the super's responsibilities. I'm not used to someone tracking my movements and don't particularly want to be accountable to you. Thank you for wanting to share your supper, but I've already eaten. And if you don't mind, I'd like to be by myself." With that, he entered his room, closing the door softly but firmly behind him.

CHAPTER 8

The beauty of being self-employed was the ability to work where he wanted. He wanted to work at ODAAT. That's what the original intention was when the organization received an influx of donations. Rooms would be renovated to accommodate Sid and a group of other artisans, mostly Indigenous men. They'd be able to create in a space where alcohol wasn't permitted, protecting them and preventing them from giving in to temptation. However, ODAAT had hit a construction snag, and the studios weren't available. CSEC had great spaces, but he didn't want to interact with the well-meaning but too chatty staff eager to know more about his carving.

The first class had gone okay. He wasn't expected to teach by himself; an accomplished older artist who sort of reminded him of Bob Ross had basically interviewed Sid while he worked. Asking him about the wood, his tools, and his process. The high school kids bused up from the Muckleshoot tribe had been interested and respectful. They'd each been given a precut block of cedar and a set of tools. By the end of the four-week session, they should be able to make a recognizable animal figure. No one got injured on the first day, which Sid considered a win, but it was exhausting. Connie's coffee hour and being late for it hadn't made the day any better.

Could he have been nicer to her? Probably. He'd caught the wounded look in her eyes when he closed the door on her. He'd wanted to apologize and explain, then hug her to make up for the sting of his words. If he'd done that, held her in his arms, he wouldn't have wanted to let her go. She was sweet and soft and smelled so damn good. But they *were* just roommates, and it was better that Connie understood that.

He set about preparing to work from home. He hadn't told Connie, knowing she would jump right in, trying to make everything perfect for him. No doubt she would have rearranged the furniture to ensure he had the best natural light.

He covered the table with an old sheet on which he'd laid out his tools and the chunks of cedar he intended to carve into three nesting bowls. He wished his grandfather could see him. He'd taught Sid how to carve as a way to keep him busy and out of trouble. He now had the opportunity to make a good living from something he enjoyed doing—if he didn't screw it up.

He put that thought aside and picked up the smallest piece of cedar, cupping it in his hands. He closed his eyes and inhaled, taking in the scent and envisioning the finished product. A fat bowl with a wide base, maybe with an indent in the lip for pouring liquids. He reached for a tool, preparing to make the first cut.

A knock sounded, and the knife slipped. "Shit." Sid looked at the blood welling from the pad of his thumb. He sucked on it to stop the bleeding.

The knock came again, more insistent this time. Passing through the kitchen, he grabbed a paper towel and pressed it against the wound. He pulled open the door. "Yeah?"

"You're not Cal," a woman said in an offended voice. She

came up to his shoulder, her pale pink scalp shining through iron-gray hair pulled into a tight bun. She peered at him from behind thick lenses.

"No, I'm not."

She drew the edges of her sagging cardigan around her and crossed her arms. "When is he going to be back?"

Sid resisted the urge to roll his eyes. "He moved out a few weeks ago. This is my apartment now."

She looked him over from top to bottom, then walked away, calling over her shoulder, "Fred's not home, and my microwave isn't working." At the elevator, she pushed the button and turned back. "Well? Are you coming?"

He wanted to blame Connie for the interruption, but he'd agreed to taking on this responsibility. Mind you, if he hadn't opened the damn door, the woman would have left a note, and Connie could have handled the problem. "Yeah," he muttered and closed his door. He strode down the hallway to join the woman. They rode down to the second floor and silently walked to her apartment.

He followed her into the kitchen, and she pointed at the offending appliance.

"When did it stop working?" he asked.

"Sometime this morning. It worked for a few seconds when I was heating up my breakfast and then stopped."

Small appliances, a bread box, and a set of canisters in the shape of panda bears cluttered the countertops. He pressed the top of the electric can opener to see if it worked. Dead as well. Oddly enough, the clock on the stove worked.

"Let's, umm, let's unplug the microwave and plug it back in."

The woman huffed. "I tried that already."

"Humor me," he softened the order with a tight smile. He unplugged the microwave and plugged it back in. Nothing. That was the extent of his electrical expertise, and inwardly, he cursed Connie.

Her voice came to him from the open front door as if summoned by his thoughts. "Hello, Mrs. Land? It's Connie Ortega. May I come in?"

"Great. Tweedledum is here." In a louder voice, the woman, who was apparently Mrs. Land, called, "Come in."

Carrying a toolbox, Connie entered the kitchen looking like a professional. She smiled at them and said, "When I got home, our neighbor said you were having a problem, so I thought I'd come and see if you needed help."

Mrs. Land pointed at Sid. "He certainly does."

Connie flicked a sympathetic glance at him, further escalating his irritability. She put the toolbox down, propped her hands on her hips, and looked around at the crowded kitchen counters. "Was anything else plugged in?"

Mrs. Land shrugged. "Probably."

Connie tried again. "Were you running another appliance? The coffeemaker, maybe?"

"Hmm." The old woman tapped a gnarled finger against her arm. "The coffeemaker was on, and I was using the electric can opener."

Connie looked at the outlet behind the microwave and pressed a button. The microwave beeped, and she pushed it back into place, grunting in satisfaction. "The circuit was overloaded." She beamed at Sid. "It can't handle so many items operating at the same time."

"Thank you. I'll take that note off Fred's door so he won't come by," Mrs. Land said gruffly.

"Fred is in Hawaii for the next few months." Connie pointed to a folded pink paper on a stack of unopened mail on the dining table. "Either my roommate or I can help you if you need anything."

"I'll keep that in mind." Mrs. Land uncrossed her arms and led the way to the door.

Sid grabbed the toolbox before Connie did. "I've got it." At least there was something he could do.

The door to the apartment across the hall was open, and another older woman stood there with bright eyes. "Hello," she chirped, looking at them inquisitively. "I'm Clarice. You must be Sid and Connie. Everything all right? What did you do now, Evelyn?"

"Mind your own business," Mrs. Land glowered at the other woman, then closed her door behind Connie and Sid with a slam.

Clarice emerged fully from her apartment, wearing a baggy cardigan and thick glasses. Sid wondered if it was a uniform for women in what he assumed were their seventies. She differed from Mrs. Land in that her iron-grey hair curled tightly against her scalp, and her skin was the color of aged ivory. "Don't mind her. Cranky is her reaction to everyone and everything."

"I'll keep that in mind," Connie replied. "It was nice to meet you, Clarice. I'm expecting a phone call and need to get back to the apartment."

"Nice to meet you, dear. I'm so sorry I didn't make it to your coffee hour. I had a doctor's appointment at the same time," she explained.

"Not a problem." Connie shook her hand and then headed off.

Clarice turned to Sid with her hand extended.

"Nice to meet you, ma'am." He accepted her hand, careful not to squeeze it.

She tsked and took his hand in both of hers, poking at the paper towel wrapped around his thumb. "What did you do? Do you need a bandage? Stitches?"

"It's fine." He tried to pull away, but she was leading him into her apartment. She'd probably tumble to the floor if he snatched his hand back. Maybe break a hip. Sid sighed quietly and allowed her to lead him.

"Sit, sit." Clarice forced him into a chair at her table then turned the stove on underneath a teakettle. She left him alone and headed off to what he assumed was the bathroom. Her apartment was the opposite of her neighbor's. Her countertops were bare, the sleek Scandinavian furniture did not overwhelm the room, and nothing cluttered the surfaces besides a book on an end table.

She returned carrying a container filled with first aid supplies and put it on the table. "I went through this stuff last month and threw out anything that was expired. Wash your hands, and let's take a look at that."

"Thank you, but that's not necessary. I doubt I even need a bandage."

Clarice waved a dismissive hand and moved toward the stove. She pulled the whistling teakettle off the burner and set about making tea in a pot she'd unearthed from a cupboard. "Nonsense, it's no trouble at all."

Sid swore to himself and headed to the bathroom. By the time he washed his hands and returned, the old lady had placed the teapot, milk and sugar, mugs, and a plate of store-bought cookies on the table. She'd set out gauze, tape, and antiseptic ointment and was snapping latex gloves on her hands. She beamed at him from her seat at the table.

He took his own seat and placed his injured hand on the table, palm up. "See, it's stopped bleeding."

Clarice peered at his thumb, then squeezed it, looking triumphant when blood welled up. She wiped the blood away, applied the disinfectant, then wrapped and taped his thumb.

"I think you've done this before," Sid stated. He'd expected a bulky bandage but could move his thumb easily.

"I have three sons, ten grandchildren, and two great-grandchildren. So, yes, I've kissed a booboo a time or two. And I used to be an emergency room nurse." While speaking, she cleaned up the detritus, then settled back down to pour the tea. "Milk and sugar?"

Sid doctored his tea and accepted a cookie, recognizing that it would be a while before he could escape.

Clarice sipped her tea and looked at him expectantly. "It's lovely to have a young couple in the building. Have you and your girlfriend been together long?"

"We're just roommates."

Peering at him over her glasses, Clarice said, "I sense there's a wee bit more between you two." Then she patted his hand. "Don't look alarmed, dear. I've been around the block and am pretty good at reading people."

"That may be, ma'am, but I think you're reading too much into that."

Clarice sipped her tea and waited.

"We're really just acquaintances who agreed to share an apartment. You know what rents are like in this city."

She waited some more.

He wasn't about to bare his soul to this stranger, but if he didn't satisfy her curiosity, he wouldn't be leaving. "I think Connie is very...." What could he say? That her competence and energy overwhelmed him? That he was trying to maintain a distance but perked up when he heard her footsteps down the hall? That her presence calmed him and excited him at the same time? "Nice."

"Nice? The weather is nice. These cookies are nice. My pastor is nice. Nice is the lamest, blandest, most overused descriptive in the human language." She wagged a finger at him. "Try again."

Sid played with the handle of his mug, looking everywhere but into the perceptive eyes of the woman sitting across from him. "I am...attracted to Connie. But now is not the time to act on it. I've had limited experience with relationships, as in zero. And I've got a lot of sh—I mean crap to sort out. When I do...." He wagged his head from side to side. Would he act on it? And if he did, would Connie be receptive? Only if she were a glutton for punishment. He didn't want to hurt her, so being civil was the best thing for both of them. He finished his tea and rose from the table.

Clarice rose as well. "Thanks for indulging me. It's nice to meet a new face."

Sid cocked an eyebrow at her. "Did you just say nice?"

She laughed. "You caught me."

Sid smiled and picked up the toolbox before heading toward the door. "Nice to meet you, Clarice."

onnie opened the big binder to the repair log section.

She detailed Evelyn Land's problem on the first page in neat block letters. Using a ruler, she made a few columns. She debated whether to enter the apartment number or the tenant's name. In the end, she decided on both. She labeled the last column, Resolved. Under it, she put the date and her initials. Just as Sid entered the apartment, she capped her pen and hurried into the hallway to greet him.

"That went well, don't you think? Our first tenant issue resolved."

He nodded, lifting up the toolbox with a raised eyebrow.

"Oh, that can go in the closet. I used to keep one just like that under the concierge desk at The Arches and decided, what the heck, I'd get one for here. I figured it would be faster to have basic tools on hand, and if we need anything more than that, we can get them from Fred's closet."

Sid put the toolbox in the closet, then brushed past her to go through the kitchen to the table. He started to pack up his carving tools.

Connie stood in the doorway to the kitchen and chattered away, watching his deft movements. "You were gone for a while. Did Clarice have a problem? If so, you can write the details down in the notebook I started. I think it's worthwhile to track these things for Fred."

Sid didn't turn around, instead folding up the sheet that had covered the table. "She didn't have a problem. She gave me a bandage, and then we drank tea."

"Oh." She blinked at his brusque tone. "Oh! You should have told me you needed a bandage. I have a first aid kit under the bathroom sink. It's got antiseptic, gauze, bandages of all different sizes—"

"I know where it is. I didn't have time to get one before answering the door."

"I didn't know you were going to be working here today. How did it go? Make much progress? I see you were using a bed sheet to protect the table. I can probably find a fitted vinyl tablecloth if you'd like."

"No, thank you. The sheet works just fine." He gathered his supplies and went into his bedroom, closing the door firmly behind him. Moments later, he was back out and heading for the front door. He didn't look at her as he yanked his jacket out of the closet. "I'll be back later."

She stared at the closing door. What had she done? She returned to the table, closed the binder, and put it away. All her energy and enthusiasm left the apartment with Sid. Being roommates with him no longer seemed like a great idea, and she wasn't sure how much longer she could handle it.

CHAPTER 9

"Hey." The furrow between Cal's eyebrows belied his relaxed greeting. He opened the door to the apartment he shared with Delia and waved Sid inside. Aware of his muddy shoes and the gleaming hardwood floors of his cousin's home, Sid toed off his boots and placed them to the side. Cal took his jacket and hung it in the closet before leading the way to the living room.

"Thanks for letting me come over."

He'd taken the bus down to ODAAT only to discover that he'd missed one meeting and the next wouldn't take place for another two hours. Too restless to wait, and with no one around he wanted to talk to, he started walking. The cacophony of the evening rush hour jangled his nerves, and he hunched his shoulders against the press of other pedestrians. The mist hovering all day turned into rain, and he pulled his hood up. In front of him, someone opened the door to a restaurant and held it open for others to enter. Inside, people were smiling and laughing. The lights of the interior glinting off the bottles displayed behind the bar. It looked warm and inviting, and Sid had money in his pocket, and it was so tempting. He stood rooted to the sidewalk, staring at the bottles until the man holding the door open called out, "You going in?" Sid shook his head and turned in the opposite direction. He called Cal.

"Delia's at a client's place, and I'm done working for the day, so it's not a problem. Happy to see you. Want something to eat? I'm heating up some stew I found in the freezer."

The days Sid had lived on the streets, Cal, more specifically Jimmy's Joint, had been his port in a storm. Usually hungover, Sid would clean up in the old bookstore's bathroom, changing into clothes Cal kept on hand just for him. He'd eat whatever was on hand, drink bad coffee, and leave with a new-to-him backpack full of supplies. Cal never pressed, simply provided.

Sid took a seat at the kitchen counter and gusted out a breath. "Sure. Thanks."

Cal moved around the kitchen, getting out bowls and utensils, moving to the stove to taste the stew. "A couple more minutes," he decided. He filled the kettle with water and placed it on a burner. Opening a cupboard, he pulled out a box of Tetley tea and glanced at Sid. "I hear you had to get a new teapot."

"How did you know?" At Cal's smirk, he realized Connie must have told Delia, who told Cal.

"What are you going to make with the pieces? I know you didn't throw them out."

Sid shrugged. "Not sure yet." He'd found all the pieces except for the button on the lid. When he realized it was missing, he got down on his hands and knees, searching along the baseboards. He even looked under the stove and fridge. Like discovering a piece was missing in a jigsaw puzzle, the incompleteness nagged at him. Then Connie found it, and he'd been carrying it around in his pocket, rubbing his thumb across the rough edges.

Cal grunted, then handed placemats and cutlery to Sid. "Make yourself useful and set the table."

Sid complied, wondering briefly what Connie would have for dinner. He felt a pang of guilt for leaving so abruptly. He dismissed the thought, knowing the competent woman was capable of feeding herself.

Cal brought over the bowls of stew, and they settled down to eat their meal. When they finished, he poured tea into mugs and handed one to Sid. "You gonna tell me what's up?"

"Nothing's up," Sid muttered.

"Sure, that's why you're here eating leftovers at my place. Nice Band-Aid, by the way."

Staring at his thumb, Sid said, "A tenant knocked just as I was making the first cut on a project."

"Ouch." Cal winced. "Somebody trip a breaker?"

"How'd you know?"

Cal shrugged. "Happened all the time. You press in the GFCI button, and you're out of there."

"How come everyone knows these things except me?" Sid grumbled.

"Not everyone knows, especially if you've never had to reset one."

Sipping his tea, Sid mulled that over. That made sense. It also made sense that Connie would know. He thought about the binder she'd put together. If he'd bothered to read it, no doubt he would have figured it out. "Well, shit."

"What?"

He smoothed a hand over his head and tightened his ponytail. He told Cal about the tenant and Connie's easy competence.

"And?"

"And I walked out of the apartment feeling like a useless idiot."

Cal refilled their mugs with tea. "What exactly did she say to you?"

Closing his eyes, Sid thought about the exchange, the

smile on Connie's face. What had she said? "'Our first tenant issue resolved.' Or something like that."

"Did she gloat?" Cal asked.

Sid shook his head.

"Say something to belittle you?"

"No." Sid rose from his chair and walked to the window. Night had fallen and behind his reflection, Cal watched him, drinking his tea and not saying anything. Something niggled at the back of Sid's consciousness. Taunting him. He spoke to Cal's reflection, "She is constantly making lists and writes everything down in notebooks. She's got one for CSEC, one for personal stuff, and she made a big binder for the apartment building. It's got details about who to contact when things break down and information about the tenants. She was real proud of it when she showed it to me."

Cal pointed toward the home office he shared with Delia. "Oh, I know. Delia has a shelf full of notebooks. I've heard her and Connie geek out over them."

No doubt there was something in Connie's binder about GFCI buttons. Too bad he couldn't be bothered to look through it. She certainly had the right to say, "I told you so!" but he'd left before giving her the opportunity.

"God, I miss Connie!" Delia exclaimed.

In the reflection, Sid watched her close the apartment door, shrug off a coat with jerky movements, and stalk into the living room. Cal shifted in his chair, holding his arms open. The tension in her frame disappeared as she stepped into his embrace, leaning down to kiss him. She stood with a sigh and shifted to sit on Cal's thigh. "It's good to be home."

Cal pushed her blonde hair to the side and nuzzled her neck. "It's good to have you home."

Sid watched their easy intimacy, happy for his cousin but not wanting to be a voyeur. He cleared his throat. "I'm gonna get going."

"Oh, hey!" Delia grinned at him. "It's good to see you. You don't have to take off."

Cal lifted Delia off his knee and stood. "Yeah. Keep her company while I get supper for her."

Delia joined Sid by the window. She removed her boots and wiggled her feet on the carpet, smiling. In her stocking feet, she was the same height as him. Sid had been awestruck and slightly intimidated the first time he'd met her. He still thought she was gorgeous but had relaxed around her and could now carry on an intelligent conversation without blushing.

"How are things going with you and Connie?" Before he could answer, she went on, "For purely selfish reasons, I wish she were still the concierge here." She twisted to include Cal in the conversation. "Remember I was waiting for that package to arrive? It should have been here two days ago. I stopped at the desk to see if it arrived, and Michel said no. I called the company to find out what had happened, and they sent me the signed acknowledgment that it had arrived. So I stop at the concierge desk just now and ask again. Michel says, 'Oh, you mean this package?' He hands it to me and sniffs. He sniffed!"

"He *is* French," Cal pointed out.

Delia looked at Sid and rolled her eyes. "When Connie was here, everything ran like clockwork. She has the patience of a saint when it comes to maintaining my website —never condescending. I think she just genuinely likes helping people. Not everyone is like that. Especially Michel."

"All right, I'm done complaining." She blew out a sigh and walked over to the chair Cal held out for her. She kissed his cheek before sitting. "Thank you, babe."

"You're welcome." He pushed her chair in, then kneaded her shoulders.

She turned and smiled up at him, murmuring something that made Cal lean down and kiss her again. It was definitely time to go. Sid said his goodbyes and headed to the front door. He stepped into his boots and was reaching for his jacket when Cal joined him. "You okay?" he asked.

"I will be. Thanks, man."

"You're welcome. You going to be at Thanksgiving dinner?"

The holiday was a week away and would be Sid's first time at a family Thanksgiving meal since Pops had passed. "Absolutely. I'll catch a ride up with you."

Cal scratched the side of his nose. "I won't be there. I'm going to Delia's parents' place for Thanksgiving."

That made sense. Cal was no longer a single man. "Yeah? Can they put on a spread like your mom's? Her mashed potatoes are the best."

Cal stepped closer and lowered his voice. "Delia's cooking the turkey. It's her first time, and I'm a little nervous."

"You'll survive." He clapped his cousin on the shoulder and headed out the door.

The rain had stopped, so he decided to walk back to the apartment, thinking Delia was correct. Connie just seemed to like to help people. She'd been excited about fixing the outlet and hadn't done anything to hurt his feelings. It was his own damn fault.

With the exception of the light over the stove, the place was dark when he returned to the apartment. Sid's shoulders slumped. He'd practiced his apology the whole way home, and now he'd have to wait until tomorrow. Canned laughter came from Connie's room, and a light shone beneath her closed door. Normally, she watched TV on the big screen in the living room. He knocked on the door.

"Yeah?"

"Hey. Umm, it's Sid." He winced. Who else would it be?

"Come in."

He opened the door and leaned against the frame. Dressed in baggy flannel pajamas and thick fuzzy socks,

Connie sat cross-legged on the bed, propped against a mound of pillows. Her laptop was open in front of her, a notebook and pen to her side. Blank-faced, she stared at Sid. "Yes?"

"I, umm, whatcha doing?"

"Watching a show."

"Right." He nodded, his gaze ping-ponging around the room. She left the door open during the day so he'd seen the interior, but her bedroom was at the end of the hall, and there was no reason for him to go inside it. "You've moved the furniture around."

"Yes. I was too cold at night with the bed underneath the window."

He nodded again. This was harder than he thought it would be. Maybe he could write a note and leave it on the kitchen counter. They could put a small whiteboard on the fridge and communicate that way. No muss. No fuss. No brown eyes narrowed at him. No guilt swirling in his gut.

"What do you want, Sid?"

He shifted from one foot to the other and fixed his gaze on a spot over her left shoulder. "I'm sorry."

"For what?"

"For walking out of here in a huff." There. He'd done it. He could look at her now. Her arms were crossed, and her gaze hadn't softened. "I felt like an idiot for not knowing about the GFCI reset button and took it out on you."

"Oh." The hard lines around her mouth disappeared, and the tension left her frame.

"So, yeah. I'm sorry for being a jackass." He raised and dropped one shoulder. "Is there something about them in that binder you put together?"

Her lips twitched. "Yep. Fred left a note about a few tenants who can't seem to grasp that they can't run all their appliances at the same time."

"Ahh. Well, good night."

"Sid," she spoke quickly as he turned to leave. "I was really worried about you. That you would...."

He met her frank gaze. "I thought about it. I didn't want to wait around at ODAAT for a meeting, so I went to see Cal. So, I'm good."

She rose from the bed and came to stand near him, the scent of her shampoo drifting toward him. Her hair was still damp from her shower, and she'd run her fingers through it at some point, making it stand up in tufts. He shoved his hands in his pockets to refrain from smoothing it down.

"If I'm worried about you again.... If you take off and I don't know where you are...would it be all right for me to call or text you? Not to pester you. Just to know you're okay?"

He'd never wanted to hug someone so much in his life. She'd been worried. "I'm sorry for that, too," he said in a softer voice. "I didn't think about that. That you would worry about me." He managed to keep his hands to himself and not stroke his thumb against the furrow between her brows until it went away. He kept his eyes locked on hers. "Absolutely. You can text or call me anytime."

She relaxed and gestured behind her. "Do you umm, want to watch something with me?"

The rest of the apartment was dark, and her room was warm and inviting. Was this really a good idea? How would he keep her at arm's length while sitting beside her on the bed? He looked down at the floor and saw her rubbing one fuzzy-sock-covered foot against the other. Allowing his gaze to travel back up over her baggy pajamas, past the silky-looking skin of her neck to focus on the apprehension in her eyes, he knew that saying no was not an option. He'd hurt her once today and would not do so again.

"Sure," he forced himself to say lightly like he didn't want to kiss her and explore the softness of her lips. "But only if you let me choose what we watch."

CHAPTER 10

Connie pulled the sticky note off the door and tried to decipher the spidery handwriting. She turned and held it up to her neighbor's peephole. "It looks like the toilet isn't working in 111. Should I be worried? Is the tenant an axe murderer?" There was no response, so she added, "If I'm not back in an hour or so, maybe call the cops."

She waved and headed to the stairwell, figuring she'd check out the situation before getting the toolbox. The peephole at 111 was framed by a wreath of autumn leaves and fake acorns. Beneath the door was a sisal mat decorated with more autumnal themes.

She smiled and raised her hand to knock as the door opened. A stout woman with carefully curled, thinning white hair frowned at Connie. The woman poked her head out to scan the corridor and asked, "Who are you?"

"Hi, Mrs. Dubchek, I'm Connie."

The woman glared at her. "How do you know my name? And where's Sid?"

Connie pasted on a smile. "Before he left, Fred gave us, that is, Sid and I, a list of all the tenants. Would you like me to look at your toilet?"

"I think I'll wait for Sid."

In the exclusive apartment building where she'd worked as a concierge, Connie had dealt with many absurd requests. This one barely registered.

"That's up to you, Mrs. Dubchek. However, Sid went out of town and won't be back until sometime tomorrow."

The old woman looked deflated. She sighed and pulled her door open. "Well, you're here. You might as well look at it."

Connie pressed her lips together and entered. Passing the galley kitchen, she spotted the china place settings on the dining table. A teapot, matching cream and sugar bowl, and a plate of cookies sat in the middle. Two delicate teacups sat on equally delicate saucers, with tiny spoons beside them.

The wall-to-wall carpeting muffled her footsteps as she followed Mrs. Dubchek. She stopped at the bathroom door while Connie went inside to assess the situation. She pulled the lid off the toilet tank and peered inside, then adjusted the ball cock until the water stopped running and replaced the lid.

"All fixed." She smiled. "I'll get out of your hair before your company arrives."

Mrs. Dubchek didn't look particularly pleased. "Fine," she huffed. She walked Connie to the door and mumbled a thank you before closing it behind her.

Connie headed back to her apartment feeling like she was missing something. On the floor in front of her door was a box of bandages with a sticky note attached to it that read, *It was <u>nice</u> meeting you.* A happy face was drawn on the note as well. She held the box up and addressed the peephole. "What do you think? Bandages or something else?"

Not expecting and not receiving an answer, she went inside and kicked off her shoes. She tossed the bandages onto the dining table and pulled out her phone to take a picture of it. She texted the photo to Sid, asking **know anything about**

this? When he didn't respond right away, she put the phone down and set about making dinner.

It was a long trek by bus to CSEC, and work was still being done on the studios at ODAAT, so Sid was still carving in the apartment. She didn't know if he was being considerate or was a naturally tidy person, but she never saw as much as a piece of sawdust. Everything would be packed up and stored on a shelf of their wall unit by the time she got home. Something had changed between them since the night he'd apologized about the microwave. He was still quiet but more relaxed and seemed comfortable around her.

One evening, she'd brought home Thai food and offered to share it with him. He, in turn, shared the stir fry he'd made. This led to them routinely eating together.

Once, after having some of the chicken soup he'd made, Connie declared, "This is so much better than takeout! Thank you."

Sid lifted a shoulder, looking pleased. "It's easy to make. I could…if you'd like…cook for both of us." He flicked a glance at her before looking down at his soup bowl. "Save us some money, and save you the hassle of stopping for food on your way home."

"Really?"

"Sure. I can have it ready for when you get here." He rose to clear the table. "You work some pretty erratic hours, and I thought this would be helpful to you."

Her heart went pitter-pat at his thoughtfulness and the way his cheeks pinkened up. Having dinner together, because that's what it sounded like, was something *he* wanted. "That would be awesome," she said, pleased with his generosity.

"Yeah?"

"Hell, yeah!"

He turned from the sink, his lips quirked up. "Good."

"But I'm paying half, and I'll do the dishes." She stepped up beside him and nudged his shoulder.

He smiled down at her. "How about we do the dishes together?"

It had been Connie's turn to blush. "Okay."

The memory made her smile as she opened the fridge. Chicken pot pie was left over from the night before, and a container of vegetable soup sat beside it on the shelf. Sid hadn't given her many details about his trip that week, something to do with looking at rounds of old-growth cedar that had been cut down near the Skagit River.

The emptiness of the apartment surprised Connie. His presence, and not just his cooking, was something she looked forward to every day. She worried she was too much of a chatterbox, but he'd reassured her, saying he was interested in what she did and happy to listen.

She pulled out the soup, knowing it would be good but not nearly as tasty as if she were eating it with him. She looked at her phone, but he still hadn't texted back. A knock sounded, and she headed to the door with a sigh. This landlord thingy was more work than she thought it would be.

She opened the door to three gray-haired women. "Hi," she said with more energy than she was feeling.

"Hello, dear," Clarice said. "You've met Helen Dubchek, and this is Mona Tseng. May we come in?" Without waiting for an answer, she patted Connie on the arm and pushed past her. The other two women did as well, Mrs. Dubchek shooting Connie a suspicious glare.

Connie watched the three shuffle their way into her living room. She addressed the peephole across the hallway. "Looks like it's a party. Wanna come?" A shadow shifted below the door, but there was no answer. "Suit yourself." Connie shrugged and went inside.

Mrs. Dubchek was firmly planted in the center of the couch, arms crossed over her substantial bosom. Mrs. Tseng sat next to her, hands primly folded in her lap. Clarice stood in front of the wall unit, holding the bowl Sid was working on.

Connie strode over and plucked it from her hands. "You have no business looking at that."

"Sorry," Clarice murmured, looking anything but.

A knot was forming between Connie's shoulder blades, and she forced herself to relax. "Now, how can I help you?" she asked again.

"You told Helen that Sid was out of town. Is everything okay?"

"He's definitely coming back? You didn't chase him away?" Mrs. Dubchek grilled her.

Connie sidestepped to block Clarice from entering the hallway to the bedrooms, shaking her head at the nosy woman.

Clarice sighed and went to sit in a chair.

"Sid is definitely coming back. Now, what is this all about?"

The three interlopers held a conversation that consisted of raised eyebrows, frowns, grunts, head shakes, and shrugs before Clarice spoke again. "Sid told me that you two aren't in a relationship."

Connie blinked. "Umm, no. We're roommates."

"He's not dating anyone?" Clarice pushed.

Connie shook her head.

"He may have a chickie she doesn't know about. You know, one of those friends with subsidies things." Mrs. Dubchek said to the others. They nodded and turned toward Connie.

It was quite possible. They'd discussed overnight guests in their apartment but not spending the night with someone somewhere else. The thought deflated her. She didn't want him to be smiling at someone else. To be cooking for someone else. And definitely not sending those unexpectedly heated looks at someone else. She could only answer honestly. "I suppose. He could be."

"Hmm. We'll have to clarify that." Clarice slapped her thighs and stood. "I sure hope not because I think Sid and my granddaughter would make a lovely couple."

Connie gaped at her. "What?"

Clarice turned a satisfied smile her way. "My granddaughter is moving here from Chicago and could use someone to show her around. Sid would be perfect for that, and if they hit it off, well, that would be great."

"I wonder if he likes to dance." Mrs. Dubchek looked excited. "The Saturday after Thanksgiving, the Romanian Community Center is having a Polka and Poker night."

Mrs. Tseng beamed and spoke in a voice too low for Connie to hear. The others chuckled and headed for the door.

"If it doesn't work out with my granddaughter, your great-niece is next, Mona," Clarice replied. "We'll find someone perfect for Sid."

After the women left, Connie settled on the couch, no longer hungry. She'd wanted to point at herself and say, "What about me?" Yes, they were just roommates now, but it could develop, couldn't it? She picked up her phone and saw that Sid had read her text. He didn't respond. Granted, they didn't text very often. They didn't have long, rambling conversations or exchange silly memes like she did with Delia and her sisters. She looked back at their brief texting history. Except for him asking her if she liked coconut—which she didn't—Connie initiated their conversations.

Was he with someone right now? Was that why he wasn't answering? Flinging the phone aside and grabbing a pillow, she curled into a ball. A single tear trailed down her cheek as a sense of rejection settled over her like a heavy blanket.

❄

With each step down the corridor, tension eased from Sid, and his shoulders, hunched around his ears for the last twenty-four hours, resumed their natural position. He was pleased with the wood he'd purchased from the Skagit sawmill. He'd trekked through the woods with an old woodcutter, looking at fallen trees and envisioning the pieces he would make. He'd helped the old man and his grandsons saw the wood and haul it back to the sawmill. The price was fair, and they'd agreed to store it for him, which was good because he didn't think Connie would like it if he stacked chunks of cedar next to the dining table.

It was nice to have a choice about the wood he worked on. Less than a year ago, he'd be given warped and cracked pieces of cedar and told to carve breadboards for tourists. Which he gladly did to pay for his stay at the recovery center. Not for the first time, Sid wished Pops was still around, and Sid would tell the old man that he was right. Working with his hands did save his life.

He had spent the night in Tulalip at his aunt and uncle's house. If he'd stayed with his mother instead of Cal's parents, his sobriety would have been sorely tested. He couldn't avoid her completely, so he'd taken her out for dinner. Fortunately, Aunt Angie and Uncle Dan joined them. Knowing that Sid would be footing the bill, Violet chose the most expensive restaurant in the casino and insisted they be seated at a centrally located table where everyone would be able to see her.

Having worked at the casino off and on for years, Violet knew many employees. Each time she saw someone she knew, she'd brag loudly about Sid's stuff being in the gift shop and the money his carving brought in. He'd never liked being in the spotlight as a kid and hadn't learned to like it as an adult. His discomfort increased as the evening wore on. While his mother couldn't see it, his aunt and uncle had.

They'd come to his rescue, Uncle Dan declaring he'd forgotten his heart medication and needed to get home to take it right away. They'd dropped a disappointed Violet off before heading to his aunt and uncle's house.

He'd pulled into their driveway and sighed so loudly he fogged up the windows.

Aunt Angie leaned forward from the back seat to place a hand on his shoulder. "What do you need, sweetheart?"

Connie's face flashed before him. He wanted to drive back to Seattle. Walk into the apartment to see her sitting on the couch with her feet in fuzzy socks propped up on the coffee table. She'd be pounding away at her laptop, her curly hair in disarray because she was forever running her hands through it. He wanted to sit next to her and inhale her shampoo. Instead, he pulled the keys out of the ignition and smiled at his aunt. "A cup of tea and a game of cribbage would be nice."

His aunt won all three hands before heading to bed, leaving him and Uncle Dan alone in the kitchen.

"Another game?" Sid asked.

"Hell, no. My dignity can't handle being stomped on again." Uncle Dan packed up the cards and stowed them away. The underside of the crib board had a slot for the pegs and playing cards. Sid had carved the board and given it to his aunt and uncle when he'd been in high school. It was shaped like an orca leaping out of the water, its original black and white paint flaking away in spots.

"Thanks for bailing me out tonight." Sid wished there was a way to visit his aunt and uncle without having to see Violet.

"Not a problem. I've been dealing with your mother for more than forty years. I can put up with her."

"I wish you didn't have to." The words were out before Sid realized what he'd said. "I mean—"

"I know what you mean." The chair creaked as Uncle Dan shifted his weight. "I don't know what goes on in Violet's head, and I often wonder how she and Ange came from the same parents. You got a shitty deal when it came to mothers, and I wish we could have done more for you." He raised his hand when Sid opened his mouth to protest. "Let me finish. Could we have stopped you from addiction? Maybe yes, maybe no. But we could have done more so you didn't wind up on the streets."

"No, you couldn't. I knew you were here. I knew I could reach out, but I didn't want you to see me like that. It was bad enough that Cal did. I needed to find my own way to sobriety. I needed ODAAT, and I found it." He pulled the ponytail holder out of his hair to loosen the tightness in his scalp. "Nights like tonight, being around Violet, makes it hard to stay sober, but I'm doing it."

"Yeah, ya are. Good job."

Warmth washed through him, and he swallowed past the lump forming in his throat. He'd caused so much worry for his uncle over the years that it felt good to hear his words of praise.

He'd gone to bed feeling better and thinking about their conversation. Violet was headed to Puerto Vallarta with her newest boyfriend for Thanksgiving. Her not being present at his first family dinner in years was a huge relief and well worth the money Sid shelled out at her request. He pulled out his phone to look at the text Connie had sent hours before. He should have replied earlier but didn't know what to say. Telling her about the box of bandages was too complicated to explain by text. In the end, he sent a lame thumbs-up emoji.

Now he was home, and she was on the other side of the door, so he'd tell her about it now. Shifting his duffel bag to his other hand, he pulled out his keys.

The door across the hall opened, and Sid twisted to see his neighbor. "What's wrong?"

"Your girlfriend is trying to stop a fight."

"Where?"

"By the dumpster."

Sid dropped his duffel and raced to the stairwell. "Call 911," he shouted.

Heart pounding, he leaped down the stairs, rounded the corner, and charged down the corridor and out the door leading to the courtyard. Fortunately, there was no bloodshed. Unfortunately, Connie had gotten between two bickering septuagenarians. Arguing loudly, no one had noticed his presence.

Not knowing what was going on, Sid hung back and looked around the courtyard, trying to assess the situation.

In addition to the dumpsters for garbage and recycling, two large bins for composting had been added to the courtyard. The city had started a pilot program to encourage people living in apartment buildings to compost, and Connie had volunteered their building. Beside these bins, she'd set up a folding table for sorting recycling. Above it, she'd added laminated posters detailing what went into which category and how to prepare it. Each tenant received a small bucket for collecting food scraps. Two buckets sat on the table, one on its side; its contents spewed over the surface and onto the ground.

The two sisters, Jean Sinclair and Grace Thompson, were clutching cardigans around themselves and glaring at Connie, who stood between them, a wilted piece of lettuce draped over one shoulder.

Mrs. Sinclair said something in a low voice that Sid didn't catch.

"You don't know everything, Jean," Ms. Thompson hissed.

"Maybe not, but I know that plastic is not compostable."

Ms. Thompson sniffed. "It is if it touches food. Tell her, Connie."

Connie grimaced, clearly not wanting to take sides. "Sorry, Ms. Thompson. Your sister is right."

"I told you so!" Mrs. Sinclair crowed. She beamed and turned to clean up the table.

Ms. Thompson stuck her tongue out at her sister's back. "Fine, but I was still right about that meatloaf." She included Connie in the conversation. "I tell her that Tony Chachere's makes everything better, but she refuses to listen."

Mrs. Sinclair waved at the spilled bucket. "Are you going to stand there talking, or are you going to help me clean this up? The news is about to start, and you know I don't like to miss that."

"I'll help you." Ms. Thompson looked at Connie. "Will you please get me a broom and dustpan?"

Connie smiled, looking relieved. "Maybe Sid should do it. If you two start fighting again, someone might have to intervene, and I'm already dirty."

"Oh, Sid." Ms. Thompson twisted to smile at him. "How good to see you. I was just telling my niece—you remember Vivian. Such a smart girl. I was saying to her how nice it was to have you around the building. We just don't see you enough." She nudged her sister with her shoulder. "Didn't I say that, Jean?"

"Um hmm. Yes, you did." Mrs. Sinclair nodded.

Ms. Thompson crossed her arms and turned her full attention toward Sid. "Vivian should be here on the weekend. She's good about stopping in when Fred's out of town. How about you come up for coffee when she's here?"

Sid swallowed.

Connie's grin looked forced, and her words came out in a tight voice. "I'll go get the broom."

She smirked at him and disappeared into the building, leaving him alone to be interrogated.

"Don't be so pushy, Grace," Mrs. Sinclair scolded. "Remember what Helen said? He might be seeing someone."

Ms. Thompson snipped back, "Well, we won't know until we ask him. So, Sid, are you seeing someone?"

He was stuck between a rock and a hard place. He didn't want to lie, but as pretty as Vivian was, he didn't want to pursue her. He darted a glance at the closed door and spoke quietly, "There is someone I'm interested in."

"Oh, poo." Ms. Thompson pouted.

"What did he say?" Mrs. Sinclair asked.

Connie came through the door at the same time Ms. Thompson replied loudly, "He said he's got the hots for someone."

Once upstairs, he knocked on his neighbor's door. He really needed to go through Connie's binder to learn her name. When the woman opened her door, Sid said, "Thank you for telling me, but I wasn't needed. Did you call 911?"

"No. I just thought your girlfriend needed backup."

Sid didn't bother arguing with her about his relationship with Connie. Muffled steps came from the stairway, and assuming they belonged to Connie, Sid thanked his neighbor again, picked up his duffel, and entered the apartment. He'd just dropped it in his bedroom when he heard Connie enter and close the door behind her.

"Hey," he greeted her.

"Hey, yourself." She shuffled past him to head toward her bedroom.

"How were things while I was gone?" He followed her.

"Fine for the most part, but you saw that lovely little set-to. Who knew composting food scraps would lead to a food fight?"

"It's probably a good thing those two don't live together. I bet they've had a lot of arguments over the years."

"You're probably right." She gestured at her filthy shirt. "I'm going to take a shower. I smell like compost."

"How about I handle all the tenant issues for the next week?"

"Sounds good." Her smile was weak and didn't reach her eyes as she opened the door to her bedroom.

This was not the same Connie who'd bounced past him to get the broom. She'd been grinning like a loon, clearly enjoying seeing him on the hot seat. Now she was subdued; even her curls were sad and droopy. He knew she'd overheard his answer to Ms. Thompson. Had it upset her? They were becoming friends, and he didn't want to mislead her. "I'm not seeing anyone."

"What's that?"

"I don't want to be set up with Vivian, so I said that."

She cocked an eyebrow at him. "That you have the hots for someone?"

He shoved his hands in his front pockets and scrunched his shoulders. "Those were her words. I said I was interested in someone."

Her bedroom was dark, and the light from the living room barely reached them. He couldn't see her expression, but he could see the tension in her shoulders.

"But you aren't. You just said that to get her off your back?"

It wasn't a direct question, but it was still damn awkward. He pressed his lips together to keep from blurting *It's you. You were all I thought about while I was gone.* He'd wanted to argue about what music to play in the car. He wanted her beside him when he selected the wood to carve. He'd wanted to introduce her to his aunt and uncle. Violet flashed into his mind. He did *not* want her to meet his mother.

It was way too soon to start something. Too much shit to sort out, and someone would get hurt. He didn't want it to be Connie. She was beginning to mean a lot to him.

"Yeah." It wasn't really a lie.

She nodded, looking a little bit lighter. "I'm glad you're back."

"Me too." He didn't want her to disappear on him and put a hand out to stop her before she could enter her bedroom. "How about we go out for something to eat after you clean up? My treat." He watched a wave of color rise up her throat and stain her cheeks.

Her gaze flicked from his hand to his eyes. "S-sure," she stammered. "Just, umm…give me a few minutes." She speed-walked into her bedroom.

CHAPTER 11

After the fastest shower known to humankind, Connie stood before her closet, chewing on her lip. She flipped through the clothes Delia and Tommy had insisted she buy when they'd dragged her shopping. She'd recognized the importance of making a first impression in the business world and was happy for their expert advice but hadn't been sure she could *afford* their taste. Fortunately, all the shopping was done at consignment and thrift shops. She now had a wardrobe that could take her through any corporate situation, but…that didn't help at the moment. How was she supposed to figure out what to wear when she didn't know if this was a date or two roommates going to get something to eat?

She settled on skinny jeans, a bulky pink sweater, and a pair of booties with enough of a heel to give her height, but she could easily walk in. She ducked into the bathroom and stared into the mirror, wondering how much makeup was needed. Sadly, there wasn't time to consult with Delia or Tommy; *they* would know. "Give your head a shake," Connie told herself. This was *Sid*. Twice now, he'd seen her wearing food scraps; he wouldn't care about smoky eyes and perfectly lined lips. She swiped on mascara and lip gloss and called it good.

They decided to walk to an Indian restaurant six blocks away that they'd ordered takeout from but had never been to. They zipped up their heavy coats against the cold air and walked side by side, Sid shortening his strides to match hers.

She removed her coat inside the restaurant, and he took it, draping it over the back of the chair he'd pulled out for her. It was unexpected and charming, and she was touched by his considerate actions. No one had ever done that for her before. Surprise must have shown on her face because Sid rolled his eyes like it didn't mean anything and explained, "My grandparents drilled manners into me."

"They'll come in handy when you have tea with your fan club." Connie laughed at his pained expression.

A server arrived with menus and water and asked if they'd like something else to drink.

Connie hesitated, and Sid said, "It won't bother me if you order a drink."

"Really?"

He nodded. "Yeah, I'm good."

"Maybe another time." They each ordered club soda, and Connie asked for a wedge of lime in hers. The restaurant wasn't busy, and the server was soon back with their drinks and took their food orders.

Connie asked, "How was your trip?" while Sid wanted to know, "What do you mean fan club?"

He gestured for her to go first and raised his glass to take a drink.

She sat back in her chair and crossed her arms. "I think the tenants in our building, who are exclusively older women, are smitten with you."

Sid choked, put his drink down, and coughed into his napkin.

Alarmed, she stood from her chair.

Sid waved her back down. "I'm fine. You just…caught me by surprise. What do you mean?"

"I had a lot of tenant traffic while you were gone, and they all seemed disappointed to see me and not you. Clarice and two others demanded to know if you and I had had a fight." She laughed. "Seriously. They barged into the apartment, and two of them interrogated me while the other tried to access your room. I guess they wanted evidence you were still around."

"Oh…that's…I don't know what to say."

"But that's not all. They were particularly interested in whether you were seeing anyone because Clarice has a granddaughter she wants to set you up with." She pressed her lips together to prevent the laughter that bubbled up at Sid's horrified expression. "What was it Mrs. Dubchek said? You might have a chickie on the side. A friend with subsidies."

"Subsidies?"

"I think she means benefits." Connie sipped her drink, peering at him over the rim of the glass. She hadn't exactly asked a question, and he wasn't required to answer her, but the thought of him having sex with someone had nagged at her since the old woman put the idea in her head. He'd said he wasn't interested in anyone, but that didn't mean he didn't have a friendship with benefits. His hair was loose and fell to the top of his shoulders, shadowing his face so she couldn't read his expression.

Shifting in his seat, he ran a hand through his hair, and the light hit his face. "I don't have any friends with benefits. That's not something I've ever wanted." Color rose up the side of his neck, darkening his bronze cheeks. "I don't want to be fixed up with anyone. How do I get out of that?"

"Make plans for Thanksgiving. Be gone for the whole weekend. Otherwise, be prepared to go polkaing at the Romanian Community Center."

Sid winced. "Seriously?"

Connie nodded, feeling lighter. She could joke *now* but hadn't slept much the night before, wondering who he was with.

He huffed out a laugh. "Not so long ago, they'd have crossed to the other side of the street if they saw me."

Looking at the man before her, Connie had a hard time picturing Sid in the depths of his addiction. His face was weathered from his time living rough, and his hands were scarred with knicks, but they were steady, and his eyes were clear. He dressed simply in clean clothes, and his dark hair was lustrous and shone in the light. He carried himself well and had caught the eye of other women in the restaurant, who clearly appreciated his good looks as well.

"That may be," she agreed then pointed out, "but a lot has changed since then. You've changed. Did you visit with your family? They must be proud of you."

"Yeah." He shrugged. "My aunt and uncle are awesome. They wanted to know about the galleries I'm working with and if I've had a lawyer look over the contracts. Aunt Angie sent me home with food, by the way. She doesn't want me to waste money on takeout. My mother...." He frowned down at the tabletop. "She hit me up for money."

Connie had no idea how to respond. Her family was in each other's business. A lot. But there was a generosity of spirit. Helping each other out. Not expecting a handout. She sipped her drink, waiting for Sid to say more if he wanted to.

Their food arrived, and they ate family-style from the platters of biryani and butter chicken. After eating her fill, Connie asked, "Do you want to tell me about it?"

"Not particularly." Sid placed his utensils on his plate then looked up at her. "But allowing this to fester isn't going to do me any good."

Laughter erupted behind them as a large party was seated at another table.

"How about you tell me on the way home?"

"Sounds good," Sid replied, looking resigned.

He insisted on paying the bill and carrying the boxed-up leftovers as they headed out into the cold night air. Waiting at an intersection for the light to change, Sid spoke without looking at her, "Violet—she doesn't like me to call her mom —has been married three times. I don't remember much about living with my father, they split when I was three or four. He's from Alaska and moved back up there. When he *did* come down, Violet made such a scene that eventually, he just sent the child support checks. I've been up to see him a few times, but he has a new family, so...."

They crossed the street, and Sid picked up the story on the other side. "Violet is self-centered and believes the world should revolve around her. She didn't want me around when she found a new guy, so she would pawn me off on different relatives. My grandparents had Violet late in life and couldn't look after me, so it was usually Aunt Angie. She and Uncle Dan would take me to Jimmy's Joint, the old bookstore. Cal's grandparents, Gram and Pops, owned the place. And that's where I learned to carve." He grinned down at Connie. "Keeping up?"

She nudged his shoulder with her own. "I think so. You may have to draw a family tree though."

"I liked living with my aunt and uncle. Cal's a lot older than me, so I didn't see a lot of him, but his sisters spoiled me rotten."

They walked in silence for a bit, enjoying the night, the bite of the chill in the air, and each other's company. Then Connie watched the smile slide from his face.

He stared straight ahead. "I came home from school one day—I think I was ten—and didn't see Violet sitting at the kitchen table. Aunt Angie always had a snack waiting for me because I was always hungry. Uncle Dan called me 'the stomach that walked like a man.' I remember hugging my aunt, and the next thing I know, Violet yanks me by the arm and shoves me out of the room, telling me to pack my stuff. I protested and she got into my face real close, saying, 'I'm your mother, and you will do what I tell you.' I could see Aunt Angie over Violet's shoulder gesturing me to go. I tried to get to her, but Violet grabbed my arm and took me to my room. I had a real nice room...." He cleared his throat. "It used to be Cal's room. One day, after I'd been at Aunt Angie's for a few months, I came home from school and saw that she'd taken all of Cal's old things—posters, books, trophies—and boxed them up. She told me the room was mine now, and I could make it mine. So we went to Fred Meyer, and I picked out paint and new bedding. I even got to choose the floor rug.

"Violet swore a blue streak when she saw my room. She went back to the kitchen, and I heard her yelling, 'If you wanted another kid you should have had one of your own. He's mine, and don't you forget it.' She came back with a bunch of big garbage bags and started shoving all my stuff into them. Clothes, shoes, comforter, sheets, even the pillows. She hauled that out to her car and told me to hurry up. I went to get my backpack from the kitchen and saw Aunt Angie shoving food into it. She was crying, and I was crying, and she hugged me, and then I left."

They'd reached their building, and Connie unlocked the front door and led the way to their apartment. It had become a habit to wave at the peephole across the hall. She did so before going inside and removing her coat and boots. In the kitchen, Sid put the leftovers in the fridge then put the kettle on for tea.

"What happened next?" Connie stood close, seeing the tension in his shoulders and the tightness around his eyes.

"Violet drove me to this crappy apartment in Everett. Some guy she was shacking up with. Told him I was her sister's kid and would be staying for a while."

Connie must have made a noise because Sid turned his head to look at her. "Yeah, I might have been a kid, but the irony wasn't lost on me."

The kettle whistled, and Sid poured the boiling water into the teapot, then went to sit on the couch. The curtains hadn't been drawn, and in the streetlight's glow, she watched the emotions chase across his face for a few quiet moments. Not for the first time, she wanted to reach out and smooth away the furrows on his forehead, take his hand in hers, and let him draw comfort from her. Instead, she went into the kitchen to get them each a mug of the now steeped tea.

Sid accepted the mug with an absent nod, wrapping his hands around the warm ceramic. She closed the curtains and turned on a table lamp before settling into the corner of the couch, tucking her legs beneath her, and angling to face him. She studied the room in the soft light, sipping from her own mug. The mug that Sid had bought for her.

"Where did that come from?" She pointed to a crocheted afghan on the back of the recliner.

"Aunt Angie made it as a housewarming gift for us."

For us? Connie let that slide for a moment. "It's lovely." And it was. The sunburst pattern in light and dark shades of green brought life to the room, contrasting while blending at the same time with the bold throw pillows on the burgundy couch. "It's like she knew exactly what we needed."

"Kind of. I sent her pictures of the place when we moved in."

"That was nice of her. Aren't you going to put it in your room?"

Sid shook his head. "You can use it when you're working."

Connie was touched by his thoughtfulness. She smiled. "Thank you!" The recliner had become her favorite place to work when she was at home. The floor lamp behind it gave her more than enough light, and there was room on the bookshelf for her to put a water bottle or coffee mug. The afghan was better for wrapping up in than using her bathrobe. She poked Sid's thigh with her toe. "Do you want to finish your story?"

"Do you want to hear it?" He rolled his eyes at her mock glare. "Fine."

Shifting around to face her, he slung one arm along the back of the couch. "Violet threw my stuff into the second bedroom and then ignored me. She joined the guy—Dennis was his name—in the living room. After a while, she convinced him to take her out somewhere. And…I was by myself."

"For how long?"

"A few days." Sid glanced at her, then away. His hand curled into a fist. "I ate all the food Aunt Angie gave me and found a note at the bottom of the pack wrapped around a one-hundred-dollar bill. It was their address, phone number, and instructions to call at any time. So I did."

Connie scooted closer and took his hand, her heart going out to ten-year-old Sid.

As if reading her thoughts, Sid added, "It could have been worse. Violet would have found the money if she had gone through my backpack, and I'd be screwed. Instead, I walked to the nearest 7-11, convinced the cashier to let me use the phone, then ate a bunch of junk food while I waited for my aunt and uncle."

The tension in his grip belied the matter-of-fact words. Her own mother was a pain at times but stalwart in her love and totally reliable. Julia Ortega was in her element when her family was gathered together. She'd already started reaching out about plans for Thanksgiving. "Will your mom be there for Thanksgiving dinner?" Connie asked.

Sid relaxed his hand and let hers go before reaching for his tea. "No, thank God. She and her boyfriend will be in Puerto Vallarta. That's what she wanted the money for."

"Seriously?" Connie gaped. "But that's…that's…."

"That's my mother." His eyes glittered, his lips forming a thin, tight line. "Now that I have something to offer, she's all over me."

Connie's mother had taken to Sid and asked after him often, genuinely interested in his carving, the food he made, and whether he had warm clothes. If her mom ever found out how Sid's mom treated him, and they met, Connie would lay odds on her mom delivering the tongue-lashing of the century—in two languages. "Will she come here to see you?"

He shook his head. "I wouldn't do that to you. I doubt she has the address, and my family knows not to give it to her. Don't worry about it."

Connie snorted. "Oh, I'm not worried. Just thinking what my mom would do to her if she ever found out."

"Yeah?"

She twisted to put her elbow on the sofa back and propped her chin on it. "She's kind of a mother bear and thinks you need looking after."

His mouth relaxed, and his eyes lost their hard glint. "I don't need looking after, but I appreciate it. I also appreciate you as a roommate. Best decision I've made for a while."

He clinked his mug against hers, and she wasn't sure what was warmer, the tea or her face. Gazing at her over the rim of his mug, his eyes seemed to focus on her mouth, and she wondered what he was thinking. She wanted him to be thinking about kissing her. She wanted him *to* kiss her. She could kiss him, but would that be rushing things?

Nowhere in the roommate agreement templates did they say anything about what to do when you became attracted to your hot roommate.

If she were smart, she'd say goodnight and head straight to bed. Alone. Instead, she picked up the remote and aimed it at the TV, kicking her feet up onto the coffee table. "My turn to pick what we watch."

"Fine," he grumbled good-naturedly and settled close

enough beside her that a lock of his hair slid over her shoulder and tickled her neck. She didn't move it.

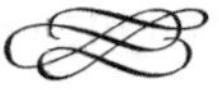

"Perhaps we should wait for Connie."

Sid stared at the water oozing out of the base of the faucet, thinking the same thing. It was also kind of insulting that Ms. Thompson didn't believe he could fix it. "No, I've got this. Just let me get the toolbox," he said, trying to project a confidence he wasn't quite feeling.

"Are you sure?" Mrs. Sinclair looked as doubtful as her sister. "I'd rather put up with a leaky faucet for a few hours than have a geyser come out of my sink."

"No problem." He hustled out of the apartment, down the corridor, and up to his own place, hoping the Building Bible would have a section on fixing faucets—with illustrations. It did not. It did have a phone number for a plumber, though. He was sorely tempted to call the number, even going so far as to pull his phone out of his pocket. Instead, he went to YouTube. Hallelujah! He scrolled through multiple videos to find a faucet that looked similar to Mrs. Sinclair's. Fortunately, he had the same model in his own kitchen sink. After watching the video all the way through, he searched through Connie's toolbox. He found a pipe wrench but no O rings. If Fred didn't have any in the maintenance closet, he'd have to trek to a hardware store. Once again, the gods were smiling. He grabbed an assortment and a tube of plumber's grease and went upstairs to practice.

Fifteen minutes later, feeling cocky and confident, he stood at Mrs. Sinclair's door with the toolbox. Ms. Thompson answered and led the way into the kitchen. Three women were gathered around the dining table, looking at him expectantly.

"He certainly looks like he knows what he's doing," Mrs. Tseng said.

"He's not wearing a toolbelt, though," Mrs. Dubchek pointed out.

Ms. Thompson scoffed, "Carpenters wear toolbelts, not plumbers."

Mrs. Sinclair pulled her walker toward her and stood up. She scolded the others as she walked toward him. "Leave him alone. This is his first faucet. Sid, dear, do you need anything?"

He placed the toolbox on the counter and opened it. "No, ma'am, I've got everything right here."

"What about a towel to mop up spills?"

"Well, almost everything." He shot her a grin.

The repair took twenty minutes under watchful eyes and with a running commentary from the women seated at the table. Then he had to stay for coffee and cake.

The cake was good, the conversation was uncomfortable. Ms. Thompson was bound and determined to pry details from him about his "romantic interests." Trapped behind the table, he could only squirm and deflect. He wasn't about to tell them his only romantic interest was Connie, and he was moving at a snail's pace because he was afraid he'd screw it up. Every day, thinking of her as only his roommate was getting harder. That morning, she'd come out of her bedroom clearly distracted. A flash of pink bra peeked through the gaping material of the shirt she hadn't buttoned correctly. Tongue-tied and face flaming, he'd pointed in the general direction of her cleavage. She whipped around and rebuttoned her shirt. That flash of pink had been teasing him all day.

To throw them off the scent, he told the nosy women about Cal and Delia. They oohed and ahhed and cooed, "Isn't that nice," clearly tickled that his cousin had found his happy ever after. That led to a discussion about love stories and what were the elements that made a book a romance novel. Sid sat back and listened and ate more cake.

An hour and a half later, he was back in his own apartment. With a satisfied grin, he entered the repair in the Building Bible, eager to tell Connie about it. She'd be happy for him because that was who she was. Instead of begrudging the accomplishments of others, she took pleasure in them.

His phone rang, jolting him from thoughts of Connie's curls and bright smile. He took the call and punched the air in jubilation when he hung up.

It called for a celebration, and he knew just how he wanted to do it.

❄

*H*er phone pinged with a text message as Connie climbed into her car. She'd spent most of the day in meetings at CSEC and if the traffic gods were in her favor, she'd be home in less than half an hour.

The text was from Sid, and her face softened with a smile. He'd learned about the GIF keyboard on his phone and now made a point of texting her daily, usually to tell her what was for supper, using GIFs and emoji. This time, he was using words. In full sentences.

I had a good day and I want to celebrate with you. Can I take you out to dinner tonight? Let me know and I'll make a reservation at Mateus Rosé.

Connie sucked in a breath. Mateus Rosé was *the* hot restaurant in Seattle. Tommy and his partner Kevin had been there and raved about their tapas to Connie, who'd then told Sid about it. She reread the text. The words *take you out* and *reservation* popping out at her. As if reading her mind, he texted again: **Just to be clear, I am asking you on a date.**

The phone slipped out of her sweaty hand and down into the space between her seat and the console. Cursing silently, she fished it out and hoped she hadn't accidentally sent him an eggplant emoji. Very carefully, she typed in: **Sure!!!** She deleted two of the exclamation points and hit send before she had a chance to overthink it. This time, he responded with a high-five emoji.

The traffic gods were not in a good mood, and Connie inched along in the bumper-to-bumper traffic, mentally trying on and discarding every item in her closet. Finally pulling into a parking spot near their building, she took a few deep breaths to calm her nerves, wanting to present herself as cool and collected when she entered the apartment.

The place was quiet when she unlocked the door. Was Sid even home? He'd texted her the time of their dinner reservation, and she figured she had an hour and a half before they had to leave. Turning the corner of the short hallway leading to the bedrooms and bathroom, she stopped in her tracks.

Sid stood beside his bed, shirtless and frowning. He wore charcoal grey slacks that fit like they were made for him and held two dress shirts up by their hangers. His expression cleared when he saw her. "Which one do you think?" He presented first one, a plain, dark burgundy, then the other, forest green with a faint paisley pattern, for her opinion.

"Uhh...." How was she supposed to think when all that smooth bronze skin was on display? He quirked an eyebrow at her, and she pointed at the green one. Really, the man could wear a wet paper bag and look good. He nodded, tossed the other onto the bed, and donned the green shirt.

"How was your day?" he inquired while buttoning it up.

"Good." Talking to him when he was fully clothed was so much easier. "But apparently not nearly as good as yours. Gonna tell me about it?"

He grinned and shook his head. "Nope. You're gonna have to wait."

"Fine." She scowled at him. "I'll get changed."

Sid had set the bar high in those slacks and that shirt and Connie stood in front of her closet agonizing over her choices. She'd showered quickly and shaved her legs, careful not to get her hair wet because taking the time to dry it was out of the question. Now, with her makeup on and her curls as tamed as they were going to get, she selected her one and only dress and the shoes that went with it. Fortunately, it was clean, and as she smoothed it over her curves, she hoped it wasn't too much.

He looked up as she entered the living room, his eyebrows winging up. "Wow, you look…amazing."

She ducked her head at the compliment, pleased that she didn't trip when she walked. Wearing high heels wasn't a regular thing, and landing ass over teakettle was a definite possibility when she did put them on.

She went to retrieve her coat, but Sid's voice stopped her. "I have it." He held it ready for her to slip her arms into it, then scooped her hair out from under the collar and smoothed his hands over her shoulders before letting go.

A little thrill shot through her at the intimate gesture. "Thank you."

"You're welcome," he replied. He put on his own coat, then held the door open for her.

Clarice was standing by the mailboxes when they exited the elevator and headed for the front door. She clucked and smiled broadly. "My, don't you two look nice. Have a good time!" Connie wasn't sure, but she thought Clarice winked at Sid.

They took an Uber to avoid the hassle of parking near the waterfront. The interior of the small car forced them to sit close together, making Connie aware of Sid's muscled thigh against her softness. It was unnerving and exciting, and the drive ended far too quickly.

Inside the restaurant, the hostess took their coats, led them toward a table at the back of the crowded space, and handed them menus once they were seated. The food smelled amazing and, from the looks of appreciation on the faces around them, tasted good as well.

After receiving glasses of water, Connie couldn't wait any longer. "So, what are we celebrating?"

Sid grinned. "I fixed a faucet all by myself today."

"That's awesome, and congratulations. But I think that's hardly worth getting dressed up and" —she pointed a finger at him—"did you buy new clothes?"

He smoothed a hand down his shirt, looking a little self-conscious. "Yeah. Tommy met me for lunch and helped me pick some things out. A gallery in Bellevue is giving me a one-man show, and my agent suggested that I wear something other than jeans and flannel."

"That is freaking fantastic!" Connie reached across the table to squeeze his hand, pleased for his success. He squeezed hers back and grinned.

A server arrived at their table, greeted both of them, then addressed Sid as if Connie didn't exist. "It sounds like you're celebrating." The woman was staring at him like he was a snack and a half, and she was hungry. Connie snickered, thinking that the woman's mouth would water if she'd seen Sid shirtless.

"Yes." Connie gestured at Sid. "His artwork will be featured at a swanky gallery very soon."

"Well, that is cause for celebration. Shall I bring some

sparkling wine?" The woman looked duly impressed and even more interested in him.

Sid shook his head while Connie looked up at the server. "Do you have anything non-alcoholic?"

"We do indeed." The woman bobbed her head.

"Then I think a bottle of your finest, please," Connie said grandly.

The server swayed her hips so provocatively as she walked off that Connie thought she would put her back out.

Sid didn't even look at the woman. His gaze was focused on their hands. He turned hers over to link his fingers briefly with hers before letting go.

The touch left her jittery, and she covered it up with conversation. "That really is impressive. What did your aunt and uncle say? They must be so proud."

He smiled up at her. "They don't know yet. I wanted to tell you first."

"Oh." He was telling *her* before the most important people in his life. Her toes curled at the level of significance in that. Then they uncurled. "What about Tommy? What did you tell him?"

"I made up a story about needing something to wear for Cal and Delia's engagement party." Sid's eyes danced. "Which will happen sooner than later, I expect. So it wasn't *really* a lie."

"I assume you don't want me to say anything to Delia about your gallery showing?"

Propping his forearms on the table, he leaned closer. "I plan to tell my family at Thanksgiving. Can I trust you to keep it secret until then?"

"Absolutely." She mirrored his movements, enjoying their little conspiracy.

He smiled and pointed at her. "That's the dress you wore when I first met you."

"You remembered?"

"Of course." His eyebrows came together. "You looked great, and I couldn't stop looking at you."

"I can't remember if Tommy or Delia picked it out and insisted I buy it. I don't need to wear dresses often, and this is only the second time I've worn it." Clearly, she had to send them each a thank-you note.

"I'm glad you wore it tonight. I like you in pink."

The warmth in his eyes was making her so soft and gooey. If he kept it up, she would melt into a puddle.

"You also had a Band-Aid on your arm. What was that from?"

She laughed, thankful for the change in conversation. "Wow, you have a great memory. I got bit by one of the damn dogs I was taking care of at the time. I'm so glad I don't do that anymore." She held up her arm to show him the slight scar.

An unnerving shiver through her as Sid traced a finger over the mark. Connie was relieved when a burst of applause went up in a corner of the restaurant as their server returned. She showed the label to Connie for her approval before opening the bottle and filling the flute glasses she'd brought.

"What are they celebrating?" Connie asked, indicating the large group. A white-haired couple seemed to be the center of attention. The man took the woman's hand and smiled fondly at her before kissing her cheek to more applause.

"It's their engagement party. They've lived across the hall from each other in the same building for three years and fell in love." The server sighed. "Isn't it lovely to find your happy ever after at that age?" She positioned the bottle in an ice bucket and left them alone.

Seeing Sid's faint smile as he watched the group, Connie asked, "Do you think this is the first time falling in love for them?"

He shook his head. "One of the other guys looks so much

like the old man, I'm betting that's his son. So I think this is his second time around for love."

"They're about the same age as most of our tenants," Connie observed. "I wonder why none of them have married again."

"We don't know how many marriages they've had," Sid pointed out. "Mrs. Dubchek was married twice. Widowed once, then divorced the second man when she realized he wanted her to look after him—you know, fetch his pipe and slippers and clip his toenails in his old age."

Connie curled her lip up. "Eww, how do you know that?"

"I overheard her say that today when I was fixing the faucet." Sid grinned. "None of those women seem to think marriage is the be-all and end-all for themselves. Although, they do like the idea of other people being in love. They seem obsessed with fixing up their grandchildren."

"Are they still trying to fix you up?"

"I keep giving them the slip. I told them about Cal and Delia today. That kept them going for a while."

She'd been on the sidelines as their relationship developed and was truly happy for Delia. Delia's face would light up when she spoke about Cal, and Cal acted like there wasn't another woman in the room. Kind of like the way Sid was looking at her.

"It's going to be all over the building that you and I went out tonight," she said softly, toying with the base of her wineglass.

"I'm okay with that," he replied, looking at her steadily. "I like being with you, and up until recently, I haven't had much to celebrate. You are at the top of the list of people I want to celebrate with."

"That must be a pretty short list," she joked.

"It is." He shifted in his seat, treating her remark seriously. "Cal, his parents, and his sisters will be happy for me, but I wish Gram and Pops were alive. They'd…." His eyes gleamed with unshed tears, and he looked away.

Connie took the hand that wasn't clutching the wineglass in both of hers. "They know. They know and are very proud of you." She couldn't make the pain of loss disappear, so she held his hand.

He cleared his throat and shot her a watery smile. "They'd like you."

She shied away from the intensity in his gaze and tossed her curls. "Of course, they would. And seeing as how they were part of making Cal, I'd probably like them, too."

Sid laughed, and she grinned.

Connie's anxiety kicked up as the Uber got closer to The Firs. Dinner had been wonderful, and Sid couldn't have been more attentive. But this was a *date*. A *good* date. And good dates ended with expectations, like good-night kisses. The idea of Sid holding her, looking deep into her eyes, and touching his lips against hers made her swoon. He would no doubt be very good at kissing.

Sid helped Connie out of the car when they arrived at The Firs and walked beside her to the front entrance. The building was quiet, and they were as well, taking the elevator to the third floor in silence.

Inside the apartment, he took her coat and hung it up in the closet, and she tingled with anticipation, knowing this was the moment. When she turned around, he would look at her, cradle her face between his hands, and pull her close to—

She jolted at a sudden noise.

"Are you going to get that?"

"What?" She stared at Sid dumbly.

He pointed to her purse. "Your phone. It's ringing."

"Right!" She fumbled to pull out the phone and glanced at

the call display. She let the call go to voicemail and looked up at Sid, eyes filled with apology. "It's my sister Teresa. She's away at college and never calls. I need to—"

"Of course." He smiled and squeezed her shoulder gently before letting go. "Take your time. I'm not going anywhere."

CHAPTER 13

Clarice pounced on Sid in the lobby the next morning. "So? How'd it go?"

Sid skirted around her to get to the recycle containers, thinking about playing dumb but knowing that wouldn't work. "Fine," he answered without looking at her. And it had been fine, although it didn't end the way he'd hoped.

Connie's sister had had an epic battle with her boyfriend and needed to hash it over. Connie had smiled apologetically at him, then disappeared into her room, where he heard her murmuring into the phone for ages. Eventually, he'd given up, texted her a goodnight, and gone to bed.

Clarice blocked his access to the corridor. "Fine? Just fine? What did you do wrong?"

He sighed. "I didn't do anything wrong. We had a great time."

"When are you going to see her again?"

"You know we live together? I saw her this morning at the coffeemaker." He dodged around Clarice to head out to the courtyard and dump the recycling.

She followed behind, refusing to be deterred. "You know

that's not what I meant. What's your next move? You've got to do something romantic to up the ante."

Up the ante? The old woman was making him nervous. Connie had enjoyed the scones he'd made for her this morning. Was that romantic enough? Maybe not, but he wouldn't ask Clarice's opinion. She'd probably want to bring the rest of the tenants into the conversation.

"Look, I don't want to blow it, so I'm taking it slow." As disappointed as he was that the night had ended so abruptly, that was the truth. Connie meant something to him, and he was afraid to screw it up. If he made a move sooner than she was ready, he could scare her off, and the apartment would become very small very quickly. Ignoring Clarice's pursed lips, he held the door open for her to precede him into the building. She muttered a thank you before saying, "That girl's a keeper, so don't go too slow, or someone else is gonna sneak in there and scoop her up."

His aunt preferred to talk on the phone rather than text and called the next day. It was the Sunday before Thanksgiving, and Aunt Angie had lots on her mind. Sid tasted the sauce he was making for the ziti while listening to her tell him the names of those who'd be there and that Violet was already in Mexico. He heaved a sigh at the news. He'd worried she'd change her mind, pocket the money, and show up for dinner.

"Cal's lending me his Jeep again. I'll pick it up Thursday morning and should be there by noon," he informed his aunt. "What can I bring?"

"Just yourself, sweetheart."

He made a mental note to pick up flowers because showing up empty-handed was just plain wrong.

"You'll be helping your uncle with the deep fryer, so a warm jacket would be good."

"What does he need help with?"

Aunt Angie laughed. "Nothing really. He just wants the

company. And to keep the grandkids away. Last year, one of them tried to put an ice cube in the deep fryer."

"Oh shit. That would have been bad."

"Dan nearly had a heart attack. So help with the rugrats would be great. Do you want to invite Connie to join us? We might be a little crowded, but there will be plenty of food."

Sid peeked around to where Connie sat at the table, headphones on and frowning at her laptop. He'd love to have her join them, but knew she would be with her family. "Thanks, but she's got plans. Her mother has a to-do list a mile long for Connie to take care of."

"Too bad. I wanted to pick her brain about grant writing. There's one available for a health clinic the tribes are applying for, and I don't understand the wording." In addition to running an insurance agency, Aunt Angie was active with the Tulalip tribes.

Sid put the spoon down and propped a hip on the counter, angled to watch Connie work. Her frown turned into a scowl as she pounded away at the keyboard. "I can ask her to give you a call."

"No worries," Aunt Angie replied. "I'll reach out to her after the holiday. You have a good week, and I'll see you Thursday."

Sid disconnected and put the phone down, thinking about what his aunt's reaction would be when he told her about the gallery show. No doubt hugs and squealing would be involved. Connie hadn't squealed or hugged him, but her evident pleasure on his behalf was satisfying. When his agent had called, she was indeed the first person he wanted to tell.

Swearing loudly, Connie removed her headphones and tossed them onto the table.

"What's up?" he asked.

"Someone was supposed to review the data for the application, and I just received an email that he's out of town for the holiday and won't be available until next Monday. The application is due Tuesday." She pushed her hands through her hair until it stood on end, and she glared at the computer. "I should never have agreed to work with someone else. You can't rely on them."

Sid made a sympathetic noise but didn't know what to say, so he refilled her glass of water. She mumbled a thank you, and he squeezed her shoulder and returned to making supper. It was a new recipe he'd gotten from Mrs. Sinclair at book club.

He'd opened the door one afternoon expecting a complaint that he might or might not be able to address. Instead, he found Mrs. Dubchek at his door and Clarice knocking at 3B's door.

"I know you're in there Wanda. It's time for book club," Clarice spoke loudly.

"I'm not coming, and stop bothering me." The grumpy voice came through the closed door.

"Oh, poo," Clarice huffed then turned to beam up at Sid. "Excellent. Did you take notes? You look like the kind of person who takes notes while reading the book. Helen practically writes a synopsis of each book we read. How many notebooks do you have now?"

"Five." Mrs. Dubchek smiled smugly. "I keep them in chronological order."

"Let's go." Clarice made shooing gestures. "Or the tea will be cold, and there won't be any cookies left."

Now he remembered. Ms. Thompson had cornered him in the laundry room, alternately lecturing him on the proper way to fold his clothes and talking about their book club. It met every two weeks, rotating between the apartments of the eight members. "What book were you reading?" he asked.

"One of the ACOTAR books by Sarah J. Maas. Which one was it, Helen?" Clarice asked, headed for the elevator.

"*A Court of Silver Flames*," Mrs. Dubchek answered.

"I haven't read it. I won't have anything to say about the book."

Clarice ignored his protest. "Who cares. Just come and be social."

He had no excuse for not going other than he didn't want to. He opened his mouth to say exactly that, but the hopeful expression on Mrs. Dubchek's face stopped him. He locked the door and followed her to the elevator.

Sid had met all the women gathered in Mrs. Sinclair's apartment and nodded politely before wedging himself into a corner of the couch. Ms. Thompson took the seat beside him while Mrs. Tseng sat in a dining chair at right angles to him. It was tight quarters, and he wouldn't be leaving any time soon.

"How long has the group been together?" he asked.

Ms. Thompson sipped her tea before answering. "I can't tell you exactly. It was going when Jean and I moved into the building. Helen would probably know. She writes down everything." She raised her voice to ask Mrs. Dubchek the question.

Mrs. Dubchek riffled through her big bag and flipped through a composition book. "The first meeting was held ten years ago. The original members were Clarice, Wanda, Evelyn, and myself."

"I didn't know that Evelyn used to come to book group," Ms. Thompson said, looking surprised.

Clarice snorted. "She only wanted to read political biographies, and when Wanda suggested we read Michelle Obama's book *Becoming,* Evelyn said it didn't count. An argument ensued, and Evelyn stormed out. She hasn't been back since."

"From then on, we decided we'd just read fiction," Mrs. Dubchek stated before tucking her notebook aside.

"That's not to say we haven't had any heated discussions.

Remember the *Wuthering Heights* fiasco?" Clarice asked the group.

There was a collective shiver before Mrs. Sinclair sighed. "And I've apologized for suggesting that book. Let's not bring it up again." She'd then turned the conversation toward the new cookbook she'd bought.

Now, tasting the ziti sauce, Sid thought he could handle another book club meeting. He hadn't felt that cosseted since Gram had passed.

Behind him, he heard Connie closing her laptop and muttering to herself. The grant was all she'd talked about recently, and he knew it was a big deal for both her and CSEC. He'd seen her spreadsheet of the grants she'd applied for and their amounts. So far, she'd had a hundred percent success rate, but they were small potatoes compared to the one she was working on. He didn't blame her for being grumpy and, other than making sure she was fed, vowed to stay out of her way.

She rose from the table with a groan. "How long until supper is ready? I'd like to take a walk and maybe clear my head."

"We've got lots of time. Go for it."

She trudged down the hall, and he heard her opening and closing the closet. A knock sounded and he hurried to the door, wanting Connie to get her downtime and not have to deal with a needy tenant. She beat him to it and stood in the open doorway, listening to Evelyn Land harangue her.

The red-faced woman stood over a basket of laundry, one fist on her hip, wagging a finger in Connie's face. "I waited two hours for a dryer to be free, and then it ate my money and didn't dry my clothes. You need to fix this now!"

Connie held out a placating hand. "Mrs. Land, you're going to have to be patient. When—"

"I am not going to spend my night going up and down to the laundry room waiting for that—woman to empty the dryer. I want the keys to Fred's apartment. I'll use his dryer." She thrust her hand out expectantly.

Connie's back stiffened. Sid stepped up beside her to provide support. She glanced at him and back to the irate woman.

"We can't do that, Mrs. Land."

"Nonsense. He's my son-in-law."

"Connie's right, Mrs. Land," Sid spoke up. "We can't let you in without his permission."

Mrs. Land picked up the laundry basket and thrust it at Sid. "Then you take care of it. I want those dried and returned to me tonight." She stalked off to the elevator.

Sid stared after her, then followed Connie into the apartment carrying the wet laundry. The sound of pages being flipped and Connie muttering in Spanish came to him. He put the basket down and returned to the kitchen. She had the binder out and was running a finger down a page. "Ah-ha!" Picking up her phone, she dialed a number.

"Repair guy?"

"Yes. But God knows when they're going to get here." She ran a hand through her hair. "I don't need this right now. Another problem for me to take care of."

"Maybe it's something we can fix ourselves."

Connie rolled her eyes and snapped at him. "Right. And how much experience have you had with commercial laundry machines? Consulting the university of YouTube is not going to work this time. I will—"

Someone picked up on the other end, and her tone changed. The biting sarcasm was replaced by that of a competent professional. "This is Consuela Ortega calling on behalf of Fred Thompson at The Firs apartment building."

While Connie spoke to whomever, Sid grabbed a handful of quarters from his bedroom and headed to the laundry room. None of the washing machines were in use, and three of the four dryers tumbled away while the door of the fourth yawned open. He inspected the insides before closing the door and standing back, hands on hips. He checked the lint trap, but it was empty. He inserted four quarters and pressed start. The machine started up, and Sid figured he'd give it a few minutes and then see if the interior had heated at all. Thanks to the janitorial crew, the room was clean. He drifted over to the bulletin board near the door. At the top was a notice of operating hours: 8 a.m. - 7 p.m. It was now six-thirty. Even if they could get a repair man here tonight, that wouldn't get Mrs. Land's laundry done. Two laminated papers with instructions for operating the machines were posted on the board. At the bottom of each was written: Problems? Contact Fred. Sid snorted. Like that was helpful. He opened the dryer door and stuck his hand in. Stone cold. And that was the limit of his expertise.

The apartment was empty when he went upstairs. He hadn't a clue where Connie was and, at the moment, wasn't interested in finding out. Her dismissive attitude pissed him off. He found Fred's keys, grabbed the basket of wet laundry, and headed for the stairs. The building owner occupied the entire fourth floor. On one side of the landing was the entry to the apartment. On the opposite side was a door to an office suite and one to a workout room. Sid and Connie had been up there once to check which key fit which lock, but they hadn't looked around. Sid entered the apartment, fumbled for the wall switch, and gaped. To his left was an expansive open area with a wall of windows and French doors that opened onto a rooftop patio. The living room seating area flowed into the dining area, which was separated from the kitchen by a large island. The light furnishings and woodwork further brightened the room. On his right were doors that he assumed led to bedrooms, bathrooms, and the laundry room. Choosing the door closest to the kitchen, he scored on his first try. Unlike the well-maintained but well-used equipment downstairs, Fred had top-of-the-line machines beneath windows at one end of the room. The sides of the room held counters and cabinets that Sid was tempted to explore but wisely chose not to. He loaded the clothes into the dryer, set the timer, and headed back out. He might be unable to fix the dryer, but at least he'd get Mrs. Land off his back.

He took the stairs all the way down to the first floor, figuring he'd lock up the laundry room. Connie's laugh came to him as he got closer. He slowed his pace as the laugh turned into a giggle, and he heard a man's low voice.

Who the hell was that?

He came to a stop in the open doorway of the laundry room to see Mrs. Tseng folding her laundry on one side of the island. Lips pursed, bristling with disapproval, she looked over at Sid. In front of the broken dryer, a bulky blond man was removing his jacket. Muscled biceps strained against the confines of a black T-shirt with Speedy Appliance Repair printed on the upper left chest. Connie stood beside him, wearing a goofy grin and all but twirling her hair like a smitten schoolgirl.

"Hey," Sid made his presence known. He wasn't sure what to do with himself. Choose a wide-legged stance with his hands on his hips? Cross his arms and lean nonchalantly against the door? He settled for shoving his hands in his front pockets and lifting his chin in greeting.

"Oh, Sid." Connie's eyes were bright. "Sven just got here. He thinks it's an issue with the thermostat and should be able to fix it tonight."

Sven put a way too familiar hand on Connie's shoulder and directed her to move to the side. Connie shuffled around to stand by a washer. Mrs. Tseng passed in front of her, holding her laundry basket. She stopped by Sid's side, directed pointed looks at Sven and Connie, and murmured, "Some people know how to move quickly," before exiting the room.

Well, shit. It looked like Clarice was right. He'd dragged his feet all weekend to give Connie time to think of them as a *them* and not just roommates. Now she was looking at another man with the smile Sid thought belonged to him. "Do you need a hand with anything?" he asked.

The brawny repairman grasped the dryer and pulled it away from the wall without breaking a sweat. He didn't even look at Sid. "No, man. I got this." Then he winked at Connie. Sid watched the flush creep up her neck until her cheeks bloomed with color. That was supposed to belong to him as well. He felt heat rise in his own face. If she liked big muscle-bound blonds, he didn't stand a chance. There was no reason for him to stay. No one noticed his departure.

Connie tore the check from the ledger and handed it to Sven, all but pushing him out of the apartment. He was cute, but oh my God, if he said one more condescending thing to her, she was going to kick him in his nicely rounded ass.

He stood in the hallway, zipping up his jacket. "Maybe I should call you tomorrow. Check that it's working properly."

"Thanks, but I'll call the service number if necessary." Connie stood inside the apartment, ready to close the door.

"Why don't you give me your number anyway? Just to be on the safe side." He winked. *Again.* He'd winked so often that she thought he had a nervous tic.

"No. I don't think so."

"Come on, *chiquita.* I'm sure you've got other things that need checking out." His gaze roamed suggestively up and down her frame before lingering on her chest.

"What's the name of the company you work for?" Sid stood in the hallway outside the apartment, slightly behind Sven, holding a basket of laundry. It looked like he wanted to use it as a bludgeon. His tone was mild, but his white-knuckled grip gave him away. His eyes glittered with a glare hard enough to cut glass.

"Speedy Appliance Repair. Why?" Sven looked him over dismissively.

"I bet they have a policy against harassing customers."

Sven moved closer to Sid, forcing the shorter man to look up at him. "Who are you?" he sneered.

Sid didn't bat an eye. "I'm the guy telling you to back off and leave her alone."

"What if she doesn't want me to?"

"Connie," Sid didn't raise his voice, didn't shift his gaze away from Sven, "do you want to give him your phone number?"

"No."

"There's your answer." He advanced, forcing Sven to step back until Sid could enter the apartment. "Do I need to show you the way out?"

Red-faced, Sven shook his head and stomped down the hallway. He banged through the door to the stairwell and clomped down the stairs.

A disembodied voice came from across the hallway. "I recorded that on my phone."

Connie looked at the cracked door, unable to see anyone. "Umm, thanks. I'll let you know if we need it."

She found Sid standing, arms crossed, staring out the front window. She joined him in time to see Sven fling his toolbox into the back of his van. As if sensing the attention, he raised a middle finger to the window before climbing inside. The engine started, and the truck pulled away from the curb on squealing tires.

Sid stepped back with a grunt. He crossed the room to retrieve the laundry basket. "I'm taking this to Mrs. Land. Help yourself to the ziti. I've already eaten." And he was gone.

He'd already eaten? She'd definitely spent too much time dealing with that muscle-bound idiot. She got herself a plate of food and sat at the table to pick at it. It was delicious; she just didn't have an appetite.

At first, it had been fun being the recipient of all that flirting; Sven was easy on the eyes. Even Mrs. Tseng seemed to appreciate his physique. When he started explaining the working parts of the thermostat, the differences between home and commercial appliances, and why he preferred European over American-made washing machines, Connie was done. The job might have been finished faster if she hadn't stayed in the laundry room. But the machine was fixed, and Sven was gone.

The door opened and closed, and Sid entered the kitchen. Retrieving a glass from the cupboard, he filled it from the tap and drank it down. She watched the smooth muscles of his throat as he swallowed.

"Was Mrs. Land appreciative?"

"No idea. I put the basket by her door, knocked, and left."

Connie watched him refill the glass. "Probably a good idea. That woman's a piece of work. What's Fred's apartment like? Did you check it out?"

"Nope. I started the dryer, saw you in the laundry room, and came here to finish the ziti."

"Which is very good, by the way. Thank you." She took a quick bite to prove her sincerity.

He rinsed out the glass and put it in the drainboard. "You're welcome. I'm gonna take a shower." He left the room without looking at her.

That was weird. Now that she thought about it, they hadn't made eye contact since she saw him in the laundry room. Tense and jittery from her interaction with Mrs. Land and then with Sven, she felt like she was missing something but didn't know what.

Teresa's phone call couldn't have come at a worse time,

but her sister's first real boyfriend had delivered the "it's not you, it's me" speech when he broke up with her, and she was devastated. Connie'd then spent almost three hours consoling her, careful not to trash talk in case Teresa and the jerk were to get back together.

On Saturday, Sid took off to meet with his agent to brainstorm which pieces to include in his upcoming show, so they'd barely done more than say good morning at the coffeepot. Although he had made scones for her, which was sweet.

A door opened and closed, and she looked up, but Sid didn't appear, which was probably for the best because she had data to review and couldn't afford to be distracted by more of his sweetness.

She was working on her laptop when she registered a presence. Sid took the seat across from her, wet hair hanging loose about his shoulders, dampening the fabric of his shirt.

"Hey," she said, surprised by his sudden appearance.

"Got a moment?"

"Yeah. Let me finish this sentence, though." At his nod, she quickly typed in a few words, clicked enter, then closed the laptop's lid. "What's up."

He folded his hands in front of him, took a deep breath, and looked her directly in the eye. "We're roommates, right?"

"Yes."

"And partners in handling the super's duties?"

Since the GFCI incident, she and Sid had been sharing the responsibilities, although most tenants requested Sid. She didn't blame them. He was patient and kind, took the time to listen while drinking endless cups of tea, and his rare smiles lit up the room. He'd made a point of going over the Building Bible, as he referred to it, to learn the idiosyncrasies of the units, the tenants, and fast fixes for most problems.

"Absolutely," she agreed.

He ran a hand through his hair, staring off to the side for

a bit before looking back at her. "It hurt my feelings when you dismissed my suggestion tonight."

Connie's stomach dropped. "What?"

"You were on the phone to call the repair service immediately after Mrs. Land dropped her laundry on us."

"Well…appliance repair is beyond the scope of our responsibilities and skill set, no doubt." She squirmed in her seat.

"That may be. The point I'm trying to make is that I made a suggestion, and you didn't even take a moment to consider it." He raised his chin and stated his case without raising his voice.

In her head, she relived the old bat yelling at her, going through the binder, and then calling the repair service.

"I don't remember it that way. I thought it was a time-sensitive matter and that calling the repair service was the correct response." She spoke firmly but was feeling less certain about her answer.

Sid's nostrils flared. "I don't disagree with that. What I'm saying is that I would have liked to have been part of that decision."

She was shaking her head before he finished speaking. "I've dealt with this before. Fix the problem and keep the tenant happy."

"You could have talked to me before making that call."

"Why?" She waved a hand dismissively. "That would have only delayed Sven from showing up."

"Right. *Sven.*" His lip curled.

"What's that mean?"

"You hang all over him while he's fixing the dryer and then blow him off when he asks for your number." Sid gripped the table until his knuckles went white.

"I did not hang all over him," she protested, ignoring the twinge of guilt in her spine.

"Then what were you doing? You didn't need to be there."

Heat crawled up her throat to her cheeks. "I was…supervising."

Sid snorted.

Perhaps she'd admired the fit of his jeans, and maybe she'd been mesmerized by his twinkling blue eyes, but that had quickly worn off. "I was! At The Arches, we didn't leave repair services in apartments unsupervised if the tenant wasn't home."

"Well, this isn't The Arches, and that was the *communal* laundry room."

Connie opened her mouth to argue, then snapped it shut. He was right. Dammit.

Sid rose from the table and pushed the chair in. "We're roommates, so if you want to ogle repairmen, have at it. My point still stands, though. When it comes to things that happen in the building, we make those decisions together."

He was gone before she could respond.

CHAPTER 14

"What are you doing here?"

Sid looked up at Frank, his mentor and former roommate, and pointed at his mug. "Drinking coffee."

"I can see that." The older man settled into a chair across the table from Sid. Around them, ODAAT community members bused tables, clearing the remains from Monday night's dinner in the center's dining room. The clatter of cutlery and the occasional laugh came to them in the corner of the room. "You've got a pretty skookum setup in that apartment, so why are you drinking coffee here? Ya moping?"

"No," Sid said defensively.

Frank crossed his arms and waited in silence. They'd been in this position so many times that Sid knew he wasn't off the hook. So he talked. About the date. About not being able to follow up on it because of Connie's busyness. About the washing machine, and Sven, and the conversation afterward.

Talking about it left him drained. Cradling the mug that had long since lost its warmth, he smiled wanly at Frank. "'Help me, Obi-Wan. You're my only hope.'"

His craggy eyebrows coming together in a frown, Frank

shook his head before sighing. "Ya done good."

Sid snorted.

"No, hear me out. You got your heart stepped on but didn't hide in a bottle. You defended your position about managing the building and set down reasonable ground rules instead of sulking and again, hiding in a bottle. Like I said, you done good."

A meeting was about to start, and the dining room was now empty except for them. The frustration and disappointment that had coiled into a tight ball in his belly loosened, and Sid breathed a little easier. "Thanks," he muttered.

Frank dipped his chin in acknowledgment. "So, what's your plan? Coming back here?"

That hadn't occurred to Sid. As uncomfortable as things were with Connie, he had no desire to return to ODAAT. "We agreed to share the apartment for six months. I'll stick with that. She's a decent roommate, and I just have to remind myself that's all she is." *And all she wants to be.* He let out a humorless laugh. "Though, you might see more of me when she does start dating."

Something that looked like disappointment flitted across Frank's face. "You're not going to try again with her?"

"Do you think I should?" His poor, battered ego couldn't handle another rejection.

Frank extended his arms to the sides. "I've been married and divorced three times and now live with a bunch of whiny drunks. Ya think *I'm* an expert on relationships?"

Sid smiled as he knew that was what Frank wanted. He may have not been an expert on relationships, but he was damn good at helping a person stay sober.

After yet another fitful night's sleep, he awoke to the sound of rainfall. Sid stretched and blinked, then reached for his phone to check the time. Seven a.m. He didn't have to leave to pick up Cal's Jeep for a few more hours, but he wasn't inclined to stick around the apartment any longer than necessary. Icy politeness was the best way to describe the current atmosphere between him and Connie. Perhaps he'd stop at a diner for a leisurely breakfast before heading to Cal's to avoid seeing her.

He couldn't look at her without thinking how badly taking her on a date had screwed things up. But now he knew she wasn't interested in him, and he would get over it. Eventually. And only if he moved out.

Despite his assertion to Frank, he didn't want to be *just* roommates with Connie. Sid wanted a relationship, and he wanted it with her. Seeing her every day and knowing she didn't feel the same way would be too damn painful. When he got back from the weekend, he'd tell her that he'd cover his half of the rent until New Year's, but he'd be out as soon as he could find something else. No doubt she'd be relieved.

It was early, his bed was warm, and yes, he was hiding from his roommate, so he set an alarm for eight o'clock and sank back into his pillow. A loud crash followed by car horns going off got him out of bed. He couldn't see anything from his bedroom window, so went into the living room. Pulling open the curtain, he craned to see the source of the noise. A bus was sideways, wedged between parked cars at the bottom of the street. The driver got out of the bus and immediately slipped and landed on her butt.

Sid retrieved his phone to call 911 and collided with Connie in the hallway.

"Oof!"

"Sorry," he muttered and returned to the window, Connie trailing behind him. The bus driver was up on her feet and rubbing her backside, talking to a passenger who stood in the open door of the bus. The passenger stepped down from the bus, grabbed the driver's hand, and they penguin-walked to the sidewalk. A blast of a car horn drew everyone's attention. Below their building, a car skidded and slid down the hill backward in a slow-motion ballet. With its passenger side almost kissing the bus, the car came to rest. The driver got out looking shaky but uninjured. He stared at his car and the bus and pulled a phone out of his pocket.

"Oh shit!" Connie exclaimed.

"No kidding," Sid agreed. "This is not going to be good." He'd heard from Clarice that except for Evelyn Land, who didn't get along with any of her children, and 3B across the hall, who never left her apartment, all the tenants were expecting a loved one to pick them up for Thanksgiving dinner. Sid had good boots, and if he took his time and walked carefully, he shouldn't have any problem getting to Cal's place. Provided Cal was still willing to lend him the Jeep. Depending on road conditions, he could even give Connie a ride to her parents' house. His phone rang before he could vocalize the thought.

"Hey," Cal said. "I can't lend you the Jeep today. The gate for the parking garage is frozen shut. With the roads being what they are, it could be a while before they can get it repaired. Sorry, man."

"Not your fault." Sid stared out at the ice hanging from the electrical wires. He disconnected and looked at the weather app on his phone. Freezing rain was expected until noon, with the possibility of snow. Icy conditions and Seattle's hills meant no one would be going anywhere for a while. He walked into the kitchen to make coffee and found Connie at the table talking on the phone in Spanish too quickly for him to understand what she was saying. She didn't look happy. Sid started the coffee brewing and went to get dressed.

He returned to the kitchen as the coffeemaker finished sputtering. Connie was still on the phone, now writing on a notepad. He poured coffee for himself and then one for her. He set it on the table before her and waited to catch her eye.

She smiled her thanks and pulled the phone from her ear while her mother rattled on.

"Your mom upset?"

She blew out a sigh. "She's taking this personally. Like the weather gods conspired to ruin her Thanksgiving dinner. Dad is supposed to pick up the turkey this morning and can't get to the store. And I won't be there to make the sweet potato casserole. Like *no one else* can do it. Hang on." She said her goodbyes to her mother and hung up. Picking up the mug, she blew on the hot coffee before taking a sip. "Thanks."

Sid drank his own coffee, staring out at the gray day. "Does Fred have salt or sand or whatever for the sidewalk?"

Connie nodded. "Yeah. He's got deicer and snow shovels in the maintenance closet."

"Okay. I'll go see how much we have. I figure we should do the front walkway and around the dumpsters at the minimum. What do you think?"

"Are you going to walk to Cal and Delia's after that?"

He shook his head and told her about their parking garage.

She winced. "I'm glad I don't have to deal with that. Those tenants are going to be pissed."

"Our tenants aren't going to be much happier. There's going to be a lot of disappointed faces around here." He pushed off the counter. "I'll go talk to the bus driver. Find out if she has an estimate for when the road will be cleared."

Connie took her coffee to the window to look over the frozen landscape. Icy rain had coated parked vehicles and weighed down leafless tree branches. Unless it warmed up quickly, it was going to be a mess. Below her, outside the window, Sid picked his way gingerly over the icy walkway. He slipped, righted himself, and turned to look up at the window. He grinned up at Connie and gave her a thumbs up. She returned it, feeling warmer. Three days of not speaking to him had been exhausting.

She watched him take careful steps down the street toward the bus. He stopped where the bus driver, passenger, and driver of the stranded car huddled under an overhang. They stiffened at Sid's approach but then slowly relaxed, and the conversation became animated, accompanied by a lot of head shaking and arm waving. Then a burst of laughter shortly before Connie's phone dinged with an incoming text. She read it, returned a thumbs-up emoji, and hustled to get dressed. Sid was bringing guests.

The building's carpeted lobby was warm. Its big windows provided a much better view of the trapped bus than the window in Sid and Connie's apartment, so after using the bathroom and accepting a cup of coffee, Sheila, the bus driver, decided to stay in the lobby. Connie brought the light, stackable chairs from the laundry room for the impromptu gathering.

Sheila removed her coat and slung it on the back of her chair. "There are accidents all over the city, and because this street isn't a main thoroughfare, it's not a priority. SDOT estimates at least three hours before they can get here." She raised her coffee mug in trembling hands and took a sip. "Sorry about that. I've been driving the same route for five years, and this is my first accident." The middle-aged woman's face was as pale as her white shirt. Connie didn't think she had anything to be sorry about and said so.

Kumar, the other occupant of the lobby, was a hospital pharmacist who worked the graveyard shift and was often Sheila's lone passenger that early in the morning. The tall, thin, stooped man spoke in a Middle Eastern accent and shifted his chair closer to Sheila's, absently patting her shoulder.

Sid had laid down deicer on the walkway and the length

of sidewalk in front of the building. Kenny, the driver of the stranded car, smoked and paced in front of the building. Connie hadn't learned his story, but the bulky guy looked like he was barely out of his teens. She guessed the sleek BMW belonged to his parents.

"Oh, lovely. Are we having a party?" Clarice smiled, her hands clasped in front of her as she surveyed the gathering.

Sid spoke low into Connie's ear. "I think she has an internal radar for sensing what passes for excitement around here."

Connie turned her head to meet his gaze. Humor crinkled the corners of his eyes, and she realized how much she'd missed it the last few days. Pride was such cold comfort in comparison to the warmth of his smile.

Sheila and Kumar were explaining the situation to Clarice, who was making sympathetic noises. She walked back to Connie and Sid with a gleam in her eye. "It looks like no one will be going anywhere for a while, so I suggest we have a party."

"Here?" The lobby was cramped with just five people. Connie couldn't imagine there'd be room for all the tenants.

"No, dear." Clarice clapped again and held her hands in front of her. "We'll have a progressive dinner!"

Neither she nor Sid was familiar with the idea of a progressive dinner and looked at each other with puzzled expressions while Clarice explained.

"We used to do it all the time in my neighborhood. We had young families, and it was too expensive to go to restaurants for dinner and pay for babysitters. It was so much fun." She sighed, clearly lost in memory.

"How did it work?" Sid asked.

"We'd meet up at the first house where we'd have a cocktail. Then, we'd walk to the second house for appetizers. We'd have the first course at the third house, move on to the fourth house for the second course, and have dessert and coffee at the last house."

Connie could see it in her mind and thought it was a great way to bring a community together.

Clarice went on, "Sometimes there'd be a theme. It might be all Italian one night. Another night, oh this was funny, everything served had to start with the letter B." She poked Sid in the shoulder. "You know, like the cocktail would have Bailey's in it. Or the appetizers were, ohh, broiled beets on bread. Now, that won't work here. We'll have to visit each tenant to find out what dish they've prepared." She fluttered her hands. "I need to write this down. I think better when I make a list."

"You're speaking my language. How can I help?" Connie asked, glad for something to do.

With a stop at their place for Connie to pick up her laptop and notebook, they followed Clarice to her apartment. Clarice's phone rang as she opened the door, and she hurried to pick it up.

"What are we getting ourselves into?" Sid whispered to Connie.

She grinned at him. "I haven't a clue, but this is kind of fun." It would certainly be better than moping around the apartment, hoping the weather would improve enough for her to get to her parents' place.

Clarice waved them to take a seat in the living room while she spoke on the phone. There was a loveseat and a recliner that was clearly Clarice's chair, so she and Sid took the loveseat. Sid's shoulder brushed against hers as he sat down. She'd been avoiding him for the past few days, which was awfully hard when you shared a bathroom.

Guilt and frustration and the awareness that she hadn't treated him like an equal had swirled in her head and in her gut. No amount of ibuprofen or Pepto Bismol would take care of it. To make matters worse, he was so damn polite.

He'd made dinner for both of them; *she'd* chosen not to eat with him. He didn't say a word, though. Just let her stew. And it took so much energy. And she was so over it, and with Clarice on the phone, now was the time.

Staring down at her interlaced hands, Connie sighed, "I'm sorry for snapping at you." She felt, rather than saw Sid turn to look at her. "I was worried about my sister and frustrated about the grant, then angry at Mrs. Land and took it out on you. You were right. It would hardly have delayed the process for me to talk to you first before calling the repair service."

All he said was, "Thank you."

She looked up at him. "That's it?"

"What do you mean?"

"You're not going to lecture me? Gloat about you being right and me being wrong?"

He twisted and put one hand behind her on the back of the couch. "I don't see any point in doing that. To me, it wasn't a matter of who was right and who was wrong. Just that I think we should work together. Make decisions together. How does that sound?"

"I'd like that."

His expression softened, and his hand skimmed the back of her neck for a second before coming back to settle in his lap. She would have been happy to sit there for hours with his shoulder pressed next to hers, and she wondered if she'd screwed things up so badly they couldn't go back to Friday night when he'd looked at her with so much warmth.

Clarice got off the phone and came toward them with a pad of paper and a pen. "Right. This is what I think we need to do."

CHAPTER 15

Growing up, Sid had never lived in one place long enough to know his neighbors, except for when he stayed with Aunt Angie and Uncle Dan. Their community seemed to revolve around them, and their house was always full of people. With how Clarice described them, progressive suppers would have been fun in his aunt's neighborhood. He also imagined there'd probably have been a few hangovers the next day. He hoped there wouldn't be a lot of alcohol present at today's progressive dinner, though. If so, he'd stick close to Connie for support, but sticking close to her was what he wanted to do anyway.

Thinking back on her earlier apology, he realized it was good to know she wasn't perfect; it was also good to know she didn't hold on to her mad for too long. Violet had turned holding onto anger and bitterness into an art form, and he'd had enough of that for a lifetime.

Clarice and Connie created a flyer that contained the details of the day's activities. Sid held a stack of them, ready to hand them out one by one and ask tenants if they wanted to participate. He'd been assigned his own floor, which was good because it was one less door to knock on, and now stood before Ms. Thompson's apartment. Her sister, Mrs. Sinclair, had the apartment next to hers.

He knocked once, and the door was opened almost immediately. Both sisters stood before him. "Oh. Umm. Hi."

"Good morning, Sid. Can we help you?" Ms. Thompson asked, eyeballing the papers in his hand.

He peeled off two flyers and thrust them out. "Yes! With everyone stranded because of the icy roads, there's going to be a progressive supper this afternoon. Would you like to participate?"

The women took their time reading over the information. "Please come in," Ms. Thompson said. "Jean and I have some questions."

Sid fixed a polite smile on his face, understanding now why Clarice said it would take an hour or so to inform all the tenants.

3B was his last stop. The tenant's name was Wanda Woods. He'd thought of her as 3B for so long, Sid worried he'd call her that. Wearing another Snoopy sweatshirt and an expectant look, she opened the door.

"I've heard your spiel with the other tenants, so you don't need to bother."

"Oh, good." He really didn't want to go through it again. "What dish have you made, and would you prefer to host tenants or deliver your dish to another apartment?"

"I won't be participating."

"Got it." Sid made a note beside her name and turned away.

"You're not going to try to convince me?"

Sid turned back. "Ma'am, I don't see the point. I understand you prefer to be by yourself."

She huffed. "Well, give me one of those flyers, so I'll know what all the noise is about."

Keeping his face expressionless, Sid did so before turning and leaving.

He found Connie and Clarice huddled over a spreadsheet in Clarice's apartment. They looked like generals plotting a battlefield strategy.

"Hey, what took you so long?" Connie asked.

"My back teeth were floating, so I stopped to go to the bathroom." He held up a hand as Clarice picked up the teapot. "If that's for me, no thanks. Except for 3B, every tenant insisted I come in for tea or coffee."

Connie stuck her lip out. "Nobody asked me in for coffee."

"That's because you carried a clipboard like a woman on a mission. They didn't want to slow you down," Clarice pointed out before looking up at Sid. "Everyone on board?"

He settled into a chair and set out his own paperwork. "All but 3B."

Clarice nodded. "Not surprising. Now let's figure out what we've got."

Sid and Connie, Evelyn Land, and 3B were the only ones without food to share. Altogether, there would be eighteen people, including Sheila, Kumar, and Kenny. Clarice came up with a schedule that had the top floor hosting first, then people splitting up and being sent to different apartments on the next floors. After that, Sid stopped paying attention, assured that he would be told where to go and what to do. From the sounds of it, the tenants were excited and looking forward to it.

"I'm surprised you've never done this here before," Connie said.

Clarice grimaced. "When I first moved here, there was a lovely woman who was quite the Julie McCoy, arranging outings, board game nights, all kinds of things. She had to go into care, and it hasn't been quite the same." She drifted off into silence that neither Sid nor Connie attempted to interrupt. She cleared her throat and then beamed at them. "Right, now, what's on the menu?"

Side dishes. Lots and lots of side dishes. Candied yams, scalloped corn, roasted vegetables, and jellied salads.

"Is there any protein?" Connie worried her bottom lip with her teeth.

Clarice perused the list. "Mona Tseng's pork dumplings and Helen Dubchek's cabbage rolls. She gave me the recipe years ago, and I think she combines ground beef and ground pork. Oh, and Jean Sinclair makes a charcuterie board that's to die for. So, yes, but not a lot. This will definitely be a different Thanksgiving dinner."

Connie shrugged. "I worked last Thanksgiving and came home to a plate of leftovers. This will be fine."

Both women turned to look at Sid.

"I can't remember which one," he said with a shrug, "but I ate at one of the shelters…. The food was good, and I woke up the next morning with two turkey sandwiches in my pocket. So it was all right." Noting their careful expressions, he went on, "I haven't a clue what a charcuterie board is, but I will happily eat it."

Clarice laughed and patted his hand. "Right. Now. We must discuss the fly in the ointment. Evelyn will no doubt stand in her doorway glaring at people and telling them to be quiet."

"What is her problem? She's always unpleasant, or is it just me?" Connie asked.

"She's Fred's ex-mother-in-law and has been here a long time. She was perfectly pleasant when I moved in—not terribly social, but pleasant. Something happened about three years ago, and her kids stopped coming around. I've heard her yelling at Fred, but I don't know what about. He and Debra divorced ages ago, but he still looks after Evelyn. She doesn't get along with Grace and Jean either—Fred's aunts. It annoys her that her granddaughter, Vivian, visits them as often as she visits Evelyn. That girl should be nominated for sainthood."

"And 3B—I mean Wanda Woods. Does she ever leave the apartment?" Connie inquired, wincing.

Clarice's lips tipped up at Connie's fumble. "Remember I mentioned the woman who arranged all the social events? That was Wanda's partner. She had a stroke and never recovered. Wanda was out of town when it happened...."

Tears gathered in Connie's eyes, and she blinked them away. Sid felt a tightening behind his nose. His own tears weren't far away, either. He stood and pushed his chair in.

"I'm going to go and check on the bus people. Where do you want me after that?" He grinned. "Aunt Angie and my cousins have been bossing me around for years. I'm good at taking orders."

"Excellent. Then you and Connie can rearrange the furniture for Helen. Don't let her try and do everything herself. She tends to forget she has a bad back."

❄

"I've seen him, you know."

Connie had gone to Clarice's apartment to retrieve a sweater for her and now faced a spiteful-looking Evelyn Land. "Excuse me?" Connie had no clue what she was talking about.

"The phrase is 'pardon me.'"

It was her own fault. Clarice had warned her, giving Connie specific instructions, "Get in, get out, and if you see Evelyn, do not engage." It should have been simple.

At Connie's silence and blank expression, Evelyn Land continued condescendingly. "The phrase, 'excuse me,' is used before doing something that may disturb someone. You say, 'pardon me' when you must apologize for a minor rudeness or need someone to repeat what they said." She shifted her feet, staggering slightly. "Your roommate. Everyone thinks he's so great, but I've seen him. Hustling tourists for cheap carvings and drinking out of a paper bag. I don't know what Fred was thinking, letting a drunken Indian in here. At least your kind knows your place." She waved a dismissive hand. "Go on back to your party. It must be time to do the dishes by now."

Gutted by the woman's vicious words, Connie stumbled toward the stairs. Stopping in front of her apartment, she brushed back tears and all but checked herself over for physical wounds. She'd worked with enough older people to understand that Mrs. Land's vitriol was fueled by loneliness, and Connie was simply a convenient target for her anger and frustration. But understanding didn't make it hurt less. She longed to climb into bed and have a good cry, but she should get back to the party. Hopefully, she could fake a smile and make polite conversation.

Feminine chatter rose up from the floor below, accompanied by a burst of laughter. Someone had suggested a taste-off for the five jellied salads and asked the bus people to be the judges. Kenny, the galumphing college student who'd almost totaled his mother's car, turned out to be an enthusiastic judge. He and Kumar got into a good-natured argument over whether carrots and cucumbers should be eaten combined or separately for the best tasting experience while Sheila laughed at them, refusing to get involved.

"Are you okay?" 3B stood in her doorway, frowning down at Connie.

"I'm fine," Connie sniffed. "I just needed a minute."

"Missing your family?"

The question caught Connie by surprise. In the excitement of preparing for the party and the confusion of traipsing back and forth and up and down to the different apartments, she hadn't thought about them. She was even more surprised by the question and the caring tone in which it had been delivered. "Not really," she responded truthfully.

"I talked to my mom earlier today. It might be delayed, but my family will have a Thanksgiving dinner."

"So why were you crying?"

Seriously? They'd barely exchanged a hello since becoming neighbors, and the woman chose now to show an interest? Connie forced a smile, not wanting to reveal anything to this stranger. "It's nothing. I need to get back."

As she turned to leave, 3B shared, "You remind me of Gina."

"I'm sorry?"

3B—Wanda cleared her throat. "Gina was my partner, and you have her same sort of energy."

Connie thought she saw the ghost of a smile on the older woman's face. "I'm hoping that's a good thing."

"For the most part, it is. Before I needed this"—she thumped the frame of the walker—"we were out and about all the time. If she had her way, we'd have been on the go constantly. Sometimes, I wanted to nail her feet to the floor."

Connie laughed. "You two sound like my mom and dad. When he finishes work, my dad wants to park himself in his recliner and stay there for the rest of the day. Mom works just as many hours as he does, but she still has energy to spare when she comes home."

Wanda nodded knowingly. "She draws energy from being around people."

"I never thought of it that way." Connie cocked her head. "That's a great way to describe it."

"Is your father around people all day?" Wanda asked.

"Yeah." Connie propped a shoulder against the door frame. "He runs a janitorial business with a lot of staff and has to deal with business owners as well."

"Sounds like he uses his evenings to recharge his batteries."

"Is that the way you and Gina were?" She hoped the question wouldn't send Wanda back behind her door, but the woman smiled again, this time a little sadly.

"For the most part, yes. I'm a psychologist—well, I *was* a psychologist. I had my own practice, which was rather draining. So I was pretty much done peopling by the end of the day."

"What did Gina do?"

"She was a speech therapist in an elementary school. She loved her job and came home with some great stories." Wanda lapsed into silence, staring off into the distance.

A murmur of voices came from the stairwell before Clarice stepped into the hallway, closely followed by Sid.

"There you are, dear. We'd thought you'd gotten lo—oh, hello, Wanda."

"Clarice." The front part of Wanda's walker poked out into the hallway, but she remained behind the door frame and nodded at Sid. She didn't tense up, seeming resigned to talking with more people.

Carrying two covered plates, Sid came to stand next to Connie. "There's enough food here for the rest of the weekend. Ms. Wood, would you like some?"

Wanda was shaking her head before Sid finished the question.

"Are you sure?" Clarice asked. "Mona made dumplings."

Wanda perked up. "Really? I haven't had those since...." She sniffed and wiped her nose on her sleeve. "Not since Gina's memorial."

"Well then, it's about time." Clarice grabbed a plate from Sid. "How about I carry this into the kitchen for you?"

Wanda's laugh sounded rusty. "Fine, Clarice. You can satisfy your curiosity about whether I've become a hoarder." She twisted around and moved deeper into the apartment.

Clarice grinned impishly at Sid and Connie before following her.

Putting a hand over her heart, Connie sighed. Maybe ice storms weren't so bad after all.

Sid nudged her shoulder. "I thought you were coming right back. Everything okay?"

She pulled away and headed toward the kitchen. "Oh yeah. No problem."

He stopped her with a hand on her arm and gave her a searching look. "Are you sure?"

"Um hmm."

"You're not looking at me."

She crossed her eyes at him. "Yes I am."

"Hey, when I said I want us to work together, it means I want to know what's going on. And not just if someone's toilet is backed up. If something upsets you, I want to know. Did Ms. Wood say something that upset you?"

Connie's eyes rounded. "Not at all! Ms. Wood is lovely. I'm glad I got a chance to talk to her."

He stepped closer and ran his hand up and down her arm. "So, what is it? I can feel the tension in you?"

She shook her head, eyes focused on the divot at the base of his throat. His pulse beat in a slow, measured tempo. They'd been having such a good day that she didn't want to tell him about her confrontation with Evelyn. She flicked her gaze up to meet his. His eyes were warm and patient and filled with concern.

Eyes glued shut, she got it out in a rush. "Mrs. Land stopped me in the hall, schooled me on etiquette, said she'd seen you drinking out of a paper bag at the waterfront, and Fred was crazy to let a drunken Indian in the building."

"Is that it?"

Her eyes popped open. "Isn't that enough?"

"Nothing she said wasn't true. A year ago, that was me." He continued to stroke her arm, his hand warm and comforting. "Did she say anything mean about you?"

Connie wrinkled her nose. "Just that at least my kind knows their place."

Sid stepped back, lips flattened into a thin line and eyes snapping with fury. "And this ends right now."

Connie grabbed his arm as he turned away. "No, Sid. Stop. She's a lonely old woman who's angry at the world, and I just happened to be there for her to lash out at."

"Uh uh. That doesn't cut it."

She held him in place with both hands. "I agree. But it's Thanksgiving, and you know how holidays can bring out the worst in people…and I think she might have been drinking. Her speech was a bit slurred, and she was a little unsteady on her feet. We'll both say something if it happens again."

He held her gaze steady, and his tense jaw relaxed. "If that's what you want."

"Yeah." She dropped her hands to her sides.

"All right." He hugged her, then pulled back, focusing on her lips.

Her hands rose to grip his sinewy forearms, and she waited, not breathing. Wanting him to kiss her. Wanting a return of that closeness she'd felt on their date Friday night. The pulse in his throat was beating faster, and her own heart rate kept pace as she pressed into him, silently urging him closer.

He lowered his head, his breath feathering her cheek, and she held herself in check, waiting.

He brushed his lips against her temple, then released her and stepped back. His gaze shifted from her lips to her eyes and back to her lips like he couldn't figure out what he wanted to do. "I…um, I'm gonna head back downstairs."

Sagging with disappointment, she slumped against the door to watch Sid walk away.

CHAPTER 16

The temperature rose, and the threatened snow turned into light rain, and the log jam of vehicles at the bottom of the street was gone by three o'clock. With careful maneuvering and a lot of instructions from onlookers, Kenny had moved his car without damaging it or anything else and had taken off, his belly full of progressive dinner delights. Most of the building's residents were tucked back into their apartments, snoozing after the excitement. Sheila and Kumar, each carrying bags of leftovers, waved at Sid and left in the bus. Sid had no idea where Kumar would have normally sat, but today, he was in the seat closest to Sheila. Both of them were grinning broadly.

Sid pulled his toque down lower and set about clearing slush away from the sidewalks and walkway in front of the building, applied more deicer, and went around to the courtyard to do the same. Cal called as Sid was putting the stacking chairs away in the laundry room.

"Hey, how did your day go?"

"Well," Sid chuckled and proceeded to tell him about the wedged bus, the progressive dinner, and the impromptu jellied salad contest.

"It sounds like you got enough to eat," Cal said.

Sid groaned and rubbed his belly. "They wouldn't stop feeding me. The only thing missing was the turkey."

"The garage door in our building is fixed. Do you want to come and get the Jeep?"

If he left now, Sid could make it up to his aunt and uncle's in time for a turkey sandwich and stay the rest of the weekend. He thought about Connie because it was her Thanksgiving weekend, too, and he didn't think leaving her with the tenants was right. For the most part, they'd treated her like their favorite grandchild and couldn't get enough of her today, but who knew what would happen tomorrow.

He had no desire to be away from her, either. It had felt good and right to hold her—even if a little briefly. It had been so tempting to kiss her on the lips. It might have been his imagination, but it seemed like she'd wanted it to, and he needed to find out.

"Thanks, but no. I might go with Connie to her parents' place for dessert."

A muffled noise was on the other end of the line, as if Cal had covered the speaker and was talking to someone else.

"Really?" It was Delia. Her question ended with a squeal. "You're going to meet Connie's parents? What are you going to wear?"

Sid groaned again. He *would* be meeting Connie's family, but he hadn't thought about it that way. The flowers he'd bought for Aunt Angie would now be given to Mrs. Ortega. As for clothes, he looked down at his jeans and boots. "What do you suggest?"

"*R*eady to go?" Connie called out as she entered the living room.

Sid nodded, and his appreciative gaze made

Connie glad she'd taken the time with her hair and makeup. He had changed into another plaid flannel shirt, clean jeans, and a denim-colored knit sweater in soft wool. Connie resolved to adopt the sweater as soon as possible. He looked yummy, and her younger sisters were going to eat him up. She knew the flowers he held weren't bought with her mother in mind, but her mother didn't need to know that.

The cabbage rolls from Mrs. Dubchek were going with them. They weren't something her mother made, and Connie had no doubts that she'd like them. The phone rang as she was about to pick up the container.

"Hey, Fred. Happy Thanksgiving!"

"And to you as well. I hear you're having some great weather today."

Connie rolled her eyes at Sid. "Says the man lounging on the beach."

Fred laughed and then asked, "Seriously, everyone okay?"

She put the phone on speaker and moved closer to Sid so he could be part of the conversation. "Sid found the deicer and is taking care of the walkways. A bus got stuck at the bottom of the hill, and none of the tenants could go to their families for Thanksgiving dinner, so Clarice organized a progressive dinner."

"That sounds like Clarice," Fred declared. "Everyone have a good time?"

"Well...." Connie looked up at Sid. "Those who participated did."

A sigh came from the other end of the line, and Connie imagined Fred running a big hand over his balding head. "I'd be surprised if Evelyn participated. But that's why I'm calling. She's a...difficult woman and won't have anything to do with the family. My daughter and I are about the only ones she has contact with. Usually, I invite her to Thanksgiving dinner—and she always says no—so I bring her a plate of food. I'm wondering if you wouldn't mind checking in on her?"

He was such a nice man. How could he have wound up with a mother-in-law like Evelyn? Connie reminded herself that Evelyn was Fred's EX-mother-in-law.

"I talked to her earlier today, and she seemed fine." Sid nudged her, mouthing the word, *liar*. She jabbed him with an elbow, and he grinned.

"Oh good." Relief was palpable in Fred's voice.

"We've got a ton of leftovers. Would you like us to drop a plate off for her?"

Sid crossed his arms and glared at Connie. "Those were my leftovers," he muttered.

"Sorry, I didn't catch that last bit," Fred said, drawing her attention back to him, "but it would be great if you did that."

"Not a problem, happy to help." They said their goodbyes, and Connie disconnected. "What else was I supposed to do? It's Thanksgiving."

"Yeah, yeah, yeah." Sid opened the fridge door and pulled out one of the containers of leftovers. "She can have some jellied salad and yam puree. I'm not sharing the dumplings." He glared, but his lips were twitching up.

"Oh, come on. There's at least a dozen dumplings. We can share."

"There's ten. I counted them." He put a protective arm around the container of steamed goodness.

"I'll give her three from my share then." Connie found a clean takeout container and started to assemble the food.

Sid plucked up a dumpling, popped it in his mouth, and chewed slowly as if savoring the taste before grumbling, "The old bat doesn't deserve it."

"You're probably right, but someone needs to be the bigger person."

"That's not hard considering how low she is."

Connie elbowed him, and he grunted. She picked up the container. "I'll be back shortly."

"I'll come with you. Someone needs to protect you from trolls." He puffed out his chest.

"We'll leave the plate on her doormat, knock, and then run." Connie grinned.

Sid waited at the top of the stairs while she walked to the door. She put the plate down, stood, and was about to knock when she heard something. She paused, her ear to the door.

"Are you coming?"

She held up a staying hand and cocked her head to the side. She heard it again. A low groan. She banged on the door. "Mrs. Land? Mrs. Land, it's Connie Ortega, are you all right?"

Sid was at her side in a flash. "What is it?"

"I hear groaning. I think she's hurt." She tried the door. It was locked. Sid raced for the stairs as she banged on the door again. "Mrs. Land, Sid's gone to get the key. We'll be with you in a minute." Alarmed, she turned, crossed the hallway, and knocked loudly on Clarice's door.

"Hold your horses, I'm coming," Clarice called through the closed door. There was a shuffling of feet, and she opened the door. "What now, Evelyn? Oh, Connie. What's up?"

Connie pointed. "I hear moaning, and I think Mrs. Land is hurt. Sid's gone to get the key, but I don't think we should enter her apartment alone." She wouldn't have been concerned if this had been The Arches and she was in an employee's uniform.

Clarice frowned, and then her expression cleared as understanding dawned. Accidental shootings happened all the time, especially when fearful, bigoted white people were involved. "You're right. I'll go in first. We don't need to wait for Sid, I have a key to Evelyn's place." Stepping more briskly, she went back inside.

Sid returned at the same time as Clarice. Connie picked up the plate of food and stepped aside.

Clarice knocked before unlocking the door. "Evelyn? It's Clarice. I'm coming in." She entered the dark, cold apartment and flicked on the light, Sid following behind her, Connie bringing up the rear. She bumped into Sid when Clarice suddenly stopped with a gasp. A small, sleek form slunk quickly past Connie.

"What the hell was that?" Sid demanded.

"I'm hoping it was a cat," Connie answered, looking behind her. A black tail flicked before disappearing around the door.

The one and only time she'd been inside the apartment, it had been clean but cluttered. Now, it was even more cluttered and definitely not clean. The basket of laundry Sid had delivered a few days before sat on the floor with three empty wine bottles nestled into the rumpled clothing. A wad of wet dishtowels lay on the floor next to it. The apartment smelled stale and musty, illuminated only by the light in the hallway.

Clarice was undaunted, moving steadily, if cautiously, deeper into the apartment. "Evelyn?" she called.

The moan came again, and the trio followed the sound to an icy, darkened bedroom. In the glare from the muted television, Connie saw an open window through the half-drawn curtains. The covers of the rumpled, unmade bed hung over the side closest to the window. Clarice turned on the overhead light, and Connie squinted against the sudden brightness.

A bare, wrinkled foot poked out from behind the bed and twitched. "Clarice?" a slurred voice came from the floor, "I need help getting up."

"What did you do?" Moving between the oversized furniture that dwarfed the room, Clarice turned off the television before stopping at the foot of the bed by the window. "And why is this window open? It's freezing outside."

"Stop nagging and help me up. It's bloody cold, and I think I peed myself."

"Hang on." Clarice waved for Connie and Sid. Connie moved to her side and looked back. Sid remained by the door to the bedroom, shaking his head. "I'll stay here," he said firmly.

"Who's that?" Mrs. Land demanded. "Who did you let into my home?"

"It's Connie Ortega, Mrs. Land. Fred asked me to check on you, and I heard you moaning." Connie lowered her voice to speak to Clarice. "Do you think we should call 911?"

"I don't need 911. Just help me get up."

Clarice tsked. "For a woman lying in her own pee, I don't think you're in any position to make demands. Now hush, Evelyn."

Sid spoke up, "We can move the bed. Would that make it easier?"

"It's either that or drag her out by her feet."

Connie chuckled at Clarice's matter-of-fact tone. "Let's start by closing the window," she suggested, "then covering her up with a blanket." Connie did so and stood back, surveying the situation. Mrs. Land was wedged between the big bed and the wall. With little room to maneuver, they were faced with a challenge.

"If we strip the bed and move the mattress and box spring to the side, we may not have to move the bed frame." Sid had taken off his jacket and hung it on the doorknob.

Clarice tucked herself out of the way in the corner and kept up a line of chatter while Sid and Connie set to work. The smell of urine rose as the room heated up, and she wondered how long Mrs. Land had been lying on the floor.

Apparently, Clarice was wondering the same thing. "Clearly, you've been down there for a while. What happened?"

"Butters was pawing at the window, so I went to open it,

but it was stuck. I pulled and pulled, but it wouldn't open. Finally I gave it a good yank, and it opened, but I lost my balance and wound up here. My back went out, and I couldn't move. I might have fallen asleep for a while."

An empty wine goblet sat on the dusty dresser. Connie suspected it wasn't the first one Mrs. Land had had that day.

"When did you get a cat?" Clarice wanted to know. "I thought you hated them."

Mrs. Land made a derisive noise. "I don't hate cats. *They* don't like *me* for some reason."

Sid snorted and gave Connie the side-eye. She bit her cheek to keep from laughing.

"Butters lives in the neighborhood," Mrs. Land went on. "I'd left my window open one day, and he came inside. I found him licking the butter dish. So that's what I named him."

Soon enough, the bed was completely stripped, the covers folded neatly and placed in the hallway with pillows. Sid positioned himself closest to the door, jutted his chin at the other side of the bed, and gave directions, "You push, and I'll pull."

Connie moved to do so, telling Mrs. Land what she intended to do.

"Well make it quick," the old woman snapped. "I haven't got all day."

"Stop that, Evelyn. No one would know what happened if it weren't for these two. You'd probably freeze to death, and the cat would be nibbling on your corpse for weeks." Clarice nodded at Connie. "Go ahead."

They shoved the mattress and box spring aside, revealing the bedframe and an accumulation of dust bunnies beneath it.

Mrs. Land heaved a sigh and wriggled. She got her hands beneath her and rose slowly onto her hands and knees.

"Can you stand? Or do you need help?"

Ignoring Connie's question, Mrs. Land demanded, "Clarice, give me a hand."

"Not me, Evelyn. I'd probably collapse on top of you. Let one of these young people do it."

Connie glared at Clarice's innocent smile before moving closer to Mrs. Land. "I'm going to wrap an arm around your waist and support you. Put your hand on the bed frame and see if you can push yourself up."

The old woman moved her hand to comply but didn't have the strength to push up. She sagged back down, pulling Connie with her. Connie braced herself with an oof and stood back up.

"I'll do it," Sid offered, moving closer. "Even if we move the bed frame, she won't be able to get off the floor by herself."

Mrs. Land tensed up. "Don't you put your—"

"It's that or call 911. And who knows how long that's gonna take with the roads being so icy?" Sid folded his arms across his chest. "Your choice, but decide soon because I've got better things to do than stare at your piss-soaked ass."

Connie gaped at him.

Clarice gave him a thumbs up.

Mrs. Land twisted her head to peer over her shoulder at Sid. "You're no better than me. I saw you with your dirty friends, drinking from a paper bag and trying to sell shitty trinkets you probably stole from a chink tourist trap."

A muscle moved in Sid's jaw, but he spoke in a measured voice. "That was me. I spent way too much time drunk off my ass. But I got help, and maybe it's time you did, too."

The room went silent. It was all Connie could do not to hug Sid. She settled for bumping her shoulder against his and smiling up at him.

"Fine," grumbled Mrs. Land. "But don't you—"

Before she could finish the sentence, Sid bent over, wrapped his arms around her middle, and hauled her up.

Twisting around, he placed her on her feet. She clutched the dresser, and Sid let go, walking around her to the doorway.

"Let's get you cleaned up. If you two put the bed back together, I'll take care of putting the covers back on." Clarice put an arm around Mrs. Land and led her out the door and to the bathroom. She stopped beside Sid, tugged on his arm for him to bend down, and kissed his cheek. "Well done," she murmured in a soft voice.

❄

*I*t was good to be out of the building, to be sitting in Connie's car with nothing to do except hold a plate of cabbage rolls in his lap as she drove carefully and competently on the wet streets in the late afternoon gloom. They crossed the Aurora bridge, skirted Green Lake, and turned into the neighborhoods of single-family homes and small apartment buildings. Sid craned his neck as the lights of Ballard High School came into view.

"My sisters and I went there. In fact, in that parking lot to the right, next to the big Madrona tree, is where I had my—"

As much as Sid was happy that she'd had a good high school experience, he didn't want to relive her first kiss with her. He didn't want to hear that it was sweet and romantic or so hot it made her toes curl. He didn't want to picture another guy kissing her. Especially as the kiss he'd given her today was so lame. Did a kiss to the temple even count? No, but it was appropriate to the situation. He'd have been an ass to take advantage of Connie after Evelyn Land had been so cruel to her. He was still angry. It would have served the woman right to freeze to death in her own piss after being such a bitch.

"—fender bender."

"What?"

"Minor car accident. Have you not heard the term 'fender bender' before?" She shot him an amused look.

Relief coursed through him as he realized she wasn't talking about an old boyfriend. "Yes, but I—never mind. You were saying?"

"Yeah, Robbie Tran—the jerk—backed out of a parking space right into me. Then he jumped out of his car, trying to blame me for it. Yelling that his dad was a lawyer and would sue my ass off."

She was smiling, so Sid figured things didn't end well for Robbie. "What happened?"

Connie grinned. "My friend Paulie was recording a video of himself singing with the radio and got most of it on camera. Including Robbie sucking on a joint. Not a big deal now, but that would have gotten him busted back then. And his dad, the lawyer, would have blown a gasket because Robbie would have lost his scholarship to Stanford."

"How'd it end?"

"His dad came to my house to talk to my parents. Mom made coffee, and we all sat in the living room—my parents insisted I be present. Mr. Tran put a big wad of cash on the coffee table and ignored it like it wasn't even there. He mentioned the contract my dad had for cleaning his building, he then *explained* to my parents that going through insurance would be such a hassle and suggested they settle it privately. Mom and Dad looked at each other, looked at me, then politely refused. Mom said they'd already started the insurance process and asked him if he wanted more coffee. Mr. Tran declined, said goodbye, and headed to the door, leaving the money on the table. But my dad got to the door first. Again, Dad politely told him to take the money with him. They had a staring contest, but Dad won, and Mr. Tran scooped up the cash and left."

"What about the cleaning contract? Did your dad lose it?"

"Um hmm. But six months later, Mr. Tran called and

asked to renew it. Unfortunately, the business had no openings, and Mom offered to put them on the waiting list."

By this time, they had turned down a quiet residential street lined with cars. Most of the houses were older and well-maintained, interspersed with those that had undergone extensive renovations, their modern exteriors looking out of place, at least in Sid's eyes. He didn't voice his opinion aloud. It was possible Connie's family lived in one of the newer homes. She pulled her Subaru into a narrow driveway behind a Prius bearing a University of Portland bumper sticker.

"That's my sister Teresa's car. I think she brought her roommate home with her."

"Is she okay? You never did tell me what she was upset about."

Connie looked at him quizzically. "I didn't?"

When he shook his head, Connie sighed and turned off the engine. "You'll meet her in a few minutes, but I'll warn you now. Tessie can be a bit…dramatic. Her boyfriend broke up with her, and she was devastated and needed to talk through it."

"Had they been together long?"

"About a week." At his slow blink, Connie huffed out a laugh and continued. "I know, it doesn't seem like a long time, but you have to know Tessie. She throws herself into things. It's probably why she's such a good athlete. She's a fearless risk-taker. That works out a lot for her, but sometimes…" She trailed off and shook her head.

"She gets hurt?" He winced, feeling bad for a girl he had yet to meet.

"Oh, Lord, yes. Don't ask her about how many sports injuries she's had. She'll go on all night."

"Is she going to be an emotional mess?"

"I don't think so. She texted me yesterday that her boyfriend, and I quote, 'realized the error of his ways and groveled his way back into her good graces.'" Connie rolled her lips between her teeth like she was biting back a smile.

Sid relaxed and shook his head. "Got it. Don't ask Teresa about sports injuries or boyfriends. Anything else?"

Connie's expression turned solemn. "I need to prepare you."

Sid waited while she chewed her lip. "You're making me nervous."

"I've never brought a guy home, which might be awkward. They know we're just roommates, but my mom and sisters are addicted to telenovelas and might try to… make things into more than they really are."

"Why haven't you ever brought a guy home before?"

Her eyes bugged out. "Really? That's what you focus on?"

"Seriously, I want to know." If there was a chance that there could be more, he wanted to know now. If there was no chance of him getting out of the "just roommates" category, he needed to know that, too. He prayed that wasn't the case.

Shifting in her seat, she spoke in a rush, "There's never been a guy I've liked enough to want to bring home. Not a friend or…anything else."

Her hesitancy gave him hope. Maybe it hadn't been his imagination earlier, and *she* wanted more from *him*. He held back his smile. "So I should be prepared for an interrogation from your parents and your sisters to ship us together."

"That about sums it up. You ready? I saw the curtain twitch, and we can't stay out here much longer."

"Right. They might start to wonder why the windows are fogging up."

"Sid!"

Teasing her was too much fun, and he wished they had more time alone. He balanced the plate and flowers in one hand and exited the car. The front door was flung open before he and Connie were halfway up the walk. The forms of three women were silhouetted against the welcoming light. One of the women squealed and raced down the porch steps to throw herself at Connie.

Laughing, Connie wrapped her arms around the young woman who had to be a sister, rocking her back and forth. "I'm glad to see you too, Tessie."

The sisters separated, and Sid saw the strong family resemblance in their facial features. The same dark brows and big brown eyes, full-lipped smiles, and rounded cheeks. Whereas Connie was short and rounded, with curly hair framing her face, Tessie was tall, long-legged, and slim. Her dark hair hung in a heavy sheet down her back.

She pulled back and grinned at Connie. "It's been months. Can I help it if I'm excited to see my big sister?" She glanced over at Sid, and her grin turned into a cheeky smile. "And you brought a *friend* home."

"Teresa! Let them come inside. It is too cold to stand outside."

"Right away, Mom." Tessie detached from Connie and looped an arm through Sid's. "Let me introduce you to everyone."

"Sure." Sid let her lead him into the house. Meeting a girl's parents was a new experience, and he hoped like hell he didn't screw it up.

Behind him, Connie grumbled, "That's what I was going to do."

Sid greeted Mrs. Ortega and offered her the flowers. "Thank you for having me." At the look of delight on her face, he inwardly thanked Gram for teaching him to always bring a gift when invited into someone's home.

"You're giving flowers to my wife? Have you got something for me?"

Connie groaned and gestured toward the graying, barrel-shaped man approaching them. "Sid, this is my father, Edward."

"Sir." Sid stepped forward with his hand extended.

Connie's father took his hand, scowling ferociously. "Call me, *Mr.* Ortega."

"Daaad!" All three sisters chorused.

"Don't be an idiot, Eddie." Mrs. Ortega smacked her husband on the arm before sailing past him with her flowers. She walked through the living room, into the adjoining dining room, and disappeared into what Sid assumed was the kitchen.

Edward Ortega's eyes crinkled up to the point of disappearing when he smiled. "Sid, it's good to meet you." He turned to Connie with arms spread wide. "Hello, princess. How's my favorite daughter?"

Wrapped in her dad's arms, Connie stuck her tongue out at her sisters. They reciprocated. "Everyone knows I'm the favorite," Tessie proclaimed with a toss of her hair before following her mother.

"You must be Samantha." Sid turned to a slight girl with her hair in two perfect French braids. "I'm Sid."

The youngest and smallest of the Ortega sisters smiled shyly. "Hi." She followed Tessie.

"What have you got there?" Mr. Ortega pointed at the container in Sid's hands.

Connie scooped up the container. "You're gonna love these. But I want to show Mom first."

And just like that, Sid was left alone with Connie's father. The older man gazed at him frankly. "Your people are up near Everett?"

"Tulalip, actually. On the reservation."

"I'm thinking of bidding on the cleaning contract for the casino. You got any pull?"

"Ah, no sir. I can't help you at all."

Mr. Ortega shrugged massive shoulders and led Sid into the living room. "It was worth a try. Let's get you a drink. I don't touch the stuff, but I know there's wine and maybe some cans of those mixed drinks. The girls like those."

"Just water for me, sir. I don't drink."

Connie's father gave him a once-over and a slow nod. "You got it." Laughter rose from the kitchen, and he smiled. "Let's go see what they're up to. And Sid? Call me Ed."

Tension leaked out of Sid as he followed the older man into a room full of laughing women.

CHAPTER 17

He seemed to be having a good time. If he wasn't, he was doing a darn good job pretending to. After eating turkey, mashed potatoes, and gravy—they'd already had massive amounts of side dishes—under the watchful eyes of Connie's mother, the table had been cleared, and the playing cards brought out.

Her mom shuffled and dealt like a pit boss; all of the Ortega girls were good at card games. Growing up, Sundays were considered family time. They would attend church, and while their dad would have an afternoon nap, the girls played board games or cards with their mother, read, or did homework. No cell phones or electronics were allowed. The sisters never argued with their parents about it because Sundays had always been that way. It was also the only day of the week their dad was home for dinner. His janitorial business meant he often worked evenings and sometimes late into the night. Her parents' hard work had paid off, and they had the contract to clean the branches of three major banks and four high-rise office buildings in Seattle. They now had an operations manager who handled the day-to-day, Connie's mom was training someone to take over the finances, and her dad rarely worked nights anymore.

Protests rose around the table as Sam turned over her last card with an innocent smile and won yet another round of Blackout. She pulled the pile of pennies toward her and made a show of arranging them into neat stacks of ten.

Tessie's college friend Casey threw down her cards and groaned. "Does she always win?"

"Pretty much." Dad winked at his youngest.

Mom pushed the cards toward Sam and rose from the table. "Please put these away while your sisters and I get dessert."

"Can I help?" Sid offered.

"Nah, that's skirt work." Her dad grinned amid outraged squeals.

"On second thought, you clean up." Mom picked up the deck of cards and rained them down over her husband's head, then she kissed his forehead and whispered something in his ear that made him blush. She turned away with a satisfied smile.

Connie felt Sid's gaze upon her and looked up to see him biting back a grin. He shot her the barest wink, and she scuttled into the kitchen, cheeks heated.

The women had formed an assembly line around the kitchen island. Connie served up pieces of pumpkin pie or apple crisp per request. Casey topped them off with whipped cream or ice cream, and Tess delivered the desserts while Mom got the tea and coffee ready.

"Your boyfriend is awfully cute," Casey said.

"We're just roommates," Connie said. "He's not my boyfriend."

"But he wants to be," Tess sing-songed as she returned from the dining room. "The way he looks at you? Yum."

Connie made a scoffing noise, concentrating on making precise cuts in the pie while suppressing a smile. Something had changed today. There was a hum of energy between them. An awareness of possibility. "You're just making stuff up."

"Uhh? Hello? Obviously, you weren't watching. He hung on every word you said. Oh, and Casey? Did you catch how he offered her the food first? Kept her water glass full and gave her his napkin when hers fell on the floor?"

"Umm hmm. He was so attentive." Casey swooned dramatically.

Tess poked Connie in the shoulder. "And who gave you his sweater when you said you were cold?"

"He was just…just.…"

"Exactly!" Tess cackled and picked up the last of the dessert plates. She and Casey headed back to the dining room.

A hand reached around her and plucked the knife from Connie's hand. She looked up to see her mother's soft eyes on her. "He's not—"

"Teresa is right. He wants to be."

"But we haven't…he's never.…" But he'd tried, and she'd backed off. Talking long into the night with Teresa, then burying herself in work. Fearing that she was just convenient and not enough for a relationship. Sid didn't push. Was he waiting for her?

"Really?" Her mother crossed her arms.

Connie tucked her hands into the sleeves of her sweater. Sid's sweater. She was enveloped by his scent. His care for her. She'd barely uttered the words that she was cold, and he'd pulled it off and given it to her. In their apartment, the fridge was now stocked with her favorite brand of yogurt. He cooked for her. She chose what they watched on TV.

"He puts the toilet paper on the holder," she said in wonder. Seeing the confusion on her mother's face, she explained, "When I was working at The Arches, a tenant was remodeling the bathrooms in his apartment. He was going to be gone when a worker was scheduled to tile the shower. I took her to the apartment, let her in, and showed her the bathroom. She pointed at the toilet paper sitting on the counter and split a gut laughing. She and one of the women she worked with kept a running tally of where people put their toilet paper. She said that men didn't put the paper on the holder nine times out of ten. I told Sid that story and that you were always after Dad because he would leave the paper on the counter instead of putting it on the holder."

"Sid is very considerate." Her mother pointed at the sweater. "And very thoughtful. A man doesn't act that way for someone he doesn't truly care about. No, you haven't known each other long, *but* you live together, so you have the benefit of seeing him when his guard is down. That means you need to be careful. Don't play with his heart."

"Mom! I would never do that."

"I know, sweetheart." Her mom placed an arm around her shoulder. "Definitely not on purpose. Hearts are incredibly strong, but they can bruise and break. I think Sid's offering his to you." She picked up the coffee pot and went to the dining room.

Her mom's warning not to play with Sid rang in her head. Was that what she had done with the repair guy? Possibly. Was that what was going through Sid's mind when they'd argued about the washing machine? She thought about him holding her today. His anger at Mrs. Land on her behalf. He was so protective and…caring. Connie rubbed her cheek against her shoulder. Feeling Sid and not just his sweater. She was warm all over.

They were back in the car an hour later with possibly more food than they'd arrived with. Learning that Sid had a sweet tooth, her mom had presented him with a container filled with mini pumpkin cheesecakes and told him he didn't have to share if he didn't want to. She also promised to share the recipe.

"Earth to Connie."

"Hmm?"

"The light's turned green. You okay?"

"Yep." She checked both ways, then went through the intersection. The rain was on the edge of turning into snow, and she drove carefully.

"I can drive if you'd like," Sid offered.

"No, it's fine." They continued on a little farther, but the thoughts in her head were taking up too much room, and she needed to know if her mother was right. She turned into the empty parking lot of her old high school and put the car in park.

Sid looked around, then over at her. "Did you change your mind?" He put the dessert tin on the floor at his feet, undid his seatbelt, and was about to open the car door before she could answer.

"Wait. No!" She grabbed his sleeve and held him back. "There's something I need to talk about."

He sank back into the seat and faced her.

She flicked a glance at him, then out the windshield. Fat, wet flakes landed and dissolved on the glass along with her courage. She rubbed her sweaty palms on her legs. "Do you...."

From the corner of her eye, she could see his white-knuckled grip on his knees. Apparently, he was just as freaked out as she was. She ripped off the bandage, faced him directly, and blurted, "When we got back from the restaurant last Friday, I thought you were going to kiss me. Then Tess called, and the weekend was crazy and...and...do you like me?"

He blinked. "Yes." The word came out as more of a question than a statement.

Connie was good at many things. She was fluent in two languages and was tackling Swahili; she manipulated pivot tables with ease, could pinpoint bottlenecks in organizational charts in the blink of an eye, and had no problem addressing and convincing a conference room full of stubborn tribal leaders about the benefits of sharing resources. Why couldn't she talk to an attentive, attractive man without sounding like a five-year-old? She wanted to punch him in the arm and take off across the schoolyard to see if he would follow her.

She undid her seatbelt and pushed her seat back. Holding his gaze with hers, she leaned across the console and pressed her lips lightly against his. Sid's eyes widened, and for a moment, she thought she'd made a mistake. Then he raised both hands, cupped her face, slid his fingers through her hair, and pulled her closer. He dragged his nose along hers and rubbed his lips against hers. His tongue darted out and traced the seam of her mouth, seeking permission to enter. She opened, and his tongue swept in. She clutched at his shoulders, loving the strength of his arms, wanting to crawl across the console, curl up in his lap, and kiss him for eternity.

He pulled back with a groan and a grin. "Yeah. I like you a lot."

She sighed. "I've been wanting to do that all day."

"I've been wanting to do that for weeks." He took her hand and rubbed his thumb across her knuckles.

A little thrill shot through her. "Yeah? When was the first time you wanted to kiss me?"

He answered right away. "When I found you in the dumpster. Even covered in garbage, you were just so damn cute." He grinned, then narrowed his eyes at her. "When I saw you flirting with Sven, I wanted to kiss you to let him know you were off-limits."

"I wasn't flirting."

He raised one eyebrow, silently mocking her. "Then what was that about?"

There was no escaping the intensity of his gaze, and she

needed to be honest with Sid and herself. Hoping to still her erratic heartbeat, she took a deep breath then let it out. "I was confused and a little bit afraid."

"Did I do something? Was I—" His eyes widened, and he reached for her hand, then pulled back as if thinking better of it.

"No." She laughed weakly, then took his hand in her own, tracing a fingertip across the knicks and scars on his knuckles. "You treat me *very* well. Better than I deserve, in fact. It's just—God this is hard!" She wanted to drive home, find a notebook, and write out a list of the reasons why she retreated, then another list of the reasons why he should give her another chance. Then turn that into a PowerPoint. Instead, she was stuck in the car with a sweet, patient man holding her hand and watching her with warm eyes filled with affection and maybe a touch of…. "Do you find this amusing?"

His lips twitched up. "Maybe a little. You're cute when you're flustered."

"You're not helping," she grumbled. He *was,* actually. His presence bolstered her confidence and quieted the butterflies in her belly. "I've dated some, but not seriously. Too focused on school and then work, I guess. Sharing the apartment with you was unexpected, but we've made it work, and you are such a good roommate." Was he *growling* at her? "I was afraid to change that dynamic. If we didn't work out as a…couple, we'd never be able to go back." He'd shifted in his seat, and his face was in shadows. She couldn't see his reaction, and the butterflies started up again.

"What if we did?"

"Did what?" This was not a conversation to be having in a dark car. She wanted to see his expressions and have time to formulate coherent thoughts. Sid wasn't giving either of those things to her.

"What if we tried being a couple, and it worked? It has been known to happen."

His dry response annoyed her. "But it could—"

He pulled his hand out of hers and pressed a finger against her lips. "Hear me out. We like each other. Right?"

Unable to speak, she nodded.

"And there's a mutual attraction? A desire to spend more time together and not just as roommates?" He shifted out of the darkness, and she saw his resolute expression. He was not going to let her hide. Again, she nodded, and he moved his hand to cup her jaw. "Good. Because the first thing I want to do every morning is kiss you. And it's the last thing I want to do every night."

She melted at the heat of his gaze and the fierceness of his admission, managing to squeak out, "Me too."

He heaved a great sigh and continued, "Things might work out really well, but we won't know until we try. If something bothers me, I will talk it out with you and not run away. If you agree to do the same, I think we can make this work."

Could it be that simple? She rolled the idea around in her head and thought that maybe, maybe it was.

"Yes." The word was barely out her mouth before Sid's lips were there, pressing against hers in a firm kiss as if sealing the deal.

"One last thing." He pulled back and narrowed his eyes at her. "I don't want to share you with anyone, so no flirting with repairmen."

She widened her eyes dramatically and spoke in a rush. "Mrs. Land was mad at me, and then you were mad at me, and he was *really* good-looking. But he ruined it by opening his mouth and wouldn't shut up." She leaned against the seat-back, staring at him. "Flirting with him was a dumb idea."

"I thought that if you liked them big and blond, I didn't have a hope in hell."

"Nope," she reassured him, reaching out to touch his hair, "that's not what I like at all."

Sid slid his seat back and guided her over the console until she settled in his lap. "Good." He kissed her on the nose, then pulled back, his gaze roaming her face before narrowing in on her lips. He ran his hands up her legs and under her sweater to bring her closer. Kissing his way up the side of her neck, he bit at her lower lip. "You have the sweetest mouth. I can't get enough—"

There was a tapping at the window, and a light swept the car's interior. Booming with authority, a voice came to them. "You're gonna have to move along. You can't stay here."

Connie giggled at Sid's frown. She clambered back behind the wheel and grinned at him. "I don't know about you, but that's a first for me."

"Making out in a car or being busted?"

Her giggle turned into a full belly laugh. "Both."

They pulled out of the parking lot with a wave at the security guard, and Connie drove home, two hands on the wheel and Sid's hand resting on her thigh.

❄

When Connie parked the car, he kissed her again, then he held her hand all the way from the street to their doorway. They kicked off their shoes, hung up their coats, and faced each other. She worried her bottom lip, peeking up at him through long, dark lashes. Once again, he took her hand, led her to the couch, and pulled her down beside him. She snuggled into him with her head on his shoulder like it was the most natural thing to do.

He put his feet up on the coffee table and let out a contented sigh. He couldn't remember the last time he'd kissed a woman. And definitely couldn't remember kissing someone when he was sober. Connie shifted against him, and he touched his lips to the top of her head.

She twisted to look up at him. "May I have a cheesecake?"

"Is that why you kissed me? To gain access to my cheesecake?"

"Maybe?" Her eyes sparkled as they looked off to the side and back at him.

He kissed her on the nose and then captured her mouth. Pulling back, he smiled smugly at her heavy-lidded gaze. "Fine. I'll share. But only one." He stood and hauled her to her feet. "I'll make the tea."

With tea and cheesecake, they settled back on the couch to play a round of Hallmark Christmas Movie Bingo. Connie printed out bingo cards, handed one to Sid, and queued up the movie. He ticked off the first square, "hot chocolate with candy canes," before she could, but she landed two in quick succession: "carol singing in the town square" and "cookie decorating disaster" next. She completed one entire row before Sid filled his second square.

He scowled at her when the movie ended. She'd filled in her entire card to his six squares. "Not fair, you've done this before."

She cackled. "Every year. It's the only way my dad will watch Christmas movies with us."

"That's cool. I have to tell Aunt Angie. She and Uncle Dan would love this. Any other Christmas traditions in your family?"

"Dad will put up the Christmas lights next weekend. He puts up so many outdoor lights he overloads the circuits. Mom told him to cut back. Instead, he had an electrician come out and add another circuit. People drive by just to see the display. I'm pretty sure the lights are so bright that planes get diverted from their flight paths."

"Don't the neighbors complain?"

"They used to. But now the lights go off at nine-thirty. He's got them on a timer."

"That's a lot of work." Sid's eyes widened. "Do you girls help him?"

"Uh, no. My mild-mannered father turns into a major pain in the butt. He has a plan. He has a system. And we'd just get in the way." She shrugged and rolled her eyes. "It takes him most of the afternoon, and it's usually dark by the time he's done. We grab chairs and heavy coats, sometimes umbrellas, and sit at the end of the driveway, drinking hot chocolate and watching him. Lots of neighbors join us, especially those with little kids. Dad's a bit of a ham and leads us in a countdown before turning it all on."

"That sounds awesome." His aunt and uncle's outdoor lights were nothing in comparison, and he couldn't wait to see her father in action.

"A little Clark Griswold, but yeah." Connie sighed like her father's antics made her really happy.

"Who's that?"

Connie gasped. "You don't know who Clark Griswold is?"

"Should I?"

She aimed the remote at the TV. "Absolutely. Prepare thyself."

He snuggled into the couch and pulled her close, content to watch old movies with her if it meant having her beside him.

CHAPTER 18

He awoke to the sound of rain again, but traffic noise accompanied it this time. Sid stretched out on his back and laced his hands behind his head. It had been a great night. After watching *Christmas Vacation* while Connie provided commentary, he'd kissed her goodnight outside her bedroom door and went to his own bed wearing a goofy grin.

Today, they would drive up to Tulalip. Connie had met his aunt and uncle at the party when Jimmy's Joint closed down and once again at the opening of CSEC. This time, though, this time he would be introducing her as his girl-friend. He liked the sound of that.

A noise came from the hallway, and then the sound of water running in the bathroom. He grinned to himself, wondering if she was grinning at the mirror. He got up to make coffee for her.

Later that morning, after coffee and a few sweet good-morning kisses from his girl, he took the compost bucket down to the yard waste bin. The sorting table looked a little grubby, so he retrieved a rag and cleaner from the maintenance closet and wiped it down. He'd left the courtyard door open and could hear someone huffing, so he went to help.

Mrs. Land glared at him. Two red spots rode high on her lined cheeks. "You," she snapped.

He stepped back to let her pass. "Can I help?"

"Now you ask? Where were you when I was hauling this from the elevator?"

There was no point in arguing. Was she hungover? Embarrassed? Or just plain mean?

She dragged the bag across the ground, and the plastic gave way, spilling its contents of soup cans, boxes from frozen dinners, and bottles. Lots of bottles. They clinked and clattered and rolled across the courtyard. Mrs. Land swore viciously.

Sid avoided her glare, picked things up, and tossed them into the recycle. He went to the closet for a broom and dustpan to sweep up broken glass. Returning, he found Mrs. Land stroking a muscular black cat and crooning to it. "Who's the bestest boy? Yes, he is. Does Butters want sardines or tuna?" The cat butted its head against her hand. "Tuna it is then." She turned and saw Sid at the same time the cat did.

It jumped down from the table and approached with appraising yellow eyes, and its tail held high. Sid glanced at Mrs. Land then down at the cat. He stood stock still while the cat sniffed his boots, looked up, then wove a sinuous figure eight through Sid's legs, before strolling to the open door.

"Humph," Mrs. Land muttered and stomped through the doorway.

The cat, Butters, watched her walk away then looked up at Sid. It might have been the light, but Sid could have sworn that Butters winked at him before following Mrs. Land at a desultory pace.

Hours later, Aunt Angie greeted Sid with a bone-crushing hug, giving Connie the same treatment.

"All right, Ang. It's not like they're returning from war." Uncle Dan clasped Sid's shoulder and grinned at him before greeting Connie with a gentle side hug.

"I'm just so glad they're here." Aunt Angie sniffed.

While he missed his cousins, Sid was happy it was just the four of them for lunch. Violet was still in Mexico, thank God. He came with enough baggage and didn't want to subject Connie to Violet's unpredictability. They were too new.

Connie and Aunt Angie got into a deep discussion about the hurdles of starting up a small business, which agencies and government departments were the most helpful, and which ones to avoid. Sid was in high school when Aunt Angie started up her insurance agency, and she had lots of stories about that time.

"This one," Aunt Angie pointed at Sid, "was a bottomless pit. I'd get home from work to find him standing at the door wondering what was for supper after eating everything snack-worthy in the house. There was a day when nothing went right. I had a new computer I couldn't get to work, the manual was incomprehensible, and I couldn't get hold of Cal, my usual tech support. Dan was out at sea, the girls were off somewhere, and I was so exhausted I practically crawled in the front door."

Sid groaned and covered his face. "Do we have to talk about this again? Haven't I apologized enough?"

Connie looked between him and his aunt. "I think I really want to hear this story."

"Oh, you do." Aunt Angie smirked. "So, Sid is sprawled out on the couch playing a video game at a thousand decibels."

"It wasn't that loud."

His aunt ignored him. "I'd called him earlier when I knew

I would be late, gave him my credit card number, and told him to order a pizza. Which he did. And ate the whole thing."

Uncle Dan looked up from his plate. "Don't forget the milk."

"Right. The milk. I was so damn hungry and so damn tired I didn't say a thing. I'd have cereal for supper. He hadn't eaten all of that, but there wasn't any milk left. I'm standing in the kitchen holding the empty milk jug—which he'd put back in the fridge—and he saunters in and asks if I'd brought home dessert."

"You didn't?" Connie gaped at him.

He scrunched his eyes closed, raising and lowering his hands in defeat. "I was a self-centered teenage jerk. I admit it."

"What did you do?" Connie asked his aunt.

"I threw the book at him. Literally. I grabbed a cookbook off the counter and threw it at him. Told him that if he could read, he could cook, and from then on, *that* would be his responsibility. Then I drove to the nearest fast-food place, sat in my car, and cried in my french fries." She laughed and wiped a tear from her eye. "When I got home, the place was as neat as a pin. The TV was off, and Sid was studying that cookbook like he expected to be tested on it."

Sid nodded.

Aunt Angie reached over and squeezed his hand. "It wasn't all his fault. We hadn't set up any kind of routine yet. We did so that night. We worked on menu planning, and he took over cooking supper."

"He cooks the meals for us, too." Connie smiled at him. "I really appreciate that. He makes some good stuff."

Uncle Dan snorted. "In the beginning, he had five things he could make. Don't get me wrong. They were good. But you get awfully damn tired of the same five meals time after time."

"Well, I appreciated it," Aunt Angie proclaimed. "It was one less thing I needed to take care of."

After lunch, Connie picked up the plates, but Dan snatched them from her hands. "Nah." He waved her off. "Sid and I've got this. You go talk to Ang."

"You sure?" At the nods from both men, Connie went in search of Angie.

"In here, sweetheart." Angie was ensconced in a big leather chair that hummed. "Dan gave me this for my last birthday. I thought it was a waste of money until I tried it. It has a heating and cooling unit and these little thumping things that hit my shoulders perfectly." Her voice jiggled as the massage chair operated. "Wanna try it?"

"No, I'm good."

"Would you mind taking a look at this, please? I'm not sure what they're asking for."

Connie accepted the paper from Angie and sat in the chair by the cluttered desk. She looked over what appeared to be a standard grant application. She found a paragraph circled in ink with a big question mark beside it. She read it through two or three times before inquiring, "Who is the grant from?"

"It's an organization made up of Protestant churches that oversaw Indian boarding schools in the past and want to make reparations. They recognize that there is unconscious bias and, at times, racism in how BIPOC people have been treated by the medical community. So they want to fund health clinics with staff that have all undergone equity and unconscious bias training."

"That sounds awesome and well-needed."

"Tulalip wants them to build one nearby. Our people, as well as the migrant farm workers, would certainly benefit.

I'm going to reach out to the local Black churches for their support as well. If I can figure out what that paragraph means, I can send in the application fairly soon."

"Yeah," Connie agreed. "They're using complicated legal jargon to cover their butts. Sometimes, I think these organizations want to look generous by offering grants but don't actually want to fund them. May I take this with me? Off the top of my head, I can't tell you exactly what they want."

Angie smiled. "Certainly. I would appreciate that."

Connie and Sid were on the road shortly afterward, with Sid driving while Connie dozed in the passenger seat. She blinked awake when the car stopped moving.

"Where are we?" They were in a crowded parking lot filled with Christmas trees. Twinkling lights strung around the lot shone invitingly against the gloomy afternoon clouds.

"Bothell. I think we should put a Christmas tree up in the lobby." Sid was out of the car before she could process the information.

They laughingly argued over the type of tree, the size, the cost, who would pay for it, and where to put it. In the end, they selected a short, squat fir, strapped it to the top of the car, and made their way home. They wrestled it into the front entrance of the building and propped it up in the corner of the lobby. Connie found a bucket, filled it half full of water, and they plopped the tree in it for the night. Covered in needles, sap, and sweat, they stood shoulder to shoulder to admire the tree. Sid mentioned seeing lights and decorations in the storage closet, and they agreed to put them up the next day.

"The tenants are going to love this," Connie said with a sigh.

"But do *you* love it?"

Connie plucked pine needles out of his hair and smoothed it back. "Yes. Yes, I do."

Sid kissed her nose, his eyes crinkled in a smile. "Good."

Holding hands, they headed up to the apartment. "This is going to be the best Christmas," she murmured.

After coffee the following morning, they searched through boxes Fred had collected over the years. Buried deep in the janitorial closet, they found a tree stand, some light strands, and a box of ornaments that looked like grapefruit-sized disco balls. They were so hideous; they were charming.

Sid stood to the side of the tree, hands stuffed in his pocket, gaze switching from Connie to the tree and back again.

"Well," she declared. "It's a start."

Pressed up against a window in the corner of the lobby, the tree itself was beautiful. Full and lush and redolent with evergreen goodness. In her mind's eye, Connie could see it twinkling, lighting up the night for passersby. Right now, however, it needed more lights, more ornaments, more everything.

Clarice came through the front entrance and smiled with delight. "You got a tree!" She dropped her shopping bag and came to stand by Connie. "Are you going for a minimalist theme?"

Connie laughed. "Until I can get to the store, yes. But it's a lovely tree, don't you think?"

Before Clarice could answer, there was a pop and a flare, and the tree lights went out. Sid hurried to unplug them from the wall outlet. Clarice patted Connie's arm, picked up her shopping bag, murmured, "I'm sure it will be," and hurried off.

Sid put an arm around her shoulder. "How about we have some lunch and then hit the shops?"

"Sure. I think there's a craft fair at the—" A phone interrupted. "It's my mom."

She engaged the call while following Sid up the stairs to their apartment, still thinking about decorating the tree. When they were kids, she and her sisters strung popcorn and cranberries. Could she convince Sid to do that with her? Should they get a star or an angel for the tree topper? She tuned into her mother's excited chatter when she heard the words, "leaving next Friday for three weeks."

"What?" Connie stopped in her tracks.

"We fly to Miami next Friday and will be home on the twenty-second. Your father and I have been talking about taking a cruise for years, and I can't believe he organized the whole thing by himself. Your Aunt Rosa will stay with Sam until Tessie gets home for Christmas break." Her mom sighed. "He thought of everything."

Connie looked up to see a worried expression on Sid's face. She sent him a reassuring smile that she didn't quite feel. "That's great, Mom. You deserve this. Is Dad going to put the outdoor lights up early then?"

"Oh, we'll put some lights up around the windows and front door this year. I don't want Rosa and Sam to have to worry about them. Dad will get the tree down before we leave, and those two can decorate it. Apparently, they're working on a color scheme. I can't wait to see it." Her mother laughed. "I have to go, sweetheart. I'll email the details to you in the next few days."

"Bye, Mom." The call ended, and she stared sightlessly at the phone.

Sid tipped her chin up with one finger. "Hey, what's going on?"

She sniffed. "My parents are going on a cruise."

"Oooo-kay. And that's bad?"

There was no way to explain it without sounding selfish. Yes, her parents deserved to go on a cruise, but did they have to do it now? Right before Christmas? "No. It's just…they won't be home until right before Christmas. Dad's not going to do the light display, and we're not going to decorate the tree together and, and…." She dissolved into sobs.

Sid wrapped her in his arms, and she cried into his shirt.

"Can I help?" 3B —Wanda spoke from her open doorway.

She felt Sid shake his head. "Connie got some distressing news and needs to process."

"Oh. Okay." There was a thump and a rattle from Wanda's walker, and Connie felt a hand on her shoulder. "I'm here if you need to talk to someone."

That made her cry all the harder.

CHAPTER 19

She was tucked up in the recliner wearing his sweater and wrapped in his aunt's afghan. Sid brought her a cup of tea and stroked a curl away from her face.

He had few good Christmas memories when he was a kid. He remembered getting a handheld gaming device that Violet resold and the loud drunken fights between Violet and whoever she happened to be with at the time. His first Christmas with Aunt Angie and Uncle Dan, he'd been keyed up, expecting drama. Instead, it had been fun. His cousins, Lisa and Laura, were in charge of the decorating. Lights and garlands and tinsel hung everywhere. When they finished decorating the tree, ornaments hung every which way, many of them homemade. Uncle Dan had scooped Sid up for him to place the angel on the top of the tree. The next day, they trooped to the mall. Clutching money given to him by Uncle Dan, Sid hunted through the stores for the perfect gift for Aunt Angie. On Christmas morning, she'd opened the box of coffee mugs with reindeer painted on them and cried. Sid thought he'd screwed up until she hugged him so hard that he couldn't breathe. After Christmas, Aunt Angie packed the mugs away with the decorations and lovingly brought them out each year after.

Now, Sid lifted Connie from the chair and settled her in his lap, tucking her head against his shoulder. "I thought I might carve a crèche for Aunt Angie this year."

"What?"

"She has one made out of porcelain, and Mary, Joseph, and baby Jesus are fair-haired and blue-eyed. I've always thought that's not what people in the Middle East would have looked like. If He were born here, on the West Coast, before the white man came, I wonder what animals would have been there? Not a donkey or a cow. That's for sure."

Connie had been toying idly with his ponytail and gave it a tug. "If there weren't a cow or a donkey, what would be the point of a manger?"

"It wouldn't have to be a manger. I'm picturing a woven basket lined with feathers and cedar boughs. Instead of a donkey and a cow, there'd be forest animals and sea mammals."

"What about the shepherds and the three wise men?"

"Fishermen instead of shepherds. And three *wise men?*" He looked at her in mock horror. "No. Three women in blankets, their hair braided with shells."

"That sounds beautiful. Your aunt will love it. Can I help?"

"Can you carve?"

"Nope."

Sid chuckled and tugged her closer. "How about make the tea and sweep up the wood shavings?"

"I can do that." She sighed. "I'm sorry I overreacted. Mom and Dad deserve this. It's just…I was surprised. This is our first Christmas together, and I wanted to share my favorite parts with you, and now that's changed."

His breath caught. Their first Christmas together. He wondered if she was aware of her word choices. "We could start our own traditions. Putting up so many outdoor lights we blow the circuits probably isn't a good idea, but we can certainly decorate our tree together."

"I'd like that," she said, kissing the underside of his jaw.

They headed to a local church that was hosting a "make-it, take-it holiday craft fair." The entry fee bought them coffee and two Christmas cookies each. Tables were set up for people to make wreaths, cut chains of snowflakes from paper, decorate gingerbread figures and houses, and prepare soup or cocoa mixes in mason jars. In one busy corner of the church hall, laughter rose over the sound of whirring sewing machines. Connie tugged Sid in that direction. Pieces of colorful fabric cut in the shape of large Christmas stockings were piled on a table. Next was a table full of lace, ribbons, fabric markers, buttons, and bows. The idea was for people to choose two fabric stocking pieces, glue or hand stitch on the decorations, and hand them to one of the four people operating sewing machines to stitch them together.

"Ta-da!" A man held up a finished stocking. The crowd applauded, and the man presented it to the waiting child with a flourish.

"Oh, hey. It's Tommy," Connie waved and called out, "Tommy!"

Tommy Federov found her in the crowd and waved back. He motioned them to join him in a quiet corner. He kissed Connie on each cheek before grabbing her hands and studying her. "I did not authorize the purchase of this sweater. But, hmm, I approve. It has that 'purloined boyfriend's clothing' vibe going for it." His narrow-eyed gaze took in Connie's sparkling eyes and Sid's tiny grin. "You two are just so dang cute." He turned and called, "Hey, Kevin. Connie's got a boyfriend!"

Sid knew of, but had never been introduced to Kevin Armstrong. A dark-skinned man smiled from where he worked at a sewing machine. He held up one finger and went back to conferring with a serious-faced girl who pointed at her stocking then pointed at the sewing machine. Kevin traded places with her, and the little girl sat on the chair in front of the machine, her feet dangling off the floor. The stocking pieces were put in place, and with her tongue poking out between her teeth and following Kevin's directions, the girl lowered the presser foot. Kevin said something, she nodded, and he used his hand to operate the foot pedal. The needle went up and down, slowly at first and then picking up speed. It was hard to tell whose smile was bigger, the little girl's or Kevin's. They high-fived when the stocking was finished, and the little girl scampered off with her finished stocking.

"He is going to make the best dad ever." Tommy clasped his hands tightly in front of his chest and sighed.

Kevin approached wearing a big grin and a Christmas sweater that matched Tommy's in hideousness. "Hey." He kissed Connie's cheek and slipped his hand into Tommy's.

While Tommy made introductions, Sid shook Kevin's hand and stood straight under the other man's appraising gaze. Kevin's eyes lingered on Connie's relaxed stance and hand tucked inside Sid's elbow. His lips tipped up at the same time his chin lifted slightly. Sid relaxed.

Kevin stepped closer to Tommy as a small boy ran past, clutching a fat candle coated in glitter. Tiny particles of glitter floated in the air behind him. "I hate that stuff," Kevin muttered. "It gets everywhere."

"Glitter is the best," Tommy proclaimed. "You're just going to have to live with it."

"Humph." Kevin mock-glowered at his partner.

"Changing the subject." Connie rolled her eyes. "This place is awesome!"

The hall buzzed with excitement. In one corner, a group was receiving instructions on knitting or crocheting Christmas stockings. Tables were lined up where Christmas baking was available: *lefse*, a Norwegian flatbread, *bizcochos*, and *polvorones de canele*, Mexican Christmas cookies, *Acibadem kurabiyesi*, traditional Turkish cookies, and brightly wrapped jars of jams and jellies. Soup and sandwiches were available at an open window by the kitchen.

Kevin nodded his agreement. "It was Tommy's idea. He mentioned it to my mom, and she ran with it." He pointed toward a woman with blinking Christmas lights woven into her braids, instructing a young man at the gift-wrapping station. She reminded Sid of Aunt Angie, patient, gracious, and warm.

"We used to do this at my church when I was a kid," Tommy explained. "My favorite part was afterward. The youth group would deliver cookies and sing carols with older folks at a seniors' home. My grandmother would sit in the front row and point me out to all her friends. She never wore her hearing aids and would bellow, 'That's my Tommy. He sings like an angel.'"

They laughed, and Tommy brushed away a tear. "She's the one who taught me how to sew. She'd love this."

Connie let go of Sid's hand to hug Tommy. The two of them sniffed and whispered while Kevin came to stand beside Sid.

"Is she okay? She's not looking her normal, perky self."

Sid turned to the other man and lowered his voice. "Her Christmas isn't shaping up the way she was expecting." He told Kevin about her parents' plans.

"The holidays are hard," Kevin agreed. "We all want a Hallmark Christmas, and it rarely happens. The year we lost my dad, I took my mom to Hawaii for Christmas. It was strange, but it gave us the opportunity to redefine how we celebrate and what's important. Doing things here at the church for the community is a big part of it." He waved his hand at someone. "Let me introduce you."

The woman with the blinking lights in her braids

approached them. She looked too much like Kevin to be anyone other than his mother. Almost the same height as Kevin, she had the same tilt of the head and the same high cheekbones. But the woman's dark eyes were framed by large cherry red eyeglasses matching her apron. Kevin put his arm around her shoulder and kissed her on the temple. "Mom, these are our friends, Sid Fraser, and Connie Ortega. Sid and Connie, this is Eleanor Armstrong, my mom." The pride in his voice was evident, and Sid felt a pang. He couldn't recall a time when he'd wanted to introduce Violet to anyone.

Mrs. Armstrong smiled and nodded but looked a bit stressed. "Nice to meet you. Are you here to volunteer?"

"Ah, no." Connie shook her head. "We didn't know about the event until today. But if you need help, I'm sure Sid and I—"

Mrs. Armstrong held up a hand. "No, that's fine. That's good, in fact. We have an abundance of volunteers today, and I wouldn't know where to put you. We may need some elves to help at our holiday toy shop in a few weeks. Different organizations and faith communities drop off toys and gifts, and we create a shop for parents and grandparents to pick out things for their kids. And then we gift wrap them. Here's the information to sign up to volunteer." She reached into a pocket of her apron and withdrew postcards that she handed to Sid and Connie. On the front was an illustration of a shop window framed by snow and filled with gaily-wrapped presents. On the back were a website, email address, and QR code. Mrs. Armstrong pointed at the QR code. "That was Kevin's idea. In here are links to the participating organizations, volunteer forms, and details to make donations. My son's a genius. He suggested handing these cards out to everyone present today. I would never have thought of that." She beamed.

Connie made admiring noises. "I think my parents'

church does something similar. I'm going to give this to my mom. She's always looking for ways to improve things."

During Thanksgiving dinner, Sid had learned that Mrs. Ortega chaired the facilities team at her church. If Mrs. Armstrong, Mrs. Ortega, and Aunt Angie got together, it would be quite the summit of organizing women. And *his* mother? Violet would be jeering and heckling from the back row.

W hat was that saying? *The fates laughed when people made plans.*

Sid had been choosing between different blocks of wood when the call came in from ODAAT. Now, he stood outside a hospital room, staring through a window at his friend, Frank.

He looked pale and cold, lying in a bed wearing a hospital gown and an oxygen mask, covered only with a thin sheet. He needed a blanket. Nothing was stopping Sid from entering the hospital room. He could see a blanket at the foot of the bed, still, he didn't move.

A nurse entered the room, checked the IV and the saline drip, and covered Frank with the blanket. Exiting, the nurse looked at Sid and smiled. "You can go in and sit with your father. It's good for people to know their loved ones are close."

Frank was maybe fifteen years older than Sid, but, yeah, he did look like he could be his father. Gray hair spilled over the pillow and down his shoulders. Veins bulged on the backs of his gnarled hands. Weather-beaten skin testified to his years on the fishing boats and then time on the streets. Sid didn't say anything; he just nodded at the nurse and slipped into the room to sit in the chair close to the bed. He watched the rise and fall of Frank's chest.

"Hey," he spoke to the sleeping man. "How are you?" Sid

laughed softly. "Stupid question, I know." He was hazy on the details of how his friend ended up in the hospital bed, he just knew that Frank had been found on the floor of his room at ODAAT, barely breathing. There was a big bruise on Frank's forehead. Had he tripped? Fallen and knocked himself unconscious? A bottle wasn't found in his room, and as far as Sid knew, drugs or alcohol weren't in his system.

Sid's hands shook. Not long ago, he and Frank were roommates, talking every day. Since leaving ODAAT and moving in with Connie, he'd only seen his old friend once or twice. Shame coursed through Sid. He'd been meaning to have Frank over but had never gotten around to it, thinking there was plenty of time. Frank had been instrumental in helping Sid get sober and stay that way. He was a permanent resident at ODAAT, mentoring many men over the years, and Sid wondered about Frank's current roommate. Where had he been when Frank fell?

A groan came from the bed. Frank blinked and lifted his head. Sid held his breath, but Frank closed his eyes and subsided back against the pillow.

The nurse poked his head in the door. "Did he wake up?"

Sid shook his head.

The nurse gave him a sympathetic smile. "It might be a while. But his vital signs are good, and he has a strong heart. Be patient. You've got about forty more minutes before visiting hours are over."

He left, and Sid stared at Frank, taking his hand. Sid couldn't remember ever holding another man's hand. He cleared his throat and started talking. "So, umm Connie and I are an item, and she's…pretty special." He told Frank about how they resolved their differences at Thanksgiving, that she'd been afraid, and he'd convinced her to make a go of it. He talked about meeting her family and taking her up to Tulalip. He didn't tell Frank how good it felt to make love to her, to wake up beside her every day. But he did tell him that her to-do lists made him smile. That their apartment was the first place that ever truly felt like a home. "I want you to meet her. So get better, dammit." He felt a slight pressure on his hand that was gone before he could decide if it was real or not. "I'll take that as a yes."

It was easier to process his thoughts while moving, and it wasn't raining, so he decided to walk home. Frank had been married three times. Sid had a vague recollection that he also had children but didn't know where they were. Did anyone other than the people at ODAAT know Frank was in the hospital? Would anyone visit him? He thought about finding Mrs. Land lying on the floor in her apartment and shivered. That was not the future he wanted, and was glad he had taken steps to avoid it. His phone dinged, and he stepped to the side of a building, out of the way of pedestrians to look at the text. It was Connie asking about Frank. She knew nothing about the man except that he'd been important to Sid. That was enough for her to care about him. Sid responded and carried on with a lighter step.

Waiting at a crosswalk, the spotlights in the window of a jewelry store caught his eye. A clerk was removing items from the display for the night. She picked up velvet-lined ring boxes one by one. Some held bands of hammered copper, gold, and silver. There were Celtic Claddagh rings and ruby and emerald dinner rings. Perfect for the Christmas season. A modest diamond solitaire caught his eye, and he thought of Connie. Would she like it? What they had was so new, but he could see himself standing at the front of a church waiting for her to walk down the aisle, take his hand, and say, "I do."

The light changed, and a horn honked, jerking Sid out of his thoughts. He strode along the sidewalks past shops closing for the night and bars and restaurants filled with people. He turned the corner to climb the final hill lined with apartment buildings. Approaching The Firs, he tracked the windows and their occupants. Curtains were drawn against the dark night, but light glowed behind them. He saw movement outside the window of Mrs. Land's apartment and stopped. Squinting, he made out the form of Butters. The cat jumped onto the ledge from a bare tree branch and pawed at the window. It didn't take long before the window opened, and the cat slipped inside. Sid's gaze went up and over to find his apartment to see a light in the living room. He quickened his pace, knowing Connie was waiting for him to come home.

He turned down the walkway and stopped in his tracks. A shadowy figure stood beside the building intercom, pressing each button in turn. He hurried forward, and the figure turned.

"Violet?" Dismay replaced the anticipation of coming home.

"Finally! I've been freezing my ass off here for hours, and no one will let me in."

Pissed off at her entitled attitude, Sid approached slowly. "What are you doing here?"

Flipping her long dark hair over her shoulder, she pulled her studded leather jacket tighter. Her fishnet stockings and short skirt were no protection against the cold weather. "I need to pee. Now let me in."

"That doesn't answer my question. What are you doing here?" He kept his voice low and even. No one needed to hear this conversation.

"Jesus, Sid. I'm your mother. I don't need a reason."

"Yeah, you do. Now, what do you want?"

She glared. "To use the goddamn toilet! Or do you want me to pee in the bushes?"

She would, too. He edged around her and unlocked the door. "Fine."

He hustled her through the lobby and up the stairs. She

steamed past him when he opened the apartment door and darted into the bathroom.

In the living room, Connie danced to music only she could hear, waving her arms, shimmying, and bouncing on her toes in silence. Sid crossed his arms and stood to the side to watch her. Wearing yet another set of baggy plaid pajamas, with curls bouncing around her face, he'd never seen a prettier sight. She turned and spotted him. Eyes wide and mouth open in a surprised O, she yanked the earbuds out.

"You're home." She rushed over and hugged him. "How's Frank? How are you?"

"I'll tell you later," he said with a sigh. "Right now, we've got company. Violet's here."

"Really?"

He nodded, relaxing into her, feeling the tension drain from his body. Silently, she rubbed his back. The combined scents of her shampoo and dryer sheets were the best aromatherapy in the world.

"Yeah. I'm not sure why she's here, but I'll get rid of her as soon as possible," he whispered.

"You don't need to do that," Connie whispered back.

"Yeah. I do."

Violet emerged from the bathroom and sauntered into the living room. "Ooh, isn't this cozy. Aren't you going to introduce me?"

Banging his head against the wall sounded more appealing. He'd hoped never to have to introduce Connie to his mother. Or at least not before preparing her and himself. Fortunately, she'd met the good members of his family first. He released her but kept her hand tucked into his own. "Mother, this is Connie."

"It's Violet." She narrowed her eyes at him before giving Connie a once-over and then dismissing her. She wandered about the room, picking up one object after another and putting them down in different locations. Pausing by the cedar nesting bowls, she palmed the smallest one, deftly slipping it into her jacket pocket.

"Put it back."

She pouted at Sid over her shoulder and complied. Settling into the recliner, she crossed her legs and surveyed the room like she was preparing to give an audience to her loyal subjects.

"Can I get you something to drink, Ms—Violet? Water or some tea?"

Violet inclined her head at Connie. "A glass of wine would be lovely."

"I'm sor—" Connie started.

"We don't keep any booze in the house," Sid stated flatly.

"Oh, right. Coffee then. I hate tea."

Sid raised a hand to stop Connie as she turned for the kitchen. "No, Violet. You wanted to use the bathroom, you've done so, now it's time for you to leave."

His mother's eyes glittered in the light from the table lamp. "But I just got here, and I thought we could have a nice visit and catch up."

"I'm carving, you've met Connie and seen the apartment, now go."

"Yeah, the apartment." She twirled one long carmine-tipped finger in the air. "It looks like that second bedroom is empty. There's room for me to stay a couple nights. Your girlfriend and I can get to know each other, do a little bonding."

It wasn't a request or a demand. It was a flat-out expectation.

"Absolutely not." Later, he would wonder where this newly acquired backbone came from. "I'll get you an Uber, then you're out of here. Go home to your boyfriend."

"You can't just throw me out. I'm your mother."

"You might have given birth to me, but you've never been my mother. Now go, you can wait in the lobby." He pulled his phone from his pocket to find the app. "I'm sorry about this," he spoke quietly to Connie.

"It's all right." No, it wasn't, but with her beside him, it just might be.

"I can't go back there. We had a fight." Violet picked at a thread on the arm of the chair.

"So, make up."

She made a dismissive noise. "I need a place to stay for a few nights."

"Not my problem. Head back up to Tulalip and fix it." No cars were in the area. He looked up taxi companies.

Like she'd sensed his mounting frustration, Connie suggested, "Let me get changed, and we can take my car. It might be faster."

"You can just lend me the car." Violet held out her hand.

Right. Like that would end well. Sid turned to Connie. "Thanks. I'll borrow your car, but you stay here. I need to talk to my mother."

He'd frog-marched a protesting Violet out of the building and into Connie's Subaru. The traffic gods were smiling on him, and soon, they were headed up a mercifully clear I-5. The smell of Violet's strong perfume filled the car. Sid cracked a window for fresh air, but it didn't help his mounting headache. He gripped the wheel tighter and spoke through clenched teeth, "Where does your boyfriend live?"

"I can't go back there. I told you we had a fight."

"And I said that's not my problem. And stop going through Connie's things." He reached over to snap the glove box closed, narrowly missing Violet's hand.

"Watch it! I was just looking for some gum."

Sid grunted and ran a hand through his hair.

Settling against the car door, Violet tucked a leg up beneath her and faced him. "You look good. Sleek and healthy. That little girl must be feeding you good and treating you good, too." She snickered.

He didn't bother looking at her.

"I'm hungry. Pull off at the next exit. There's a bar there that knows how to make a mean margarita and has great nachos."

"No. If you're hungry, I'll take you to a drive-thru when we get to Tulalip, but we're not going into a bar." He pressed down on the gas pedal, keeping one eye out for speed traps.

"Oh, come on. You can have water or milk or something." Not getting a response from him, she went on, "Is that too much for you? Can't handle the temptation? God, you're weak."

In his head, he heard Frank telling him not to rise to the bait. They'd had endless conversations dissecting Violet's toxic personality and her treatment of him. He remembered the last time he spent the night at Violet's place. His aunt and uncle had misgivings about leaving him with her but couldn't deny Violet access to her child. He was twelve and woke up to hear raucous laughter from the kitchen. Violet's newest boyfriend had come to visit, and a half-empty bottle of whiskey stood on the table. The man eyed Sid in his T-shirt and Spiderman pajama pants and poured him a drink.

Violet didn't protest. She laughed herself silly when Sid coughed and gasped over the rotgut whiskey. Then she added Coke to it. Sid drank that one down. Feeling fuzzy-headed and seeing the smiles on their faces, he asked for another.

He had no idea how many rye and Cokes he'd had that night. He did, however, remember waking up in his own vomit.

"Give me an address, or I'm taking you to a motel. I'll pay for one night."

She twisted in her seat to stare out the windshield. "Then drop me at the casino. I'll stay there."

"Uh uh."

"Oh, come on. You can afford it. They sell your stupid

chess boards at the gift shop for a mint." She made air quotes with her fingers. "Handcrafted by a local Indigenous artist."

His agent had recently negotiated deals with three tribal casinos to carry his work. It made sense that the Tulalip resort would have it.

"That may be, but it's *my* money, not yours. And I'm not paying for you to spend the night there." He could get cash to pay for a motel. The Tulalip resort would require a credit card, and he would not let Violet loose to rack up charges just to get back at him.

She stabbed him in the arm with a pointed fingernail. "You owe me. If it weren't for me, you wouldn't be making bank. I'm the reason you know how to carve. I introduced you to it."

They clearly had different memories. It was Aunt Angie who introduced him to Pops. On her way to Jimmy's Joint, she'd picked him up after that last night with Violet. He'd sat in the car feeling like death warmed over while his aunt chewed out his mother, then he slept during the ride into Seattle. Inside the bookstore/coffee shop, Aunt Angie told him to pick out five books while she talked with Gram and Pops. He couldn't hear the conversation, but it involved much sighing and head shaking. Pops had sat at the counter the whole time with his knife and a block of wood. Curiosity got the better of Sid, and he'd sidled over to see what the old man was making. Quietly, Pops spoke about learning to carve from his grandfather. Holding the wood and listening to it, letting the wood tell him what it wanted to be.

An exit was coming up, and Sid veered across three lanes to take it and pulled into a gas station.

"What are we stopping here for?" Violet stopped her harangue long enough to ask.

"Wait here."

He went inside to find the cash machine. Withdrawing three hundred dollars, he turned to find Violet grabbing a six-pack from the cooler. He thrust the money at her in front of the wide-eyed store clerk. "There's enough cash here for you to stay at the motel across the street and to get yourself something to eat. You don't want to do that? Then call someone to come and get you."

The watching store clerk made for a perfect audience, something Violet took advantage of. She hunched her shoulders, clutched Sid's arm, and wailed, "Please don't leave me here! I'm your mother."

Pulling away, he stepped back with both hands raised in the air. "Go ahead and make a scene. I don't care. I expect you can take care of yourself. You've always been good at looking out for number one."

The closing door cut off Violet's fury as Sid strode out of the store. Breathing heavily, he fumbled with the lock on the car door before climbing inside. He started the car and exited the gas station without a backward glance. An annoying ding penetrated his brain fog three miles down the freeway, reminding him to buckle his seat belt. A mile later, he called his uncle.

Uncle Dan answered on the second ring. "Hey. What's up?"

Sid gusted out a sigh. "I just dropped Violet off at a gas station in Lynnwood."

"So that's why she's blowing up Angie's phone."

"Sorry about that. I didn't think farther than getting away from her."

"Hang on. I'm putting you on speaker, and you can tell Ang and me at the same time."

There was some fumbling and conversation Sid didn't catch before his aunt came on the line. "Sid, honey, are you okay?"

Tears came to his eyes at the warmth and worry in her voice. "I am now."

It didn't take long to tell his story, his aunt and uncle

listening without interrupting. When he was finished, Aunt Angie spoke. "You gave her money, and she's not drunk and stranded on the side of the road?"

He was beginning to feel bad about it, thinking he'd turn around at the next exit and go back for Violet. "No. She's sober, and there's a motel with a coffee shop across the street from the gas station."

"Then I'm turning my phone off for the night. Maybe I'll talk to her in the morning." Aunt Angie's tone was determined. "And don't you go back and get her. She can sort things out with that boyfriend of hers." Her tone softened. "Sid, honey, I'm proud of you for doing that. Don't beat yourself up about it."

Staring straight ahead, he swallowed past the lump in his throat. "Thanks."

Uncle Dan declared, "Your aunt is right. You haven't done anything wrong. I'd like to think Violet will smarten up, but I seriously doubt it. You just take care of yourself. Where are you right now?"

"I just passed the exit for the U. I should be home in a few minutes."

"All right. Well, you drive safe now. And give that Connie girl a hug for us," Uncle Dan instructed him.

Sid nodded, his lips twitching up for the first time in hours. "I will."

Back at The Firs, the car had barely stopped moving before he was out and headed to the entrance. He took the stairs two at a time, and Connie was upon him before he could get his key out of the door lock. "Hey," she said, holding her arms open.

He fell into them and buried his face in her hair. Coming home had never felt so good.

She stepped back and took his hand to lead him to the dining table and pointed at a chair. "Sit." She turned a burner up under a pot on the stove and brought over a plate of sandwiches covered in plastic wrap. "I wasn't sure if you'd be hungry and figured these would keep if you weren't."

"Have you eaten?"

She shook her head. "I was waiting for you."

He snagged her around the waist and pressed his face against her belly. Waiting for him was such a simple thing to do. She pulled the covered elastic band from his ponytail and lightly ran her fingers through his hair, scratching his scalp. He groaned, luxuriating in the feel of her nails.

"Do you want to talk?"

In the warmth of her arms and the comforting quiet of their apartment, reliving the night was the last thing he wanted to do. "Maybe later. Let's eat first."

She ladled up the soup and brought it to the table. Sid plowed through two sandwiches in addition to the bowl of soup and a glass of milk before pushing back his empty plate. He chuckled. "I was hungry."

"So it would appear," she said dryly.

He smiled, his gaze darting around the neat apartment before catching on Connie's laptop at the end of the table. Beside it was an untidy pile of papers and a broken pencil. He remembered that today she was supposed to get word about the grant.

"Was that a happy dance you were doing when I interrupted you earlier?"

"Hmm? Oh." She laughed and looked away. "Not really. At least it didn't start that way. I cleaned the apartment, made soup, and still felt restless, so decided to have a dance party."

He took her hand and squeezed. "You didn't get the grant."

"No. They said the project looked promising, but there was a lot of competition that benefited a greater population, and I was welcome to apply next year."

"You?"

"I mean, the organization. CSEC could apply next year."

Connie fiddled with her spoon. Dipping it into the soup, tipping it to the side, and watching the liquid spill out. "I knew it was a long shot. The money was big and attracted a lot of interest."

Rising from the table, Sid picked up the dirty dishes and took them to the sink. He filled the kettle with water, placed it on the stove, and got the teapot down. He knew that Connie was good at grant writing, to the point she got requests from other local non-profits seeking her help. "Were you able to help Aunt Angie?"

"Oh, yeah. Not a problem." She waved a dismissive hand. "It's a small pool of applicants, and that group can't give their money away fast enough. It was just a matter of wading through the legal jargon and reducing it to plain English."

"It sounds like you've got quite the gift for this."

She jerked a thumb at the pile of papers beside her laptop. "That foundation didn't think so."

The water came to a boil, and he made the tea while trying not to roll his eyes at her pity party. Pointing out that her job wasn't on the line and it wasn't a life-and-death situation would not make life better. He dug back into his memory banks and thought about the ways Uncle Dan would lift up Aunt Angie. "How's it going with the speaker series you're working on for CSEC? Got enough interest?"

"Yeah. I originally thought we'd hold four classes. But when I put out the feelers, I got lots of volunteers. Working with small businesses, especially those with minority owners, is popular these days. I've got requests from banks, realtors, marketers, and two universities. We may target different audiences and have more than one speaker series. One for baby business owners and one for those further along, maybe thinking of multiple sites and what that entails." She stood and retrieved a cloth from the sink, then wiped the table. Looking a little happier, she went on, "Oh, and I think Delia will do a presentation."

"Really?"

"She can network like nobody's business and knows her way around social media. I think she'll do great." Connie rinsed the cloth out, then draped it over the edge of the sink. "The series is going to be awesome. We'll record the lectures and make them available online for those who can't attend in person. I just have to figure out the speaker order."

Sid doctored his tea and shifted to the side to allow Connie to do her own, glad she was perking up. He said, "CSEC is lucky to have you. You're good at your job." Leading the way to the living room, he settled on the couch and put his feet on the coffee table. Connie sat next to him. "Thanks. I like it a lot."

"How many grants did you apply for this year?" He knew it was a lot but didn't know the exact number.

"Seven," she answered. "We got six, but they were all pretty small."

"And that's a bad thing?"

She squirmed. "No, it's just.…"

He drank his tea and watched her rub her slippered feet together. He wasn't sure she was aware she did that when she was thinking.

"I wanted the bragging rights. I wanted the recognition."

"For you or for CSEC?"

Her feet moved faster, and then she stopped and sighed. "For me. Which is dumb because—"

"It's not dumb. There's nothing wrong with wanting a win. I'm just wondering if it was the right target."

"What do you mean?"

He put his mug down and twisted to look at her. "You said it was a long shot with lots of competition. There's nothing wrong with applying for smaller grants. Lots of people ignore them because they aren't shiny enough."

"Are you telling me to forget about prestige and focus on

what's achievable? That a lot of small wins are equivalent to one big win?"

"I guess so? I think what I was getting at, is asking if you want to work for CSEC or do freelance grant writing?" He was the last person who should offer career advice, but he recognized Connie's talent and wanted her to be happy in her work.

"I need to think about that." She sipped her tea, looking off to the side.

He placed a hand on her leg, idly rubbing his thumb back and forth across the worn flannel, happy to sit and be her sounding board or whatever else the amazing woman beside him needed.

"I think CSEC," she said decisively. "The organization is big enough that it can help communities in a variety of ways. Supporting small businesses is just one of those ways. If I stick with CSEC, I'll be able to see the long-term impact of their work. I think I like that better than grant writing for a whole bunch of people and never seeing the end results."

She gestured toward the unfinished nesting bowls sitting on the bookshelf. "I've never asked, but do you like doing small pieces like the bowls and chess boards, or do you want to carve larger pieces?"

"I think I like making things that are useful, not just decorative. Making the breadboards for ODAAT to sell got boring. It was the same design over and over. But I like knowing that those breadboards are functional. If someone approached me to carve something big that had a lot of meaning, I might think about it." He waggled his eyebrows. "Provided they offered me a lot of money as well."

She grinned back at him and slid a hand through his hair, tugging gently on it. "How did your talk go with your mother?"

He groaned. Connie had such great parents. It was embarrassing to admit what he'd done. Running away had never solved anything; dancing around the subject wouldn't, either. He told her what happened, concluding with, "It was a long time coming. Giving in to her just makes her more demanding. She doesn't want a relationship with me, just.…"

Connie scooted closer and wrapped him tightly in her arms. They sat like that for a few minutes before she pulled back, eyebrows drawn together. "And Frank, how did that go?"

"He's going to be okay. He fell and got a nasty cut on his head. He was in his room at ODAAT, and when he didn't come down for supper, they went looking for him."

Sid took her hand and entwined their fingers together.

"Was he…?"

"Drinking? No. That was my first thought as well. The nurse said his vital signs were good. He's unconscious, though." He darted a glance at her. "I held his hand, and I think he squeezed mine back."

"That's good." She smiled.

He thought about Frank alone in the hospital room. "When he's feeling better, would you mind if I have him here for dinner?"

"You don't need to ask me. Why haven't you asked him before?"

Was it possible to answer without sounding like a dick? Rubbing his thumb across her knuckles, he spoke without looking at her. "I think I was trying to compartmentalize, maybe keep my old life in the past. When I stayed at ODAAT, it wasn't always sunshine and rainbows. Staying sober was really hard, and sometimes I was a real jerk. Putting up with me couldn't have been easy. I think I look at Frank as a symbol of what I was, not what I want to be. Does that make sense?"

His hair had fallen in his face, and she untangled her hand from his to push back his hair and cup his cheek. Her brown eyes were filled with warmth and acceptance. "To me, it sounds like Frank helped you to become who you are, and he will always be welcome here."

The tension that had weighed him down all day released and fell away. He pulled Connie into his lap and buried his face in the crook of her neck. He hadn't gotten sober for her, but she was a good reason to stay sober.

She held him like that for a few minutes before rising and leading him by the hand. "Come to bed. It's been quite the day."

CHAPTER 20

After her parents took off for their cruise, Connie had been checking in on her sister and her aunt until Sam called her an old worrywart. They were fine. The photos her mother posted showed her parents were having a great time and would be home in the next couple of days. Tess was almost done with exams and then was headed to a volleyball tournament before coming home in time for Christmas. Pretty soon, her family would be together to enjoy the holidays.

Wreaths now decorated apartment doors at The Firs. Some tenants had added seasonal doormats, and Evelyn Land got annoyed with Clarice about the Christmas lights she'd put up to festoon her door. Mrs. Dubchek informed Connie that this happened every year and not to worry about it.

A text came in from her mom, which was a selfie of her and Connie's dad on jet skis. Would this be a new thing for her parents? Taking a vacation in December? If she still lived at home, would things be the same as they had always been? Possibly, but eventually, everything changed. Sam would graduate from high school and go to college. Her parents would retire and maybe downsize. No, change was inevitable; Connie just preferred it on her terms.

She thought about decorating the tree in the lobby with Sid. Maybe it was time for new Christmas traditions. The church that had hosted the craft fair had a concert coming up and had collected unwrapped toys for a local nonprofit. Would Sid want to go to that with her? She headed down the stairs to the lobby to vacuum up pine needles, picturing her and Sid in matching Christmas sweaters singing carols. She giggled. That might be going too far. Maybe the tenants would like to do a Secret Santa gift exchange. They could put the presents under the tree, bring chairs into the lobby, and drink eggnog or cocoa while they opened the gifts. She'd mention the idea to Clarice after she finished vacuuming. She pulled the lobby door open and stopped in her tracks.

The tree was gone.

The tree skirt she'd bought at the craft fair was gone. The lights she and Sid had put up around the picture windows were gone. A crushed ornament and scattered tinsel on the floor was all that was left.

Her knees gave out, and she collapsed against the bank of mailboxes, staring at the empty space.

"Move. I need to get in there."

Connie moved aside mechanically, allowing Mrs. Land access to her mailbox. The woman opened the box, leafed through its contents, then dropped everything into the nearby recycle bin. "Junk," she muttered, then looked Connie over. "What's wrong with you?"

Pointing a shaky finger, Connie replied, "The tree's gone."

"Good. It shouldn't have been here in the first place. Stupid pine needles everywhere and those godawful blinking lights."

"You don't understand." Connie shook her head. "Somebody stole it."

Mrs. Land crossed her arms over her ample bosom and

sneered. "Well, what did you expect? The neighborhood has gone to pot, and you put something shiny in the window. Serves you right." She stamped to the elevator, muttering about brainless young people.

Connie returned to her apartment with dragging steps. Sid wasn't home; he'd planned to check in on Frank, then head to CSEC to teach a class on woodcarving to a group of interested seniors. She wondered whether she should call the police, then thought better of it. What would be the purpose? They wouldn't be able to get the tree back. Maybe she should call Sid. But he wouldn't be able to do anything, either. Indecision warred within her. A knock sounded at the door, and she was tempted to ignore it. The knock came again, this time accompanied by Clarice's worried voice.

"Hello? Sid? Connie? Anyone home?"

Connie forced a smile and opened the door. "Hey," she said.

"Good morning dear. I noticed that the tree isn't in the lobby. Did you decide to put it in your apartment?"

"No. It was stolen."

Clarice's mouth hung open. "You're kidding."

"I wish I was," sighed Connie.

Clarice stepped across the hallway and banged on the door. "Wanda. Wanda! Get out here."

The sound of Wanda's walker could be heard, followed by her fumbling with the door locks. "For crying out loud, Clarice, I haven't had my coffee yet. What's the emergency?"

"Evelyn stole the Christmas tree!" Clarice declared.

"No!" Wanda gasped.

"I didn't say that!" Connie protested.

"That miserable old harpy." Her faded, plaid robe flapping around her tall frame, Wanda muscled her walker into the hallway and to the elevator. "She's taking it too far this time." She jabbed the call button and pointed an arthritic finger at Connie. "She is not going to hurt you again."

Connie grabbed Clarice's arm. "Mrs. Land didn't take the tree. She couldn't have. She was with me when I found it."

"That may be, but I wouldn't put it past her to orchestrate it, then hang around the lobby to see your reaction." She stalked after her friend. "I'm getting the others."

Visions of angry villagers bearing torches rallied to drive off evil forces came to Connie's mind. Should she be worried? The tenants were all sweet old women who'd probably send you into a diabetic coma from forcing Christmas cookies on you. Or stab you with their knitting needles.

Sid had taken the bus, and weekday morning traffic to and from West Seattle meant he wouldn't get back for a few hours, leaving her to deal with the impending Grinch lynching on her own. Connie said a quick prayer and headed for the stairs.

Five tenants gathered outside Evelyn Land's apartment, ready to storm the Bastille. Connie pushed through them to stand with her back to the door. She put her hands up. "Wait! We don't know that Mrs. Land took the Christmas tree. All we know is that it's gone."

"She took the Christmas tree?" Mrs. Dubchek scowled. "I thought she peed on the tree."

Clarice spoke loudly. "I told you she took the tree. Didn't you put your hearing aids in?"

Connie teetered when the door suddenly opened. Mrs. Land stuck out a hand, rocking her forward.

Mrs. Tseng gasped. "She pushed Connie."

Mrs. Dubchek grasped Connie by the arms and moved her away from the door. She got into Mrs. Land's face, waving a finger at her. "Don't you dare hurt this little girl."

"She's a grown woman, and I didn't hurt her. She stumbled," Mrs. Land snarled. "Now, what the hell are you all doing here?"

Ms. Thompson held up her cell phone. "I'm recording this for evidence, Connie, if you want to press charges."

Wanda pushed her walker forward. "Don't play innocent, Evelyn. Hand over the Christmas tree."

Once again, Connie moved to block the doorway. "She didn't take the tree!" She twisted her head to address Mrs. Land. "Sorry about this. For some reason, they think you took the tree."

Mrs. Land crossed her arms and jutted out her chin. "Maybe I did."

Multiple gasps erupted at her statement.

These women were going to be the death of her. Connie raised her voice. "Stop making the situation worse. I know you didn't do it."

"How?" Wanda asked.

Connie gestured toward the hallway with an open hand. "If Mrs. Land had taken the tree up to her apartment, there would have been a trail of pine needles, and there aren't any."

"I could have vacuumed them up."

"Now you're being difficult." Connie glared at the obstinate woman. "It would have taken two healthy people to bring that tree up here. Not one old woman with a bad back."

"Connie has a point," Mrs. Tseng said to Ms. Thompson.

"I could have asked someone to do it for me." Mrs. Land wasn't giving up. Apparently, she loved the attention.

"Then show it to us," Connie demanded.

Everyone looked expectantly at Mrs. Land. The bluster left her, and she looked everywhere but at the women. "I...I took it to a charity organization."

Clarice hooted. "That's a bunch of hooey. You don't have a charitable bone in your body. You're just trying to get us riled up."

"You started it! You're the one who banged on my door."

The rancor went out of the crowd of women, and they turned for the elevator while Clarice and Mrs. Land glared at each other.

Ms. Thompson muttered, "After all that excitement, I could use a cup of tea. Who'd like to join me?"

Mrs. Tseng and Mrs. Dubchek accepted her offer. Wanda remained silent, but Ms. Thompson put a hand on her arm. "Wanda dear, you're already out of your apartment, you might as well come with us."

"Yes," said Mrs. Tseng. "I'm having trouble choosing between—"

Wanda shushed her, and they all turned to look at Connie. "Certainly, Grace. I'd love some tea."

By then, Mrs. Land had closed her door, leaving Clarice and Connie alone in the hallway. Clarice looked rather pleased with herself.

"What was all that about?" Connie asked, feeling frustrated. "You knew she didn't take the tree, so why make all the fuss?"

Clarice turned the knob on her door and opened it, looking sly. "It got Wanda out of her apartment. Now she's having tea with the others. That will be good for her."

"Did you take the tree?"

The older woman came back to Connie. "No, dear. I have a feeling it was too much of a temptation, and someone came in off the street and took it. I'm sorry. Perhaps you can get another. A smaller one to go inside your place." Clarice's phone rang from inside her apartment. She squeezed Connie's hand, murmured another apology, and disappeared inside.

Connie stared at the closed door, feeling betrayed. All that fuss about something they didn't really care about; Clarice had done it just to liven up their day. Connie trudged down the stairs to the lobby. The tree was still gone, but now she noticed a trail of pine needles. She followed them down the corridor, past the laundry room, and out the door to the courtyard. More tinsel glittered on the ground, and sitting on the recycle sorting table was the star-shaped tree topper.

She picked it up to reveal a scrawled note. *"Thanks! The decorations are great, but you can have this ugly thing."* Beneath the writing was a poorly drawn illustration of the Grinch.

❄

Soggy takeaway wrappers were strewn across the small grassy area in front of The Firs. A crow squawked at Sid, picked up a french fry, and flew into a nearby tree to eat its supper. Sid cleaned up the mess, took it around back to the dumpster in the courtyard, and ensured the lid was firmly in place. Keeping the courtyard as clean as possible had become a point of pride. Butters sat on the sorting table grooming himself. He watched Sid through unblinking eyes and gave his tail one more lick before leaping off the table. He padded to the door and looked expectantly over his shoulder.

Sid grinned. "Let me get that for you." The grin slid off his face as he examined the door. It wasn't completely closed. There was a gap small enough to be unnoticeable to a casual glance but big enough to prevent the lock from engaging. He pulled the door open and squinted at the threshold. A marble-sized rock was wedged into one of the metal grooves. He picked up the rock and put it in his pocket, making a mental note to check for the same situation in the future. Butters slipped by him, passed the laundry room, and headed down the hallway.

The apartment was silent when he entered. He couldn't remember what Connie's schedule was for the day but thought that she'd planned on working from home. No doubt there was a message on his phone. The battery was failing, and he hadn't taken a charging cord with him. After hanging up his jacket and stowing his boots, the first order of business was to plug in his phone and touch base with Connie. He smiled at himself. He'd never believed he'd become one of *those* guys. Never imagined meeting a woman he wanted to rush home to make a meal for, talk over the day with, and plan a future together.

Once they'd successfully navigated family expectations surrounding Christmas and the holidays were behind them, he wanted to do just that. He wanted something official and wanted it with Connie.

He plugged in his phone and waited for it to turn on. His stomach dropped as he read the text messages and learned about the missing tree. Connie had called the cops and been directed to file a report, which she'd done. She'd then gone to her parents' place to get it ready for their return, only to learn that her dad had slipped and broken his collarbone. They wouldn't make their original flight and weren't sure when they'd return home. She hadn't said it, but Sid knew this probably upset her more than the stolen tree. Her last message said she would spend the night at her parents' house. Sid pressed the button to call her. The phone rang and rang.

"Hello?" A voice that was not Connie's finally answered.

"This is Sid Fraser. Is Connie there?"

"Oh, hey," came at him on a wavering sigh. "Hi, Sid. This is Sam. Samantha. Connie's sister."

"Hi, Sam. How are you?" Sid pictured the quiet young woman he'd met at Thanksgiving.

"I'm okay. And you?"

The polite exchange was driving him nuts. "I'm good. Is Connie okay? I was surprised when she texted that she's spending the night there."

Hollow footsteps came through the line, then the sound of a door closing. "Did you and Connie have a fight?"

"What? No." Sid pulled the phone away from his ear and glared at it. He wanted to pace but was tethered in place by the charging cord. He put the phone back to his ear. "Why? What's wrong?"

"She's crawled into her bed and won't talk to me," Sam whispered into the phone. "She said something about people laughing and nobody caring, and why should she bother. When I asked her to explain, she laughed—and not a this-is-really-funny laugh—and said there was no point and for me to leave her alone." There was a slight tremor in her voice.

"Sam, is your aunt there?"

"That's the thing. She and Connie had a fight. We'd just heard from Mom about Dad's fall and not knowing when they'd get home. Connie said she was worried they wouldn't get here until after Christmas. Aunt Rosa laughed and said Christmas under a palm tree beat Christmas in the rain anytime and wouldn't be surprised if Mom and Dad made the whole thing up. Connie didn't think that was funny, and told Aunt Rosa that she could just go if she didn't want to be there. So Aunt Rosa did. She packed up her stuff and went back to Yakima."

Sightlessly, Sid stared at the kitchen counter, his heart pounding. Family drama and the holidays were intertwined in his memory like holly and ivy around a tree. As a boy, he would hide in his room while his mother ranted about some imagined slight. But he was not a boy now, and Connie was not his mother. What had set her off? That didn't sound like her at all. He remembered the phone and the bewildered teenager on the other end of the line.

"Sam, did Connie bring anything with her? A suitcase?" Her laptop and planners were neatly stacked on the dining table.

"No. Just a small backpack with an afghan."

Sid twisted to look into the living room. The afghan Aunt Angie had made for Connie was gone. "Right. It might take me a while to get there, but I'm going to bring her some things. Do you need me to pick up some food?"

"No. We have lots here. Should I tell Connie you're coming?"

"Absolutely. On a white horse and everything."

Sam giggled. "That I'd like to see."

After getting the address, Sid disconnected and dropped the phone on the counter. He'd left that morning thinking he was finally getting his ducks in a row. Apparently, someone had told the ducks, and they'd scattered to the wind.

He pulled up the transit app on his phone to figure out what buses he needed to take to get to the Ortega home. Then he looked at Uber. It wouldn't be much faster and definitely more expensive. If he walked to a main through street, he could pick up a bus, which would be more direct. He went to the hall closet to retrieve his duffel. Laughter came from out in the hallway. It sounded like…Wanda?

Clarice and Wanda stood in the open doorway of Wanda's apartment, grinning like loons.

"Oh, hi Sid. How are you?" Clarice greeted him.

"I'm okay. But I got a text from Connie saying the tree from the lobby was stolen. Do you know anything about it?"

Clarice laughed. "Oh yes. And there was the biggest dust-up. Wanda blamed Evelyn and stormed her apartment. You should have seen Connie. She got between them like a protecting angel. We had the loveliest tea when we realized Evelyn didn't do it. Grace made—"

"You told me Evelyn took the tree," Wanda glowered down at Clarice.

"Did I?" Clarice played with a button on her cardigan. "I must have been confused."

Wanda loomed over the smaller woman. "No, Clarice you weren't. You distinctly said, 'Evelyn stole the Christmas tree.'"

"Well. What I meant was—"

Sid raised his voice over the bickering. "I don't care about that! How was Connie? Was she upset?"

Clarice darted a glance at Wanda and then back at Sid.

"I…guess so? Maybe. She was kind of quiet when I asked if she'd moved the tree, but then there was the kerfuffle—"

"That you orchestrated," Wanda interjected.

Clarice ignored her. "I told Connie it was probably someone who couldn't resist the temptation. It wouldn't be the first time there's been a theft in the building. Wanda, remember the—"

Sid ground his back teeth together to the point he thought they'd break off. "Clarice, please. Connie is not here, and I need to get to her. Tell me. How upset was she?" That tree had meant the world to her. She'd bought both an angel and a star for the top of the tree, intending to switch them out daily. They'd joked about which of the tenants would notice. Now, all the ornaments that she'd deliberated over were gone.

Color crept up the older woman's face. She looked everywhere but at Sid. "I…I don't know."

"I thought you'd checked on her before you joined us at Grace's." Wanda glared at her.

"The phone rang. And then I…." She stared down at her feet.

"Do you know where Connie went? Have you talked to her?" Wanda turned a worried expression on Sid.

He shook his head. "Yes and no. She's at her parents' place in Ballard but wouldn't answer her phone."

"It's just a tree," Clarice protested.

Wanda rounded on her. "No, it's not. You, of all people, know that, Clarice. It's the time and energy and memory. It's their first tree. And to have it taken away and made light of is wrong."

Clarice appeared to grow smaller with each word. If Sid weren't so concerned about Connie, he'd feel sorry for Clarice.

"Sid, is there anything I can do to help?" Wanda asked.

He sighed. "Thank you, but no. I'm gonna pack up some stuff and see if I can get a cab."

"Take my car." Clarice straightened up and blinked back tears. "It's the least I can do."

"Are you sure?" Sid hoped she wouldn't change her mind.

"Yes, she is," Wanda answered for Clarice. "It *is* the least she can do."

CHAPTER 21

Unicorns.

Smiling happy unicorns chasing butterflies, hiding behind apple trees, curled up, and sleeping on clouds. Mythical beasts sparkling and shining all over the wallpaper Connie picked out when she was ten. She'd gone with her father to a big box hardware store to buy paint, and it was love at first sight when she saw the unicorn wallpaper. She'd begged and pleaded and promised her parents that she wouldn't ask for anything else for her birthday or Christmas if they would cover just one wall with it. She'd worn them down until they agreed and spent a hot summer day sweating and swearing at each other while matching up the sheets of wallpaper. It was perfect. Almost.

Lying on her bed, facing the wall, she was nose to nose with a unicorn whose horn had been severed by whoever had cut the wallpaper panels. In that one spot, right in front of her, the seam was off by a fraction of an inch, resulting in the unicorn's horn being misaligned. Connie's head poked out of the afghan, and she sniffed and stared at the offending seam.

She hadn't told her parents she'd discovered it immediately after they'd finished. By the end of that day, they'd barely been speaking to each other. Both had sworn they never wanted to see wallpaper again.

Eighteen years later, Connie was still staring at it. Focusing on that one tiny imperfection. Why couldn't she see past it to the entire wall? She closed her eyes and sighed. Her nose was so stuffed up from crying she had to breathe through her mouth.

Sam poked her head in after knocking quietly. "Hey. Sid's here. Can he come in?"

It was tempting to pretend she was sleeping so she wouldn't have to face him, but she knew that wouldn't work. Sid would make a pot of tea and simply wait for her. She nodded. The door opened with a creak, and she heard a murmur of voices before she felt him. The air felt lighter, calmer, and more peaceful. She shifted as he lay down behind her and pulled her close. The weight of his arm and the warmth of his breath against the back of her neck released the tension in her shoulders. He didn't say a word, just held her.

She could have stayed there all night if her bladder wasn't full. She wiggled around to lie on her back and gave him a weak smile.

He kissed her gently and brushed a curl off her forehead. "You okay?"

She shrugged. "I will be, but right now, I have to go to the bathroom."

He huffed out a laugh and rose from the bed. She scurried to the bathroom to do her business and wash her face. When she returned, he stood by the bed, arms crossed, staring at the wallpaper.

"I was ten when I picked that out. I don't know why my parents haven't taken it down."

"Because it's awesome."

She snorted. "I thought so until I found a spot where the seams don't match up. Then it just drove me nuts."

He stuck out a long finger and pointed at the wall. "Right here?"

She gaped at him. "How can you see that?"

Sid grinned. "I can't, but that area has a slight discoloration. Like someone touched it a lot."

Connie moved closer, and he draped an arm around her shoulder. "I thought that if I got the wallpaper wet, I could shift it just that tiny bit so that the seams would match up."

"It didn't work, I take it?"

She shook her head. "No, and it's been driving me nuts forever."

"Why didn't you fix it?" He bent over and squinted at the offending area.

"At the time, I didn't want to bug my parents. It just about killed them hanging it up in the first place. And when I did talk to them about it, my mother dismissed it, saying I was making a big deal over nothing. I even saved up my allowance and tried to buy more wallpaper, but it was out of print. So, there it is."

Stuffing his hands in his pockets, Sid backed up, his head canted to the side. "May I try something?"

"Go ahead," she said. "You can't make it worse."

He turned to her desk and plucked a fine black marker from a coffee mug stuffed with pens and colored markers. He knelt on the bed and traced one side of the unicorn's horn with the marker. Looking at Connie, he held the marker out to her. "Here. Your turn."

Scrambling to kneel beside him, she asked, "What did you do?"

"If you thicken the outline of the horn, you'll cover up the mismatched seam."

Taking the marker, she duplicated Sid's careful outlining and sat back, stunned. "You fixed it."

He turned and dropped down on the bed, pulling Connie down to sit next to him. They leaned back against the wall, their legs stretched out in front of them. "No, we fixed it together," he countered.

"But that's…." She looked at the wallpaper and then back at Sid. "It's so much better. Thank you."

"I wish it was easy to fix everything else," he said. "How's your dad?"

"Sore and grumpy, but he'll be okay. Mostly I talked to Mom. Apparently, the cruise line can't do enough for them. Water hadn't been cleaned up somewhere, and Dad slipped. The cruise line accepted the blame, paid for the medical care, and upgraded my parents' cabin. They're going to stay on board for a few more days."

He wove his fingers through hers and brought her hand up to kiss the top of her knuckles. "I'm sorry about the tree."

He couldn't bring the tree back or fix her dad's shoulder, but his presence and those words made things so much more bearable. "Yeah," she replied. "Bad enough that it was stolen, but then Clarice turned it into a three-ring circus. I'm sure Mrs. Land hates me more than ever now." Comforting as it was to have him beside her, she still felt like she'd gone through the wringer. "Then I messed things up with Aunt Rosa. I'm going to stay here until my parents come home to look after Sam."

"Do you have to?"

"Yeah," she replied. "Sam can't stay by herself."

A crescendo of music came from the living room. The climax of an action movie probably. A *Die Hard* movie marathon was an Ortega family Christmas tradition. Connie supposed it would be just her and Sam this year.

"Does your aunt know about the tree being stolen?"

"No, why?"

He twisted to meet her gaze. "Maybe if you apologized

and told her what a crappy day you'd had, she might come back and stay with Sam. Then you could come home."

She sighed and rubbed her feet together. "I do need to do that. I know she wasn't being mean. I was just...." Her stomach rumbled.

"Hangry?" His lips twitched up as he looked at her.

"Maybe."

Across from the bed was the desk that she'd had since middle school. Above it was a corkboard-whiteboard combo. On the whiteboard was the packing list she'd made while preparing to move into the apartment. On the corkboard were index cards detailing tasks required to earn her MBA and move out of her parents' house. Each had been checked off. Beside the desk was a bookshelf holding the novels she'd started collecting since learning to read. Interspersed were awards, trophies, and knickknacks that held significance for her at some point in time. It occurred to Connie that she'd deliberately left those things behind. She'd outgrown them the same way she'd outgrown the wallpaper. Moved out and moved on. As jarring as the last few days had been, were they an indication that she needed to move on from her expectations around the holidays? Start building her *own* traditions?

A knock interrupted her thoughts, and Sam peered around the door. The lines on her forehead smoothed out, and she entered the room. "Pizza's almost done. Are you coming to eat?"

"Perfect timing," Sid replied. He pulled Connie up and tugged her toward the door. "Sam said that if I convinced you to come out of the room, I could watch John McLane with you."

"I told him we recite the dialog and fight over who gets to be Hans Gruber." Sam clasped her hands and bounced on her toes. "He thinks we're nuts."

Sid scowled at her. "I did not say that. I said your family was interesting."

"Same diff," Sam argued.

Pulling her hand away from Sid, Connie shooed them out of the room. "You two set everything up. I need to call Aunt Rosa." Hopefully, she could smooth things over with a sincere apology.

*A*fter pizza and Nakatomi madness, Connie and Sid kissed goodnight on the doorstep until Sam rapped at the front window. Catching their attention, she mimed looking at a nonexistent wristwatch and wagged a finger.

Connie giggled and pressed her forehead against Sid's. "I guess I should go back inside."

"Yeah." Sid didn't want to move, but his butt was getting cold, and no doubt Connie's was too. Cold rain hit them sporadically despite the protection of the porch overhang. He kissed her one last time and tickled the soft skin behind her ear with the tip of his nose. A shiver went through her, and he grinned. Pulling apart, he reached for the door behind her to usher her into the warmth. They said their good-nights, and when he heard the lock engage, he sprinted down the stairs to Clarice's car in the driveway. Safely behind the wheel, he waved at Sam and Connie framed in the front window, then drove off into the night, smiling.

As crappy as the day had been, it ended fairly well. Aunt Rosa accepted Connie's apology and said she'd be back the day after tomorrow and would stay until their parents returned. Tess should be home by then as well. Connie, Sam, and Sid had eaten pizza and popcorn, and Sid watched the two sisters recite the entire dialog of *Die Hard*, gleefully imitating the crisp diction of Hans Gruber. Then they had gone into raptures about the actor who played Hans Gruber. When Sam suggested that Sid stay to watch a Regency romance movie, he knew it was time to leave.

Back in the apartment, he'd written a note to Clarice and was on his way to slip it under her door. It was too late to knock and return her car keys, and he didn't want her to worry.

"I won't forget Gran. Love you, too," Vivian Thompson said softly as she exited Mrs. Land's apartment. Holding out her hand in greeting, she stopped to chat. "It's Sid, right? I'm Vivian. I was with my aunts when I met you and your fiancée a while ago."

Sid accepted her hand, not bothering to correct her. Fiancée sounded good, and he hoped to make that happen sooner rather than later. "Nice to see you again. Is your grandmother okay?"

Her big dark eyes grew troubled, and her smile diminished. "I'm not sure that Gran is ever okay. Some days she's better than others. I'm just glad that she has people who check in on her despite how difficult she is."

He schooled his expression to remain neutral. Difficult was putting it mildly. Over Vivian's shoulder, he could see Clarice's doorway. The door was framed with blinking lights and hung with a heavily ornamented wreath. A cheerful welcome mat in red and green sat before it. Mrs. Land had a mat in front of her door that said *Go Away!* And she meant it.

He nodded at Vivian. "Clarice is good at keeping tabs on people."

Vivian watched him intently, studying his eyes. She seemed to come to a conclusion and opened up her phone wallet. "Here's my card. Call me if you think she needs…someone."

It wasn't his place to judge, but he thought her grandmother needed more than someone. He took the card, offering, "Would you like Connie's number and mine?" At her grateful nod, he rattled them off, and she entered them into her cell phone.

"Thanks, I appreciate it. Especially with Dad in Hawaii.

My parents have been divorced forever, and Mom wrote Gran off years ago. I'm pretty much the only one she gets along with. She wanted me to move into your apartment and handle the building superintendent responsibilities for Dad, but that wouldn't have worked out because I sometimes have to travel for my job and didn't want to give that up. Dad told me not to move in, either. He figured my aunts and Gran would be demanding and intrusive, which could ruin our relationship. I think he was right."

Sid listened and nodded, all the while thinking Mrs. Land didn't deserve Vivian as a granddaughter.

"So I'm glad Gran has you and Connie and Clarice. Thank you," Vivian said with a small smile, then cleared her throat. "Gran said that you were an…alcoholic?"

"Am. With help, I'm able to resist. I don't know that I'll ever be able to put it totally in my past."

She shifted from one foot to the other, then peered back over her shoulder and lowered her voice. "Gran needs help. And I don't know.…"

Sid held up his hands. "In a perfect world, your gran would be willing to listen to me. But she's not. She's made it clear that she doesn't like my *kind*. And I don't know how willing she'd be to listen to you, either." He wasn't being unsympathetic. When he'd first hit rock bottom, he hadn't listened to his aunt, his uncle, or Cal and was just thankful they'd forgiven him and hadn't given up. "There are groups for people like you, though. People who have addicts in their lives and need support dealing with that. Maybe you could start there."

Vivian's shoulders slumped, and she looked down at her shoes and sighed before lifting her head and meeting his gaze. "I'll look into it. Thanks again."

He watched her head to the stairwell and turned to put the note under Clarice's door, thankful that he had been to a meeting just that morning. "One day at a time," he muttered to himself, then headed back to his apartment.

Clarice arrived on his doorstep the following day to retrieve her keys around noon—too damn early as far as Sid was concerned. She'd wrung her hands and apologized for the kerfuffle, saying she hadn't intended to take advantage of Connie's upset over the stolen tree. In Sid's mind, impact was more important than intention, but he didn't voice that aloud. After she left, he made a pot of coffee and drank it out of Connie's mug. It made him feel closer to her.

Standing at the front window, he watched the traffic go by. It was a cold, wet, dreary December day. A car with a tree strapped to its roof splashed through a puddle, and he wondered if it would be tempting fate to replace the tree in the lobby. He looked around the apartment. They could probably squeeze a small one into the corner by the window, but he might have to get an artificial tabletop tree at this late date. It wouldn't be the same, but it would have to do. He needed to take care of something else.

CHAPTER 22

Normally, their parents or Tess were around, so Connie didn't spend much time with just Sam. Now, she was learning what an awesome little sister she had. Sam wasn't a natural athlete like Tess, who'd been offered multiple college scholarships. Sam's bedroom was a bit of a disaster, with clothes, books, and art projects in various stages of completion scattered around. Connie had peeked in once and only once. Her tidy little soul longed to organize and make sense of the clutter. Instead, she closed the bedroom door and ignored the mess.

Sam was a bit of a dabbler; her grades were good but not stellar, and she had no clue what she wanted to do after high school. Like the other Ortega sisters, she worked for their parents' janitorial business on Saturdays. Sam seemed to enjoy the work, unlike her sisters, who'd simply put in their time. She liked the camaraderie of the cleaning teams, who were mostly South American immigrants. She'd become proficient in different dialects and was interested in their stories. Some of which she conveyed to Connie.

"It's heartbreaking how families can be broken up at the

border. They're coming here for a better life for themselves and their children and are willing to work. But they're greeted with suspicion like they've stuffed drugs and weapons in their pockets and their kids' toys. It's just wrong." The sisters had been working side by side to make empanadas for their parents' return.

"So what are you going to do about that?"

Sam snorted. "I'm seventeen. What can I do?"

"That depends on how deep your empathy goes. You can donate to organizations that help immigrant families. You can volunteer with local non-profits that work with immigrants. You can ensure that the people you work with know the services available to them. Things like housing or processing their immigration papers, and what rights they have so that they don't get taken advantage of." Connie put the tray of empanadas in the oven and turned back to her sister. "A language barrier is one of the hardest things immigrants face. It would be useful if you could help them practice their English and translate documents."

"Those are good ideas. I hadn't thought about that." Sam picked up the mixing bowl and baking equipment and took them to the sink. She turned on the tap and raised her voice over the running water. "Maybe I can print up something to go into the cards with the year-end bonuses Dad gives out. With a list of those services you talked about."

Connie nodded. "If you need help, let me know."

While the empanadas baked, the sisters cleaned up the kitchen. Sam got them each a pop, and she scrolled through her phone while Connie read over and responded to emails.

"Earth to Connie," Sam called.

"Hmm?"

Sam smiled. "I asked you if you had any pictures of Sid."

"Why?"

"'Cause I told Aunt Rosa about him, and the ones I have

from Thanksgiving with Sid in them, your big head is blocking his face."

"I don't have a big head," Connie protested. "The curls are growing back, and my hair is poufy."

"Whatever. So do you have any pictures of Sid?"

Connie pulled out her phone, opened up her photos, and handed the phone to Sam.

"Holy moly!" Sam's eyebrows winged up. "That's a lot of pictures. But I don't blame you. He's pretty awesome, and I don't mean just to look at."

"Yeah." Connie went squishy inside. There weren't enough superlatives to describe Sid. Awesome would have to do.

Sam laughed and turned the phone toward Connie. "What's the story behind this one?"

In the photo, Sid was leaning back against the couch, feet up on the coffee table, cradling a water bottle in his hands. He had one eye open, one eyebrow raised, and water running down his face. A balled-up pair of socks was on the couch next to him.

Connie giggled. "I was explaining my process for doing laundry, and he made fun of me. I threw the socks and nailed him right when he was taking a drink." Right after she took the picture, Sid jumped up from the couch. He'd chased her through the apartment before tackling her on the bed. Tickles turned into kisses, and shrieks of laughter became sighs of contentment as they made love for the first time. It had been a wonderful night. Feeling her cheeks warm at the memory, Connie turned her head aside to avoid Sam's perceptive gaze.

Sam was still scrolling through the photos, stopping every now and then to smile. She returned the phone to Connie and probed, "Do you think he's the one? Your happy ever after?"

So many things had happened to her in such a short time

—finishing school, landing the job with CSEC, moving away from home—that she hadn't spent time thinking about a happy ever after. Until Sid snuck up on her. The quiet wood-carver with a sly sense of humor was not who she had pictured for herself. "I think so. So much has been going on that we haven't had time to talk about it." Waking up beside Sid made her very happy, and Connie would be quite content to do so for the rest of her life.

"How does he measure up on your pros and cons list?" Sam asked with an impish grin. "I know you made one."

"Did not," Connie protested but wouldn't look at her.

"Yes, you have. You've made a pro/con list before making any big decision. Including whether or not you should cut your hair."

Connie pushed back the curls that refused to stay in place. "It's not a bad thing. I like to think things through before proceeding."

Sam picked up the phone again. "Is it on here?"

"Hey! Give that back!" Connie leaned across the table to grab the phone, but Sam twisted around and held it out of her reach. She had made a pro/con list, but no one needed to see that, especially her nosy sister.

"I wouldn't look." She handed the phone over and stood to take their empty cans to the recycle. "I'm betting the con list is pretty short."

It was indeed. But Connie didn't say that out loud.

The following day, she pulled into the parking area outside The Firs. She grabbed her messenger bag and the giant duffel Sid had packed for her. The man must have emptied her underwear and sock drawers into it. In addition, there were three pairs of pajamas, six t-shirts, and, for some reason, a pair of tailored dress slacks. She wasn't going to give him heck; she appreciated his thoughtfulness. Especially since the only thing she'd taken with her was the afghan.

Entering the dumpster courtyard, she appreciated the

tidiness of the area. The tenants had gotten on board with sorting their garbage, recycling, and compostables. Above the sorting table was a laminated poster with images of what items went where. The sorting table itself was clean, and the mat in front of the door had been swept recently. Her eye caught on a small doghouse-like structure tucked under the sorting table. She crouched to get a better look, and a pair of amber eyes blinked back at her.

"Oh!" Connie jerked up. "Butters. Did someone make you a home?"

The cat came through the clear plastic flap covering the entrance to the vinyl structure. He sniffed at Connie's shoes before leaping up onto the recycle bin and then onto the surrounding wall. From there, he watched her.

Connie looked at the cat and then back at the house. "May I?"

Butters ignored her.

"I'll take that as a yes." Connie dropped her bags on top of the sorting table and bent down. Recently filled food and water dishes occupied a rubber mat. An electrical cord ran from the back of the building to an outlet. Lifting up the flap, Connie saw a sheepskin mat covering the bottom. It was soft and warm to the touch. She stood and turned to the cat. "Room and board. Are you paying rent?" Chuckling to herself, she picked up her bags and unlocked the backdoor.

Voices came from behind the closed laundry room door to her left. That was odd. She tried turning the knob. It was locked. She knocked, the voices went quiet, then the door opened, and Mrs. Dubchek peeked out. "Yes?"

"Hi, Mrs. Dubchek, is everything okay?"

Mrs. Dubchek frowned at something or someone behind her and then looked innocently at Connie. "Yes."

"Oh, well, have a good day."

"Yes." She closed the door, and voices resumed in a buzz. Then someone scolded, "Shh!" and all went quiet.

Connie raised her hand to knock again but thought better of it. She'd only be borrowing trouble, and God knows, she'd had enough of it lately.

Pine needles were scattered on the corridor carpet, and she made a note to run the vacuum cleaner later that day. It still pained her that someone had taken the Christmas tree, but she consoled herself with the fact that they hadn't made a mess, nor was anyone hurt. Sid had told her about the back door not closing properly because of pebbles wedged in the track. She'd chastised herself for not being more diligent about locking up. When she'd told Aunt Rosa about it, the older woman replied, "Locks only keep honest people out."

Butters blinked at her from the foot of the stairs.

"Let me guess," Connie said, "you have your own door and a house? Hopefully, you won't be letting the riffraff in."

The cat trotted up the stairs, neither agreeing nor disagreeing. Connie followed more slowly, wondering if there was a rule about pets in the building. She'd have to look through the binder.

Wanda stood in her doorway to greet Butters in a cooing voice as the cat and Connie exited the stairwell. "There's that handsome boy. Did you enjoy your breakfast? I've got some new treats for you to try."

"I didn't know you were a cat lady." Connie smiled at the interaction.

Clutching the handles of her walker, Wanda straightened up and shrugged. "What can I say? He's good company and doesn't hog the remote. How are you today?"

"Better, thank you. There was just a lot going on."

Wanda studied her from under shaggy eyebrows. "Sometimes the women here act like a bunch of over-sugared toddlers in need of a nap. I hope you understand, we do appreciate you. You have an energy this place has been missing. And Sid is…a good egg."

Connie chewed on her bottom lip to keep from laughing. Sid was so much more than a good egg.

A demanding meow came from inside Wanda's apartment. "I'm coming," Wanda called over her shoulder. To Connie, she said, "I'll see you later."

$\mathcal{H}$olding his phone to his ear, Sid approached from the living room when she opened the door. "I gotta go. I'll call you later." He disconnected his call and was on her in a flash. She dropped her duffel and messenger bag and melted into his arms. Her head fit snugly into his neck, and he breathed in her scent. "I don't like it when you're not here," he muttered, kissing her on the temple before joining his lips with hers.

A shiver went through him at her sigh. "I missed you, too," she said.

Without her at the apartment, he'd slept in his own bed the last two nights but had snagged one of her pillows. He'd never thought he would miss someone so much. "You're not allowed to do that again," he growled.

Connie stiffened and pulled back. "Excuse me?"

"I didn't sleep without you here and had to put up with all the crazies by myself, so you're not allowed to go away again. Ever."

She smacked his shoulder. "Who is this Neanderthal telling me what I'm allowed to do, and where is my Sid?"

"What did you call me?"

"I said you were a Neanderthal." Connie glared at him.

"No. The other thing."

Confusion, then understanding, passed through her expression. She looked down and then peeked up at him through her lashes. "My Sid," she replied softly.

He tipped her chin up and studied her face. If he lived to be a hundred, he wouldn't get tired of looking at her. Of seeing her looking at him with those warm brown eyes. "My Connie," he murmured and kissed her again.

A knock at the door interrupted them.

Sid growled.

Connie giggled and turned to open it.

Mrs. Dubchek and Mrs. Tseng stood in the hallway. Mrs. Dubchek wore a festive green sweatshirt embroidered with poinsettias. Tiny Christmas lights hung from Mrs. Tseng's ears. Both women appeared to vibrate.

Mrs. Tseng gestured frantically while Mrs. Dubchek announced, "The washing machine needs you."

Sid squeezed Connie's shoulder as he brushed past her. "I'll take care of it while you unpack."

"No! Both of you," Mrs. Dubchek insisted. Mrs. Tseng nodded emphatically.

"Oookay." Sid held the door for Connie, closed it behind him, and they headed to the elevator.

"Is it the washing machine?" Wanda called out from behind them.

"Yes," Mrs. Tseng replied.

"Right. Coming." Wanda stumped toward them, her walker rattling with her quick, jerky movements.

Connie and Sid stood back to allow the three older women into the elevator. "We'll take the stairs," she offered.

"No," Mrs. Dubchek protested. "We can all fit."

And they did, Mrs. Tseng and Mrs. Dubchek poking and prodding each other. Connie shot Sid a questioning glance, and he shook his head. He had no clue.

Ms. Thompson stood outside the laundry room then hustled inside, saying, "They're here." There was some shuffling and banging and a loud "Shh!"

"So much for the element of surprise," Wanda grumbled.

She led the way to the laundry room, Mrs. Tseng and Mrs. Dubchek trailing behind her. Connie and Sid brought up the end of the procession.

"What do you think they're up to?" Connie whispered.

"I don't know," Sid whispered back. He hoped it wouldn't take long. He wanted Connie all to himself.

Giggling, Mrs. Tseng and Mrs. Dubchek entered the laundry room. Wanda hung back, waving Sid and Connie forward.

"Surprise!"

Except for Mrs. Land, every tenant in The Firs was packed into the laundry room. Clarice and Ms. Thompson were at the front, clutching each other's hands. Mrs. Sinclair towered over the gathering from the back. A small, gaily decorated Christmas tree stood on the island in the center of the room. Surrounding it was a pile of presents. Plates of cookies, platters of sandwiches, and a crystal punch bowl covered the appliances.

The tenants beamed.

Sid smiled.

Connie gasped and started to cry.

Tissues emerged from the cuffs of multiple cardigans and were thrust at her. She waved them off and wiped her eyes. "I'm fine." She sniffed and blinked and clutched Sid's hand. "Did you know about this?"

He shook his head, blinking back his own tears and unable to speak.

Wanda's gruff voice came from behind them. "I told you we appreciate you. Merry Christmas."

For the next hour, the tightly bunched group munched on the treats, heaping praise on each other's baking and promising to share recipes. Connie offered to collect the recipes and have them made into a book that they could give to their families. Ms. Thompson volunteered her older sister to oversee the recipe book production since Mrs. Sinclair had worked as a copy editor for a major publishing house. The two sisters quarreled quietly and briefly before Mrs. Sinclair acquiesced.

Sid stood in a corner, speaking when spoken to but otherwise watching the animated group of women love on Connie. They had pooled their resources to purchase a small, live tree for Connie to have in their apartment, and each woman had gifted an ornament. Some were brand new, others had been dug out of old boxes. All came with stories and memories. Connie teared up with each one, clasping hands or hugging the frail shoulders of the gift giver.

After that, a complicated gift exchange took place. Sid and Connie chose not to participate and simply watched. Rules were established whereby a person took a gift from under the tree and opened it. The next person could steal that gift or open one of their own. Everyone chose to take a gift from under the tree until sweet old Mrs. Tseng decided to steal a set of Christmas-themed tea towels from Clarice. Clarice then stole from Ms. Thompson, who stole from Mrs. Dubchek. This went around and around until Wanda stuck her fingers in her mouth and whistled like she was hailing a cab.

"Game over," she called above the squabbling. The sweating women clutched their treasures and glared at her. Wanda stared them down. "This isn't good for anyone's blood pressure, and besides, you're scaring Sid." She turned and winked at Sid.

"Right! Yes. This is terrifying." He pulled Connie to stand in front of him and peeked over her shoulder.

The grumbling turned to giggles, and the party broke up. With much instruction, Sid picked up the tree and followed Connie back to their apartment. He set it on the coffee table, turned on the battery-powered lights, and they collapsed on the couch.

Connie sighed and snuggled into him. "That was…unexpected."

"Weren't you planning something like that?"

"Kind of," she said. "It wouldn't have been nearly as exciting, though."

"Or bloodthirsty." Contentment settled in him as he took her hand. The light was fading, and tomorrow was Christmas Day. Last year at this time, he'd been at ODAAT. Cal had offered to drive him up to Tulalip for dinner with his parents, but Sid had politely but firmly said no, not wanting to test his newly won sobriety. Instead, he'd hung out with his friends, swapping good memories of Christmases past. Some of the men took out and examined their bad memories with frank honesty. Sid had declined, choosing to write about those memories in his journal. He didn't do much journaling anymore. If he did, today's entry would be one big happy face. Because of the woman next to him.

He nudged her sock-covered foot with his. "What's the schedule for tomorrow?"

Connie wriggled beside him excitedly. She was such a Christmas nut he was surprised tinsel wasn't draped over the bathroom mirror. "We need to be at your aunt and uncle's by eleven tomorrow." She gestured toward the neatly wrapped gifts piled on the recliner. "The ones with the reindeer wrapping paper go to your family. The ones with the wreath wrapping paper go to my family. We should put them in separate spots in the car so they don't get mixed up. I, umm, noticed there isn't anything for your mom."

"There's no point in getting her anything other than money because she'd just say something shitty about the gift. And I won't give her any more money." He'd discussed it with his aunt and uncle, and they'd agreed. Aunt Angie had talked to Violet recently, so he knew she was all right. He wouldn't call her until after the holidays, wanting to enjoy them for the first time in ages.

Connie patted his leg, wise enough to know not to say anything more about it. "We're expected at my parents' place by five. Mom texted me about an hour ago, saying they were already home and that Dad was having a nap." The relief in her voice was palpable. She'd offered to pick them up from the airport, but they'd declined, not wanting to subject her to what would no doubt be a traffic nightmare.

Just like Connie would be meeting his cousins and their families tomorrow, he would be meeting various members of her extended family. He knew he'd be subjected to scrutiny, and there was something he didn't want to do with prying eyes around. "I want to give you your Christmas present now."

Connie's eyes lit up. "Oh, good. I didn't want to do it in front of family. I want to go first." She rose from the couch and was gone before he could respond. She disappeared into her bedroom and returned, holding something behind her back. Her cheeks were bright red, and suddenly looking nervous, her steps slowed. She came to a stop before him and cleared her throat. "You don't have much of Gram other than memories and a few photos, and I saw this sitting on your dresser. It's so small I was worried you might lose it. And so —here." She held out a present.

He opened the small, gift-wrapped box and found a key chain. The finial from the teapot was mounted on the end like a jewel. He wrapped it in his hand, stroking his thumb across the smooth porcelain. His throat tightened at her thoughtfulness, and he croaked out the words, "It's lovely. Thank you."

She nodded shyly and pulled her other hand out from behind her back. "You already have mine, but if I'm not here or you ever have to go somewhere, you can take this with you." She handed him a heart-shaped form made from soft flannel.

Sid accepted it and turned it over in his hands. Embroidered in gold thread were the words, *Connie loves Sid*. He stroked a finger over the flawless stitching and then looked at her, dumbstruck with awe as realization hit him. "Wait, is this your...."

Hands clasped tightly in front of her, she bobbed her head. "My favorite pajam—"

He pulled her to him in a crushing hug, wedging the pillow between them. "I love it."

She gusted out a sigh and sniffed. "It's not much, it's—"

He stopped her words with a kiss. "It's your heart. It's everything." Nothing, nothing would ever feel this good. She could have anyone else in the world, but she chose him. Connie Ortega loved *him*. He kissed her again before reaching under the couch and pulling out a box wrapped in gold ribbon. His palms were sweating, and he swallowed thickly before handing it to her.

Big-eyed, she slowly untied the ribbon and opened the box. She pulled out the round wooden Christmas ornament with a multitude of stars carved in it. "I love it," she said with a soft smile.

Sid pointed at the largest star. "This is for our first Christmas together," he pointed at the others, "and these are for many more to come."

"It's beautiful," she breathed. "Thank you." She held it up to her face and studied it. "You made this for me?"

He nodded.

"Hang on. Does it...does it open?"

He chewed on his bottom lip and nodded again.

Connie opened the ornament into two halves, eyes shining with unshed tears. She held it out for Sid.

He took it from her trembling hands and pulled the narrow gold band from its blue velvet nest. A small diamond winked in the lights from the Christmas tree. He slipped the ring on her finger. "I know it's not much, and we can certainly get you a ring you'd like better, but I love you, Connie Ortega. I think I have since I saw you standing in that dumpster. Will you—"

She flung her arms around Sid before he could finish, sobbing incoherently. He held her to him and waited, feeling like the luckiest man in the world.

Wiping her eyes, Connie pulled back and gazed at the ring, a warm smile curving her lips.

"Gram said that when Pops gave it to her, he apologized. He said he couldn't afford to give her a diamond worthy of her and asked if she would wear this one until he could. Gram said she wore this ring every day of her life and never considered getting a different one."

"And I won't be taking this off, either." Cupping her hands around his face, she whispered, "I love you."

The ring looked perfect on Connie's hand and Sid wondered who'd be more excited, his aunt or her mother. Uncle Dan would be thrilled, and Sid thought Ed would be happy for them as well. "Do you know if your parents have plans for New Year's?" he asked.

"Not that I know of. Why?" Connie answered absently, staring at her ring.

"I thought we could invite them and my aunt and uncle over for dinner."

She was off the couch before he could finish his sentence. Grabbing one of her planners from the dining table, she returned grinning from ear-to-ear. "I am way ahead of you," she said, plopping down beside him and opening the book.

Sid leaned over her shoulder to peer at a seating chart for a dinner party. A twinge of unease went through him. "We can't fit ten people around our table!"

"We can if we borrow some tables from my mom's church. And actually, it would be twelve."

"Twelve?" Sid's eyes widened as he repeated the number.

The twinge of unease amped up. He shouldn't have opened his mouth.

Connie twisted to sit cross-legged on the couch, facing him. "Yes, twelve." She started counting people off on her fingers, "My parents, your aunt and uncle, Cal and Delia, Kevin and Tommy, you and me," in a rush she added, "Frank and Eleanor Armstrong."

"Who?"

"Your friend Frank and Kevin's mother Eleanor." She looked beseechingly up at him. "We have to invite Frank but that would make an uneven number. Kevin's mother is a widow and a lovely person and I think she would get along great with Aunt Angie and my mom." She finished up by saying, "This way, everyone who's important to us will be here."

"I've never hosted a dinner party," he grumbled and frowned at her. "Have you?"

"Nope," she replied, waggling her eyebrows. "But I've got friends in the party-planning business. They'll help us."

He pictured their family and friends all seated around the tables enjoying each other's company.

"We'd make it a potluck. I know my mom would be happy to make something."

"Did you plan a menu too?" He pointed at her notebook.

She shook her head. "I thought we might do that together and then assign something for each person to bring."

"Are you saying my cooking's not good enough?" He faked a glare at her.

"Of course not! Your food is awesome," she declared quickly. "I didn't think you'd want to do all the work."

Pulling the notebook out of her hands, he tossed it on the coffee table, then dragged her over to straddle his lap. "It wouldn't be work if we did it together," he said, tugging on one of her curls.

She draped her arms around his shoulders and smiled. "Yeah?"

"Yeah." He leaned in to capture her lips as a knock came at the door. He groaned, "Seriously?"

"I'll get it," Connie offered, climbing off his lap.

"No." Sid rose from the couch and reached for her hand. "We'll do it together."

ABOUT THE AUTHOR

Lynne Hancock Pearson writes fun, flirty, feel-good fiction that simmers at a low heat. Stories of people finding their way, even if it takes a while to get there. She lives near Seattle with two finicky felines and one long-suffering husband. She is a left-handed middle child who grew up in the Great White North and is a proud member of the Métis Nation of Canada.

For information about upcoming stories and to learn more about Lynne, go to www.lynnehancockpearson.com and join her newsletter.
You can unsubscribe at any time.

You can also follow her here:

facebook.com/lynne.hancockpearson
instagram.com/lynnehancockpearson

www.ingramcontent.com/pod-product-compliance
Lightning Source LLC
Chambersburg PA
CBHW060305310726
48976CB00007B/2214